Buddy's Blues

Nigel Hinton

Buddy's Blues

VIKING

VIKING

Published by the Penguin Group
Penguin Books Ltd, 27 Wrights Lane, London w8 5tz, England
Penguin Books USA Inc., 375 Hudson Street, New York, New York 10014, USA
Penguin Books Australia Ltd, Ringwood, Victoria, Australia
Penguin Books Canada Ltd, 10 Alcorn Avenue, Toronto, Ontario, Canada m4v 3b2
Penguin Books (NZ) Ltd, 182–190 Wairau Road, Auckland 10, New Zealand

Penguin Books Ltd, Registered Offices: Harmondsworth, Middlesex, England

First published 1995
1 3 5 7 9 10 8 6 4 2

Copyright © Nigel Hinton, 1995

The moral right of the author has been asserted

Typeset by Datix International Ltd, Bungay, Suffolk
Set in 12.5/14 Monophoto Sabon
Made and printed in England by Clays Ltd, St Ives plc

A CIP catalogue record for this book is available from the British Library

ISBN 0-670-86277-0

This book was inspired by two great musicians, Buddy Holly and Bob Dylan. And it is dedicated to two friends who have shared the music with me, Richard Lager and John Bauldie.

CHAPTER ONE

Buddy's heart was beating fast as he waited outside the office of the head of XS Records. It was over ten minutes since the secretary had asked the band to wait because Mr Rosen was on the phone to New York.

Buddy glanced at the rest of The Bosses. Were they as nervous as he was? Probably. Nobody was saying anything, just sitting, lost in their own thoughts. Then Glenn got up and walked across to the window. He raised his hands and began to click his nails against the glass. Even when he wasn't at his drums, Glenn always seemed to have a rhythm driving him to tap his feet or fingers. The clicking grew louder as Glenn tried out various beats.

'Cut it out, Glenn,' Mike snarled.

Glenn tapped once more on the glass, then turned around and perched on the edge of the window-sill. 'It's like waiting for the dentist.'

'It's worse than the dentist,' Jason muttered, bunching his long hair up into a ponytail with his fist, then letting it drop round his shoulders. 'Today is make or break.'

'Come off it,' Dave said. 'Even if he doesn't like the album, he's not going to dump us.'

'Want to bet?' Jason said.

'Shut up, Jason. There's no point in rubbing it in,' Mike snapped.

Jason grinned sarcastically at his twin brother, 'OK, Michael. Have it your way, Michael.'

For a moment Mike glared at Jason, and Buddy thought they were going to start a row. The twins argued with each other nearly all the time nowadays. They'd even had a punch-up in the recording studio a couple of weeks ago when they'd disagreed about a song. Thankfully, Mike just turned away from his brother and looked out of the window.

The lift doors at the end of the corridor slid open and Buddy glanced towards them. Whenever he was at the studios he always hoped to see some of the stars who recorded with XS, but in all the time he'd been working there he'd never seen anyone famous. The lift was empty and the doors closed again.

It was stupid, really, hoping to see stars. After all, The Bosses were stars in a way. They had a contract with XS and they'd just recorded their first album. Lots of their friends were really impressed, but Buddy just couldn't think of himself and the rest of the band as 'stars'. Sometimes, when things went wrong in the studio and their producer, Kris Dox, groaned and made them do it again, he even felt like some kind of impostor. He couldn't sing, the band couldn't play – it was all just a wild dream. They should have stuck to playing in youth clubs.

That's what his mum said. She'd been furious when he'd told her he was going into music full time.

'With exam results like yours? After all that hard work? You could go to university or do some proper training for a good job. But, oh no, you want to throw it all away.'

'Music's the only thing I want to do. I love it,' he'd argued.

'You'll end up hating it when it's a job. Better to

love it as a hobby, playing in youth clubs and places like that.'

Perhaps she was right. Perhaps he and Mike and Jason should have gone to college; perhaps Dave should never have given up his job at the bank; perhaps Glenn should have kept on being a milkman. If Bobby Rosen hated the album and dropped them from the label, they would have nothing. Like Jason said, this was make or break.

'How much longer?' Glenn groaned.

'He's showing us he's the boss,' Dave said.

'And that's another thing,' Glenn said. 'If he calls us his "boys" just once, I'll knock his teeth in.'

At that moment the door opened and the secretary came out. She bared her teeth in a smile, 'Mr Rosen is ready now.'

Rosen was on the far side of his huge office when the band filed in. He had his back to them and was looking out of the wall-to-wall window at the London skyline. Kris Dox was sitting in an armchair near the enormous desk. Kris waved his hand at them then went back to reading a magazine.

After a long silence, Rosen turned around and spread his arms wide. 'It's my boys,' he said, as if he was surprised to see them there.

Buddy glanced at Glenn, hoping that he wasn't going to explode, but the drummer was wearing the same silly grin that Buddy could feel on his own face. That was the effect Rosen had on you. He was such a legend in the music business and there was something so hard and menacing about him that you found yourself smiling and nodding at him just to try to keep him happy and friendly.

'Sit down, boys, sit down,' Rosen said, pointing to

the leather sofa in front of the desk. 'You'll have to squeeze on to this one because Sharkey wants the other one.'

He walked over to the big sofa against the wall and stroked the head of the enormous Irish Wolfhound that was spread out across it. 'You're not going to give up your bed for anyone, are you, Sharkey?'

The band sat down, squashed up tight against each other, while Rosen continued to pat Sharkey and scratch him behind his ears. Sharkey sighed and rolled over on to his side.

'So,' Rosen said, giving his dog a final pat then walking back to his desk, 'you've got your first album for me. Well, I'll tell you something – a lot of people at this place thought I was crazy signing you. But I like to trust my instinct and I had a feeling about you. You know what it was?' Rosen tapped the side of his nose. 'I could smell success. But the time's come when I've got to be able to turn to all those others and say: "Listen to this. Was I right, or was I right?" So, let's hope you've come up with the goods, eh?'

Rosen sat down at the desk and nodded to Kris Dox. Kris took a DAT cassette out of his shirt pocket and put it in the player. He pressed 'PLAY' and the tape began to spin.

CHAPTER TWO

The first track blared out from the four speakers and Buddy found himself hating it. It had been one of his

4

favourite songs when they'd recorded it, but now it sounded terrible, especially his singing.

He wondered what Rosen was thinking, but it was impossible to tell: he was sitting with his back to the windows and his face was in shadow. All Buddy could see was a glint from his glasses and the light shining on his bald head.

Bald head. Buddy's stomach lurched as he realized that the second track was starting. It was called 'Stay True' and he'd written it nearly a year ago. It was a kind of dig at Rosen for forcing them to drop Buddy's dad as manager of the band. The first couple of verses weren't too obvious, but the words of the third verse seemed to scream out the message:

> Don't sell out
> To the bald men
> Sign deals in your blood
> With a gold pen
> Stay true to yourself
> Stay truc.

He looked at Rosen but there was no sign that he'd understood what the words were saying. Buddy was almost disappointed. It would have been bad news for the band if he'd been offended, but on the other hand Buddy would never forget the day they'd signed the contract. It had happened right here in this office and his dad had been there because Buddy had been too young to sign on his own.

Rosen had shaken his dad's hand and said, 'No hard feelings, Terry. It's the best thing for the boys. Those two prison sentences of yours would only have held them back.'

His dad had smiled, but Buddy knew how hurt

and disappointed he'd been. He had pinned all his hopes on the band: it was going to be his way of showing the world that he could do something. He had worked so hard, too: he'd got them gigs, arranged publicity, made demos and videos; and he was the one who'd first contacted XS.

The truth was, Buddy had only started playing music in the first place because of his dad. He'd grown up with music all round him. Elvis Presley, Buddy Holly and all his dad's rock'n'roll favourites were always on the record player, and Buddy had learned the songs the way other kids learned nursery rhymes. It was his dad who'd bought him his first guitar. And the first songs he'd ever recorded were on a tape for his dad when he was in prison.

If anyone deserved to be part of the band's success, it was his dad. Instead, Rosen had given them an ultimatum – get a new manager or there would be no contract. As soon as his dad had heard, he'd said that he was thinking of packing it in anyway and had made them sign with XS.

Rosen had found them a new manager, Walter Shielby. He was one of the biggest managers in the business but he had so many famous clients that he never seemed to have much time to work for The Bosses. Like today. If his dad were still manager, he'd have been here to look after the band's interests; but Walter Shielby was in Jamaica, supervising a recording session for one of his other clients.

Still, it had worked out well for his dad in the end. He'd sent the videos he'd made of The Bosses to lots of record companies. One of them, Arctic Records, had been so impressed that they'd hired him and his partner, Alan, to help set up a video department.

6

He'd been working for Arctic for nearly nine months and he was having a great time.

The first thing he'd done was to buy himself a Harley Davidson Dyna Glide. It was his pride and joy and he roared up to London and back on it every day. He could have got a flat in London, but he said he didn't want to because his mates weren't there. Besides, he told Buddy, he liked living in the caravan at Des King's breaker's yard. It was home.

Buddy had immediately said that 'home' was with him and his mum, but his dad had ignored him. Buddy hadn't pressed the point.

His parents hadn't lived together for years but at least they were good friends nowadays. Sometimes he went out with them for a meal or a drink, and there were never any of the awful rows like before. In a funny way, it almost made it worse to see them laughing and chatting together. It was stupid, but he couldn't help it: if he had three wishes, his parents getting back together would still be one of them.

Buddy had been so lost in thought that he hadn't really been listening to the album, and he was surprised to realize that it was already the last song, 'Waking Nightmare'.

It was based on a dream he'd had. It had been a long, slow dream filled with pictures that didn't make any sense, but for some reason he'd felt they were about dying. He'd woken up in a sweat, heart pounding, and filled with a fear of death. He'd got up and written the song in the middle of the night. Putting the weird pictures to a tune had taken the fear away.

The last chorus now. The band sounded great – a swirling, ghostly sound. And now the slow fade.

Perhaps a bit too slow? No, just right. Dave's keyboard playing on the fade was terrific and left you wanting more. The track ended and the tape clicked to a stop.

Glenn cleared his throat and pushed against Buddy as he tried to make more room for himself on the crowded sofa. Then silence. A long, long silence.

'Well,' Rosen said at last, 'What can I say? It's brilliant. Brilliant. But there's nothing I can do with songs like that.'

Mike leaned forward urgently. 'Why not? What's wrong with them?'

'They're album tracks. There's not one song I can get played on radio or TV, not one. And if I can't get them played, I can't get a hit. And without a hit, I can't get the punters to go into a shop and buy the album. It's as simple as that.'

The band sat, stunned, as the disappointment sank in. Then there was a chuckle from the side of the room and they all turned to look at Kris Dox. He had a broad grin on his face.

'You dozy lot! I can't believe you didn't notice.' He pulled another tape from his pocket and held it up. 'You want a hit, Bobby? I've been saving the best till last. This lot seem to have forgotten about it.'

He slipped the new cassette into the player.

Which track?

The three bass notes at the start of the song gave it away. It was 'She Got'.

Even before the vocal came in, Rosen sat up straight, listening intently. Buddy almost blushed because the song was so personal. It was about Olivia, and he had poured all his feelings about her into the words.

8

She got dark curls
Sea green eyes
She got gentle voice
That can't tell lies
She got tender charm
She whisper low
She got sweet desire
To make love slow.

She know the loving truth
The others all forget
She know the more you give
The more you gonna get.

She got soft skin
And welcome smile
She got holy words
To ease my trial
She got deep soul
And time for me
She got my love
Exclusively.

The ridiculous thing was that all these other people were hearing what he felt about Olivia, and yet he'd never told *her*. He wondered what they'd say if he told them the song was about someone who right now was working, fifteen floors below them. Rosen probably didn't even know the name of the girl behind the reception desk, and none of the rest of the band ever said more than 'Hi!' to her as they went in and out of the building. But Buddy couldn't take his eyes off her.

During breaks in the recording, while the others had gone out to the pub, Buddy had often sat in

Reception, watching her from behind a newspaper he was pretending to read. She took his breath away.

And all those corny old phrases – 'take my breath away', 'feel weak in the knees' – they were all true. They were exactly what Olivia did to him. The look of her. The sound of her. He ached with wanting her.

Every time he saw her, he hoped she'd say something that would give him the chance to tell her how he felt, but it never happened. She was polite but distant – and, on top of that, he'd heard she was going out with the lead singer from a band called Tuff Tymes. He'd found that out on the day he recorded the vocals for 'She Got' – perhaps that was why, listening to the song now, his voice seemed so filled with love.

As the last note of the guitar rang out, Rosen jumped to his feet and came round the desk, shouting, 'You've done it! You big, beautiful boys! It's a hit!'

For the next two hours he hardly stopped talking. He got all the heads of departments to come and listen to the song and plan the release of the album. He sent for champagne and even dragged Sharkey off the sofa when Glenn complained that he felt like a sardine and needed somewhere else to sit. He didn't even argue much when they told him they wanted the album to be called *The Bosses: In Business*.

'You know I hate the band's name,' he groaned. 'You said you were going to change it.'

'We're keeping it in honour of Terry,' Mike said. 'It's our way of thanking him for getting us started. He was a great manager.'

'Yeah, not like the one *you* got us,' Glenn added.

Rosen took the hint and went back to raving about the album. It was the best first album he'd heard in thirty years and 'She Got' was going to explode into the charts. 'Explode' was a word he used a lot. 'Explode' and 'Megahit'. And once he'd used them, everybody else used them, too. The producers. The heads of departments. Everybody except Kris Dox.

As the band left the office, Kris took hold of Buddy's arm and said quietly, 'Bobby's on our side and that's great – but remember: this business can break your heart.'

In the middle of all the excitement, Kris's words seemed almost cruel, and Buddy's happiness drained away. Then they got into the lift and Glenn, who'd drunk a lot of champagne, started imitating Rosen, and Buddy got caught up in the laughter and high spirits again.

'Well, you great big beautiful boys,' Glenn said, 'you're going to have megahits exploding out of your ears. And probably out of other bits of your bodies, too. In fact you're going to explode so much we ought to change the band's name to The Bombs. Never liked the other one, did we, Sharkey? Oh dear, Sharkey's just exploded all over my sofa. Dirty dog.'

They were all still laughing when they reached the ground floor. Glenn was leaning against the lift doors, and as they opened he fell backwards into the lobby. He scrambled to his feet and swayed over to the reception desk. Olivia looked up, and swept the hair away from her face as he banged on the desk.

'Hello, Emma,' Glenn said.

'My name's Olivia,' she replied coolly.

'So sorry, my dear,' Glenn said, imitating her voice. 'Anyway, Emma – you're looking at someone who's gonna explode.'

He burst into fits of laughter and nearly fell over again, so Jason and Mike grabbed him and pulled him to the door.

''Bye, Emma,' he yelled as he was bundled outside.

Olivia calmly went back to her work as though nothing had happened, but Buddy tried to make some sort of apology. 'We've been celebrating. Bobby Rosen likes our album. He thinks it's going to be a hit.'

Olivia raised her head and her lovely green eyes looked at him more directly than ever before. Perhaps she was impressed. Perhaps she'd begin to take notice of him now.

'Really?' she said flatly and went back to work.

Buddy went outside. Mike and Jason were holding Glenn up against the wall and Dave was trying to hail a taxi.

'You're a stupid prat, Glenn,' Buddy muttered. 'What did you want to be rude to her for?'

'Emma?' Glenn laughed.

'Her name's Olivia,' Buddy snapped.

'No it's not, it's Emma. Emma Royd. You know why? 'Cos she's a pain in the bum. Get it? Emma Royd. Pain in the bum.'

Jason and Mike burst out laughing and Buddy turned away, trying not to let his anger show.

'Emma Royd,' Glenn went on. 'God, I pity any boyfriend of hers. She'd break your heart.'

All the way home on the train the others joked and laughed. Buddy wanted to join in their happiness, but he couldn't. Three little words stopped him.

Kris and Glenn had both used them, and he couldn't get them out of his head. It felt like some kind of warning.

Break your heart.

CHAPTER THREE

After the meeting with Rosen they expected things to happen fast. The twins and Dave got a flat in London but Buddy and Glenn decided to go on living at home. Glenn wanted to be near his girlfriend, Alice, and Buddy didn't feel like leaving home. Not just yet, anyway.

Instead, he took a concentrated course of driving lessons, passed his test, and bought a car. It was only an old banger but he loved seeing it standing outside the house, and he spent days touching up the rusty bits and polishing it until it gleamed. Nearly every day he called for Glenn and they drove round town for hours, often playing 'She Got' very loud on the stereo. He took his mum down to the sea one evening, but she kept saying he was going too fast. He laughed because she held on tight to the dashboard and slammed her foot down on an imaginary brake whenever they got near another car.

'Yes, you can laugh. As long as you don't go killing yourself, that's all,' she said rather coldly.

He went round to visit his dad at the breaker's yard and hooted loudly as he screeched to a halt outside the caravan. His dad came out, took one look at the car and burst out laughing.

'Don't leave that wreck here – the punters'll think it's a write-off and strip the engine out.'

'Dad!' Buddy said, really disappointed.

'Only kidding. It's great.'

It wasn't great; but it would make it easier to get up to London and back for all the things to do with the record.

Then, at the next meeting, Rosen told them that the single wouldn't be coming out for another six months.

'We've got a lot of work to do, preparing the ground,' he told them. 'Just trust me and be patient.'

Buddy found it hard being patient. In six months he'd be nineteen. It was such a waste of half a year. One thirty-sixth of his life. The worst thing was not going up to XS Studios. For over four months he'd seen Olivia nearly every day and he missed the excitement of being near her. He half hoped that by not seeing her the ache in his heart would go away, but it didn't. He thought about writing to her, but what could he say?

Weeks drifted by and it was like being on holiday without wanting to be. He spent most of his time with Glenn, who often came round to listen to music on Buddy's stereo because his mum wouldn't let him play records at home.

'Honest, Buddy, sometimes I think she hates my guts,' he confessed one day. 'Ever since my old man died she goes to all these prayer meetings and reads the Bible non-stop. Never watches telly or anything. She won't let me have any booze in the house. And she even tries to stop me seeing Alice.'

It was while they were waiting for something to happen on 'She Got' that Glenn discovered Blues music. He started out, buying some old Rolling Stones and Eric Clapton records, then he found out that they were based on music by even older singers and guitarists. Soon he was turning up with albums by old blues singers with weird names like Memphis Minnie, Blind Willie McTell and Leadbelly.

Buddy wasn't keen on them at first, but gradually the raw, raunchy sounds grew on him.

'Maybe we could make the next album more blue-sy,' Buddy said one day, and he began to play 'She Got' in a kind of blues style on his guitar.

'Hey, it really works like that,' Glenn said. 'Just shows what a good song it is. It's gonna be a hit, you know.'

Everybody seemed to agree. Especially his dad. Buddy gave him a tape of the whole album and he picked out 'She Got' as the best track.

'It's fan-tastic. You ought to get 'em to let Arctic make the video. I'd love to work on it.'

The only person who wasn't so enthusiastic was his mum. She liked the tune but not the words.

'It's not proper English,' she complained. 'It should be "She's got" and "She knows", not "She got" and "She know". I thought English was your best subject at school.'

It really annoyed him when she put him down like that, but a couple of weeks later she came up to his room and said she'd been playing the album every day in her car and had grown to love it.

'Honest?' he asked.

'Honest. I think it's wonderful. And the songs really say things. Like that one, "Waking Nightmare" – I don't know why, but it always makes me think about dying. It's like poetry.'

He found himself grinning in delight. She had seen what the song was about – and other people might, too. Strangers hundreds of miles away would share his feelings. He couldn't wait for the album to be released.

Then, at last, things started to happen. First there was the photo session for the album cover. The Art Director wanted to dress them in pin-striped suits and bowler hats, but the band didn't like the idea, so Buddy suggested that it would be more interesting if they were shown as workers on a building site. The Art Director fell for the idea, and the photo that was finally chosen had them standing on scaffolding, wearing hard hats and holding sledgehammers. Rosen loved it.

'You look like a heavy mob,' he enthused. 'I was wondering how we were going to sell you, especially since the single's a bit of a quiet love song. This is the perfect image for you – hard guys with soft hearts. I'll get on to the publicity department and set it all up.'

And 'Hard Guys with Soft Hearts' was the headline on the first article printed about them. It was in the magazine *Teen Stars* and it had a full-page photo of the band with just a few lines underneath:

> The buzz in the biz says that The Bosses are the Next Big Thing. So we sent our starry-eyed reporter, Natasha, to check out the boys whose first single 'She Got' is released soon. Her verdict? 'Dead hard, but cute as puppies. I want one!' Down, Natasha, down!

'Who's this Natasha? She sounds stupid,' his mum said when Buddy showed her the magazine.

'No one. It was all made up by the publicity people at XS.'

'You mean XS paid the magazine to print it?'

'I don't know. Probably. Anyway, it's only the same sort of thing as you do.'

'Buddy, I do advertising for technical magazines. I present facts, not lies like this.'

He didn't go on arguing because, in a way, he agreed with her – it was just lies. And he hated the idea of being packaged and sold as a hard guy or a puppy dog. On the other hand, if anyone could make The Bosses a success, it was Rosen and XS. He just hoped that people would soon be more interested in the band's music than in some stupid image in a magazine.

The best thing about all the activity at XS was that it gave him the chance to see Olivia again. She was obviously spending her weekends out in the sun and she had a golden tan that made her look lovelier than ever. She also seemed more friendly than before, smiling and saying hello whenever he went into the building. One day he was sitting in the reception area, drinking a coffee, when she left the desk and wandered over to him.

'I hear your single's coming out,' she said. 'You must be doing a lot of work with the publicity department.'

Now was his chance: he could tell her that he'd written the song about her. She'd love that. But when he looked up at those dark-green eyes, he froze. He didn't smile, he didn't chat. Nothing. He just said, 'Uh uh,' and looked away.

To cover his embarrassment, he picked up the plastic cup and gulped some coffee. The hot liquid hit the back of his throat and some of it went down the wrong way. He started to choke and tears came to his eyes as he gasped and coughed. He stood up and blundered away down the corridor. He burst into the nearest toilet and coughed and spluttered until it cleared.

Buddy felt so awful about what had happened that he mentioned it to his dad.

'Oh, well romantic! Still, at least you didn't splurt the coffee all over 'er!' his dad laughed. 'Nah, forget it. Give 'er a bunch of roses or somefing, girls love that. 'Ere, what a coincidence – Buddy Holly fell in love with the receptionist at his publishers. Maria Elena. They got engaged on the very first day they met.'

'Oh, cut it out!' Buddy snapped.

'What's up wiv you?'

'I hate it when you do that. "Buddy Holly was a star, you're going to be a star. He went out with a receptionist, you're going out with a receptionist . . ." It gets on my nerves.'

'All right, all right, keep your 'air on. Didn't mean nuffin'.'

His dad went to the far end of the caravan, turned on the TV, and slumped onto his bed. Buddy stood there, feeling awkward. He wanted to explain, but he couldn't – his dad would just think he was being stupid.

'I'm tired. I'm going home,' he said.

'Suit yourself,' his dad muttered, staring at the TV.

He sat outside in his car for a few minutes, daring himself to go back and tell him, but how could he? How could he tell anyone that for years he kept having this crazy feeling that, because Buddy Holly had died in a plane-crash at twenty-two, his name had a kind of curse on it? Most of the time he could push the mad idea away by thinking of all the other Buddys in the world who hadn't died young; but sometimes, like tonight, he couldn't stop the fear stabbing at his heart.

The next day he rang his dad at work and tried to make it up by telling him that he'd taken the advice and bought Olivia a dozen red roses. He didn't add that he'd pretended they were from the whole band.

'That'll do the trick,' his dad said.

He was right. It did. Two days after he'd given her the roses, Olivia stopped him on his way out and asked if he fancied going for a drink.

'Yeah, great,' he said. 'When?'

'Well, I finish in twenty minutes if you can hang on. There's a great wine-bar just round the corner.'

The wine-bar was in an old vaulted cellar, and they sat in a quiet corner at a wine-barrel with a candle burning in a bottle.

At first he was nervous that he wouldn't know what to talk about, but he needn't have worried. Olivia did nearly all the talking. He just sat and listened, drinking wine and feeling great. She talked mostly about XS Records. She'd only been there for ten months, but she was hoping to get promotion soon. What she really wanted to do was to get into the Publicity department.

'That's the world I like — newspapers, TV. Actually, I was wondering . . .' she reached over and put her hand on his. 'No, I can't ask you that.'

'What? Go on.'

'Well, you're in tight with Bobby Rosen. Do you think you could just mention that I'd like to work in Publicity?'

'Yeah, sure, no problem,' he said, feeling the wine going to his head.

Suddenly she leaned towards him and kissed him on the lips. He felt the blood pump round his body and he wanted to grab hold of her and crush himself against her.

'I thought you were going out with that guy from Tuff Tymes,' he said as she leaned back.

'I was,' she smiled. 'Past tense. He's OK, but he's a bit of a loser. They're not going anywhere, that band. Not like you.'

She took hold of his hand and gently pulled him towards her. He bent forward, and she kissed his lips again.

CHAPTER FOUR

Rosen loved the album cover so much that he decided to use the same building site for the video of 'She Got'.

'Oh, we hoped you were gonna fly us to some island in the Caribbean, Bobby,' Glenn joked, but he cut his laugh short when Rosen looked at him frostily.

The basic idea for the video was very simple: the band would be on some scaffolding, painting a house, when a beautiful girl would walk by. They would all stare at her and their paint-brushes would turn into musical instruments, which they'd play while Buddy sang to her.

Buddy thought of suggesting Olivia for the part of the girl – after all, she was beautiful and the song had been written about her – but he decided it might not be right. However, he did have a quiet word with Rosen about a job for her in Publicity.

'I'll see what I can do,' Rosen said, 'but remember – you owe me one.'

At the end of the week Olivia was transferred to the Publicity Department as an assistant to Diana Armstrong, who was in charge of the campaign to launch The Bosses. Olivia was thrilled at the new job, and even when they were out on dates she hardly talked about anything else. Most of the time Buddy didn't mind – he was so happy just to be with her and he loved to see her beautiful eyes alive with enthusiasm as she talked – but one evening, at her favourite restaurant, Cassy's, he tried to change the subject.

'Oh, come on, let's talk about something else,' he said after an hour in which she'd told him all about the magazines she'd contacted to do interviews with the band.

'This is important. You want the record in the charts, don't you?'

'Of course I do . . . but I need a break from work sometimes.'

'Work? This isn't work.' She sat back and looked at him with a disbelieving smile. 'This is power. Making things happen, getting people to do what I want. I rang up an editor today and I knew she didn't want to do a feature on The Bosses, but I kept on till she agreed. It was such a buzz!'

The energy sparked off her and he knew why the editor had given in. Nobody would be able to resist her – he certainly couldn't.

Later that night they were kissing in his car outside her flat when her mouth broke away from his and she began to kiss him across his cheek and down to his neck. Her lips played across the skin, then she bit him gently on his ear and a surging thrill pulsed through his whole body. He pressed himself hard against her, wanting to excite her, and she pressed back. For a moment a kind of wildness gripped them, then suddenly she pulled away from him.

'What's the matter?' he asked.

'I hate groping in a car – it's so juvenile. We can't go to my flat because my landlady's strict about visitors. What about your place?'

'I live at home.'

She looked at him in surprise and he felt young and stupid, so he made up a lie about how he and Glenn had wanted to get a flat but hadn't been able to afford it. Actually, the last bit was true: he couldn't afford it. He could hardly afford his car and all the expensive restaurants that Olivia loved so much. Most of the advance money the band had got from XS had gone on buying new equipment, and even Dave and the twins were finding it hard to pay the rent on their flat.

'I'll get my own place as soon as some money comes in from the record,' he told her.

'It'll be months before you start getting royalties from the record,' Olivia said, leaning forward and wiping the steam off the windscreen. The light from the street caught the soft line of her neck and the gleam on her lips. Another wave of desire rose in Buddy.

'I can't wait that long,' he laughed, reaching over to put his arm round her.

Olivia pushed his arm away and sat back. 'You'll just have to,' she said sharply.

A rush of embarrassment swept through him: he'd been so clumsy and rude. She was angry with him. He hadn't said anything about loving her, he'd just made it sound as if all he was interested in was sex. He had a wave of panic that she might stop going out with him.

'Listen, I'm sorry,' he said. 'I didn't mean it like that.'

'Yes, you did.'

'I didn't – honestly.' Buddy took a deep breath and said what he'd never said to a girl. 'I love you.'

She turned and looked at him, her big eyes staring into his to see if he was telling the truth.

'That's what all men say when they want something. But I think you mean it. Good.'

She leaned over, kissed him lightly on the cheek then opened the door and got out. Buddy watched her walk up the steps. He hoped she would turn around and wave, but she didn't. The door closed behind her.

On the long drive home he couldn't stop thinking about it. What a stupid thing to say: – 'I can't wait that long.' It made him sound sex-mad. And, in a way, he was. He couldn't deny it, he ached with wanting her. And she must want him, too. After all, she'd asked if he had somewhere to go. If only he had a flat.

He wound down the window and let the rushing

night wind pull and tug at his hair and, bit by bit, cool him down.

With the release of the record so near, the band's schedule became hectic and he didn't see Olivia for weeks, although he sent her a card or some flowers every other day. The first week was taken up with making the video. His dad wanted to come along and watch but Buddy said it might be difficult.

'Anyway, why aren't you working?' he asked his dad.

'Oh, things're a bit slack at Arctic. Everyone's cutting back on videos at the moment. That's why I 'oped Rosen would give us the job.'

'Yeah, well, XS have got their own contacts,' Buddy said, feeling guilty that he hadn't even mentioned it to Rosen. Of course he would have liked his dad to get the work, but he didn't want him becoming too involved with The Bosses' career again.

'I'd like to meet 'em – always useful to know other outfits in case I leave Arctic. I'm getting a bit fed up there. I 'ave all the good ideas, but Alan always gets to direct them, while I stand around like a nun in a strip club.'

In the end Buddy arranged for his dad to come along for just one day of the video shoot and it went really well. Somehow he always forgot what good fun his dad could be – he mucked around like crazy, making everyone laugh, yet he never got in the way. In between shots he talked to the crew about the technical problems and they seemed delighted to explain things to him. The rest of the band always liked him, of course – especially Glenn, who spent a lot of time chatting to him on his own during the lunch break.

'What's up wiv Glenn?' his dad asked afterwards.

'What d'you mean?'

'I don't know, I get the feeling he ain't 'appy.'

Buddy couldn't see it. Glenn unhappy? The opposite, in fact: he was always talking and cracking jokes, to the point where people got a bit fed up with him. Dave started calling him 'Jetmouth' and that soon got shortened to 'Jet'. By the end of the video shoot, the name had stuck.

The day they set out on a tour of radio stations all over the country, Buddy and Glenn hired the van and drove to the studios to load all the equipment. The drummer was quiet for a change and he looked tired.

'Listen, Jet, is anything up?' Buddy asked as they stacked the keyboards next to the amps.

'Yeah – you can stop calling me Jet, for a start,' Glenn snapped. 'You're supposed to be my mate.'

'I *am* your mate.'

'Yeah, you were, before you went out with that Olivia, now you're as bad as the rest. I know what you all think, I'm just the thicko milkman who didn't get no exams.'

'Glenn, no one thinks that.'

'Oh yeah? What about Rosen? What about that video director? They all crawl round you 'cos you write the songs and read books and stuff, but they treat me like I'm a moron.'

'Oh come on, Glenn, don't get paranoid.'

'I'm not bloody paranoid, right?' Glenn shouted.

They finished loading the van in silence.

Bobby Rosen had told them that getting the record on to the playlists at the radio stations was the most important element in the whole promotional push. So, for over three weeks they went from town to town, meeting DJs, doing interviews and playing live on programmes. It was hard work, but, when they finally got back to XS, Rosen was delighted: most of the stations had put 'She Got' on their 'A' playlist, and a lot of DJs were going to make it their record of the week.

Olivia had been working hard, too, and as soon as the band got back to London they were caught up in photo sessions and interviews with all the music and teen magazines. Olivia always went with them and when she told a couple of the editors that she was Buddy's girlfriend they insisted on taking photos of them together. The rest of the band didn't like the idea and Buddy felt awkward about it, but Olivia persuaded them that it would be good publicity. Even so, Buddy hated it when he saw the two magazines that printed photos of him and Olivia kissing.

The others were even more annoyed.

'Who the hell does she think she is? She keeps muscling in like some kind of starlet,' Mike sneered.

'Tartlet, more like it,' Glenn laughed. 'Emma Royd the Tartlet.'

Buddy tried to defend her but the next time they were alone he told her that he wanted to keep his private life private.

'Sure, I understand,' she said sweetly. 'Me, too. Still, if those photos help to get the song into the charts . . .'

But despite the photos, despite all the publicity, despite all the radio play, the record didn't chart. The reviews were terrific, and everyone predicted that it would make the Top 40 in its first week. It didn't even make the Top 75.

The second week the video was shown six times

26

on TV, and everybody was very hopeful. Again, 'She Got' was nowhere.

In the third week some of the radio stations stopped playing it, and it began to look as if the record had died. The marketing people at XS started to talk about cutting their losses and choosing a second single. Even Olivia seemed to have lost her enthusiasm and she kept telling Buddy that she was too depressed to go out with him in the evening.

Then, at four o'clock one afternoon, they got an urgent phone-call from Bobby Rosen. A famous American band had just dropped out of *Live with Merv Hill* and he had pulled strings to get The Bosses on as last-minute replacements to sing 'She Got' at the end of the show. They had to be at the TV studios by six o'clock, and the show would go out at seven-thirty.

Luckily, everything had to be done so fast that they didn't have time to get nervous – but, at the very last moment, it hit Buddy: they were just about to sing, live on the most popular chat show on TV. Twelve million people were watching. There was a great lurch of fear in the pit of his stomach, then he saw the floor manager give the cue and the lights came up as Merv Hill announced, 'Ladies and Gentlemen – The Bosses with their new single "She Got".'

There was a huge cheer from the audience as Glenn clicked his sticks together to count them in, and they began to play. Buddy took a deep breath and hit the opening note perfectly. Somewhere, a girl started to scream and others joined in. By the time he got to the second verse Buddy could hardly hear himself singing, and by the end of the song the screaming was almost drowning out the whole band.

When the lights went down they all looked at each other, stunned. Even five minutes later, in their dressing-room, they still couldn't say much more than 'Wow!' In all the time they'd been playing they'd never had a reception like it, and it felt fantastic.

Then Bobby Rosen walked in.

'Well done, boys – that was useful,' he said.

'Useful?' Jason said. 'Useful? That was bloody spectacular! That was mammoth! Did you hear those girls?'

'Of course I heard them. I would have been very disappointed if I hadn't heard them. They cost me a great deal of money. Now we just have to hope that I invested wisely and that the record makes the charts this week.'

CHAPTER FIVE

When The Bosses left the studios, the girls were outside, and they pushed and shouted and screamed as the band got into a taxi. Camera flash-bulbs popped and Buddy tried to hide his face.

Jason summed it all up in the taxi when he said, 'What a let-down. It's like being told that Father Christmas is a dirty old pervo.'

The following day one of the tabloid newspapers printed a photo of the girls mobbing the band. The headline was 'SHE GOT ME' and the short article said: 'Pop Sensations, The Bosses, whose song "She Got" is chartbound, were nearly "Got" by a She-crowd after last night's Merv Hill show.'

Buddy usually cut out all the articles about the band and put them in a scrapbook, but he threw this one away. And he almost had a row with Olivia about it all. She kept saying that it was fantastic publicity and that the band ought to be grateful for all the hard work people had put in, let alone the money that had been spent.

'But it's just a bloody con,' Buddy argued.

'Oh honestly,' she snapped, 'if you're going to act like some kind of virgin saint, you're in the wrong business.'

Even when the band met up on Sunday afternoon to listen to the *Chart Show*, there was still an odd mood in the air. Jason and Mike started one of their arguments about nothing, and Dave slammed out of the room, saying that he was fed up with both of them. Glenn switched on the TV and lay on the floor watching a film with the sound turned down. He kept making up bits of silly dialogue for the characters in the film and roaring with laughter at his own jokes, until Jason kicked him hard on the foot.

'Shut up, Jet,' he said. 'You're not funny – you're stupid.'

Glenn glared at him for a moment, then crawled over to the TV, switched it off, and bent down and started banging his head on the floor. Everyone laughed at another of Glenn's mad jokes – acting like a spoilt brat – but the banging went on, getting harder and harder, until the thumps were shaking the floor and Dave came out of his room to see what was happening.

'Hey, Glenn – cut it out,' Buddy finally shouted and jumped up and grabbed hold of Glenn's head to stop him.

The drummer had cut one of his eyebrows open

with the force of the blows; his forehead was red and swollen, and his eyes were filled with tears.

'God, Glenn, you're crazy,' Buddy gasped.

'No – just stupid. So stupid and thick it doesn't hurt,' Glenn snarled. He got up and went into the kitchen.

Buddy and the others looked at each other in shocked silence.

A moment later Glenn came back into the room, holding a piece of kitchen paper to his cut eyebrow. He stared at them then broke into a laugh. 'Who wants a cup of coffee?'

He went back into the kitchens and they heard him singing to himself as he clattered around. A couple of minutes later, he reappeared with mugs of coffee and handed them around as though nothing had happened, then he switched on the radio.

'Just in time,' he said as the opening music for the *Chart Show* started. 'Well, my money says we're at number 38.'

He lost the bet.

The DJ played numbers 40 and 39. They all held their breath as he announced 38, but it was a song by Michelle Mercedes. 37 . . . 36 . . . Still no 'She Got'.

Then the DJ said, 'Straight in at 35 on the nation's top chart we've got a hit by a new band . . .'

They all looked at each other.

'. . . They're called Moovie and the song is "Too Late, Too Late".'

By the time the DJ got to number 32 they realized it had happened again. Despite everything that XS had done, despite all the strings Rosen had pulled, the record hadn't charted.

'Turn it off, Dave,' Jason mumbled.

'No, hold on – I like this one,' Glenn said. 'It's got a great Hammond organ sound.'

The song ended, and Glenn got up to turn the radio off. His finger was jabbing towards the switch when the DJ said, 'And here's this week's highest new entry . . .'

Glenn stopped, his finger poised on the switch.

'. . . It's the band everyone's talking about – The Bosses. They come into the chart at number 31 with "She Got".'

Buddy would never forget that moment, as the record started to play. All the hard work, all the long, long waiting had paid off, and the joy of it burst in his chest. Everything was possible. The future was filled with excitement. Life was wonderful.

He was on his feet – shouting, laughing, jumping around and hugging four other madmen who were filled with the same thrill and hope. They were young and successful. The world was going to hear from them. They were going to be something special. Nothing was going to stop them.

On the way home Buddy dropped in to see Olivia while Glenn waited for him in the car.

'We've done it!' Olivia shouted as she opened the door.

'Wrong, Emma,' Glenn yelled from the car. 'We're the ones who did it, not you.'

'God, he's a liability,' Olivia muttered, pulling Buddy into the hallway and closing the door. 'You ought to drop him and get another drummer.'

'We can't do that – he's a great drummer. Anyway, he's my friend.'

'Don't ever let friendship get in the way of your future,' she said, then pulled him close and kissed him.

One of her hands stroked his neck and the other strayed lower and lower down his back until a shiver shook his whole body and he had to hold on to her tight to stop his knees giving way under him.

Somewhere down the corridor a door opened. Olivia broke away and stepped back a couple of paces. A tall woman in a long red dress came out of the room, carrying a tray. She glanced at them then walked away to the kitchen, followed by a black cat with its tail held straight up in the air. Buddy moved towards Olivia, wanting her in his arms again, but she shook her head.

'It's my landlady,' she whispered. 'You'll have to go.'

'I want to kiss you again,' he whispered back.

'No.'

She walked to the door and opened it. Buddy tried to take her hand as he passed her, but she pulled it away.

'I said no, Buddy. I'll see you tomorrow at the office – there'll be a lot of things to do, now the song's in the charts.'

As soon as he was outside, she closed the door without saying goodbye. Buddy wanted to ring the bell and talk to her some more, but Glenn was looking at him from the car, so he walked quickly down the steps as if he was in a hurry to get away.

The next day they had a meeting with Rosen at XS. He was in a great mood and told them that the phone had been ringing non-stop with offers for the band. *Top of the Pops* had chosen the video for one of the Chart Breaker slots, with the promise of a live appearance if the record made the Top Twenty. Best of all, though, he'd booked them as support band for the British tour of the American band, Sons of Hud, starting the following week. Although The Bosses had met regularly in a rehearsal room to keep in practice, it was ages since they'd played a live set on stage, and Buddy couldn't wait to get out on the road again.

His mum was working late on the Thursday, so he went round to the breaker's yard to watch *Top of the Pops* in his dad's caravan. They only showed about half a minute of the video, but it was still a thrill. So often, when he first started playing, he'd watched the programme and dreamed of being on it one day – and now it had happened.

'The band look great – but it's a feeble video,' his dad commented afterwards. 'We could've done a miles better job at Arctic.'

Buddy nodded, then changed the subject by talking about the places they'd be playing on the tour.

'Ace,' his dad said. 'I'll 'ave to try and get to a couple of 'em. 'Ere, by the way, now you're in the big time I don't want you stickin' needles in yerself or stuffin' fings up your nose.'

'Oh come on, Dad – you know I'm not into drugs.'

'There's always a first time, if you're nuts enough. And watch out for the birds, too – they'll be all over you.'

'Yeah, if my luck's in,' Buddy said.

His dad frowned then broke into a big grin. 'Gor blimey, I remember you when you was a nice cent little kid. Now look at you – randy tyke. Anyway, 'ave a good time!'

CHAPTER SIX

The tour with Sons of Hud began in Leeds, and The Bosses quickly found out that the crowd had only come to see the American band. The hall was less than half full when The Bosses went on stage to do their forty-minute set and the audience paid hardly any attention to them. People moved around, meeting friends and chatting to each other, and at the end of each song there was only a ripple of applause. Even 'She Got' didn't seem to spark any interest, despite the fact that it was being played on the radio a lot and had gone up to number 27 in the charts.

Afterwards the band sat, silent and depressed, in their cramped dressing-room backstage.

'Look, let's face it,' Dave said after a while, 'the Hud fans only like head-banging, power-chord stuff. Maybe we ought to play a few songs like that.'

'That wasn't the problem,' Buddy said. 'We were crap tonight. No energy, no soul – nothing.'

'Buddy's right,' Mike nodded. 'We sounded dead. Especially the rhythm section.'

'That was Jet,' Jason cut in sharply. 'He was all over the place. It's all that booze he had before we went on.'

Glenn put down his can of beer and looked at Buddy for support, but this was no time for compromise. The gig had been terrible and it had to be sorted out.

'He's right, Glenn,' he said coldly. 'Your timing's right off at the moment. You'd better get it together.'

Glenn looked hurt for a moment, then a defiant look came into his eyes. 'Or what?' he challenged.

'Or we find another drummer,' Jason replied fiercely. 'I'm not playing with someone who makes me look crap.'

Glenn was shocked by the directness of Jason's reply, and for a moment his mouth fell open. An instant later his face cracked into an apologetic grin. 'OK – you're right,' he said. 'I'm a bit rusty, that's all. What can I tell you? It'll get better. I promise.'

And it did. At the next gig, in Manchester, Glenn's drumming kicked from the very first song and it sparked the whole band. Two days later, at Newcastle, they came off stage feeling great about how they'd played and by the time they got into Scotland the audiences were beginning to listen to them. In Edinburgh they even heard some calls for an encore.

Then, in Carlisle, they arrived at the venue to set up their gear and Steve, the sound man, told them that the management of Sons of Hud had sent word that the sound level was to be kept low during The Bosses' set.

'Look, I know it's a drag,' Steve added, 'but it's a hell of a compliment – they're worried by how much the audiences like you.'

Compliment or not, The Bosses were furious and they rang Rosen to complain.

'There's nothing I can do,' he told them. 'They're the stars and they call the shots. You'll be able to do the same one day. Anyway, cheer up – I've just got the mid-week chart, and "She Got" is up to 21.'

From then on, the sound system was turned down so low during The Bosses' set that they could often hear the buzz of chatter from people in the bars at the side of the hall. All this made the band more determined than ever to put on a good show and, despite the lack of volume, the audiences still seemed to like them.

Apart from bumping into them backstage a couple of times, they hardly ever saw the members of Hud. The American band had their own tour coach, plus a huge truck for all their amps and instruments, and they stayed in the best hotels while The Bosses drove from gig to gig in their small Transit van, carrying their own equipment and staying in cheap hotels. So, one evening before the show, Buddy was surprised to see Glenn standing outside the stars' dressing-room talking to Tyrone, the bass player. Later that night, as they were loading the van, Buddy asked Glenn what he'd been doing.

'Just talking. Old Tyrone's a laugh.'

'Talking to the enemy – that's death by firing squad. Who's got a gun?' Jason said.

'Nah, I asked him straight out about the sound being turned down and he swore the band didn't know anything about it. He reckons it must've been the promoters.'

'Yeah, well, he would say that, wouldn't he?' Jason sneered. 'Honest, Jet, you're so thick you make two planks look intelligent.'

'Have it your way, Einstein,' Glenn said calmly, loading the last amp onto the van. 'I'll drive.'

Wherever they went, Glenn always wanted to

drive. Even after a gig, when everybody else was tired, he had energy to spare. Sometimes, when they had a long journey at night, the rest of them dozed off in the back of the van and woke up to find Glenn still chattering away to himself about the other drivers on the road or things he could see outside. Chatter, chatter, chatter.

Jetmouth was a perfect name for him, although Buddy was careful never to use it nowadays. He knew that Glenn was hurt by all the jokey insults, and there were times when his mood suddenly changed and he became tense and snappy. The moods never lasted long but they worried Buddy – his friend wasn't the same any more.

Perhaps this new life was changing them all. They all joked about 'being famous', but there was no doubt that there was something strange and powerful about being on stage in front of a couple of thousand people. It would be so easy to let it go to your head, and Buddy had to keep reminding himself that he was still the same person he'd always been.

Funnily enough, the one who seemed most impressed by their success was Olivia. She came to a couple of gigs with journalists who wanted to interview the band, and she was really excited by what she saw.

'You're stars,' she told Buddy after the first gig she came to. 'The guy from *Hot Sounds* was knocked out – he's gonna give you a rave review – and the crowd loved you.'

'Yeah, they'd love us more if they could hear us properly.'

'The sound doesn't matter. You've got a great image on stage. It's a perfect combination. Glenn's dangerous, a bit crazy. Jason looks mean and moody, the way his hair hangs down over his face while he's playing the bass. Mike's kind of cool even when he's playing a fast guitar solo. And Dave's the cuddly one.'

'And me?' Buddy asked.

'Oh, you're the sexy one,' Olivia said, putting her arms round him.

'Oh yeah!'

'You are. All the girls were looking at you. It was a real turn-on knowing they all fancied you but I was the only one who could have you.'

'Don't be so sure,' Buddy laughed.

'I'd better be sure,' Olivia said, letting go of him and frowning. 'I mean it, Buddy.'

'OK, OK, you can be sure,' he said, trying to pull her back into his arms. But the mood was broken, and she left shortly afterwards to take the journalist from *Hot Sounds* back to London.

After she'd gone, Buddy realized that he'd believed what she'd said about the band. He'd believed it because he wanted to believe it, especially the bit about him. But it wasn't true. It was just Olivia thinking about the image she could sell to the media. After all, if he was so sexy, how come they never got any further than kissing?

As the tour went on, Glenn became more and more friendly with the members of Sons of Hud. He often spent hours in their dressing-room and only came out at the last minute to go on stage with The Bosses. One night he even announced that he was going back with the Americans to their hotel and would travel with them to the next gig. 'You can drive yourselves for a change, instead of making me do it all the time.'

'You got a nerve,' Mike exploded. 'You never want anyone else to drive.'

'Well, you got your chance now, haven't you?'

'Yeah, well I'll tell you one thing, Jet – I'm not loading your bloody drums,' Jason shouted as Glenn walked away.

'Don't worry, genius, I wouldn't let you touch 'em,' Glenn called back.

After the show Glenn loaded his drums on to the van, then ran across the car-park and jumped on to the Americans' huge bus and sat down next to Tyrone. As the bus pulled away into the night, Glenn grinned and stuck two fingers up at them.

If he meant to annoy them, he certainly succeeded. They loaded the van in tense silence, then Mike and Jason started arguing about who was going to drive. Finally Mike jerked the driver's door open with such force that it hit Jason on the knee. Jason swore and punched Mike on the side of the head. Mike hit back, and Dave and Buddy had to try to separate the twins as they punched and struggled with each other around the van. When the fight finally stopped, Mike had dropped the keys to the van, and they spent fifteen minutes groping around in the dark before they found them.

The bad mood lasted for the rest of the tour with hardly anyone speaking to each other. The atmosphere wasn't helped by the fact that for the third week in a row 'She Got' stayed at number 21 in the chart. It began to look as if it would never make the Top Twenty.

Things cheered up a bit when they got to London

for the last three shows. They were at the Hammer-smith Apollo, and Buddy's mum and dad came to the first night. Afterwards, he introduced them to Olivia, and they all went out for a meal. His mum and Olivia seemed to hit it off at once, and they chatted about work while his dad talked about the gig.

'I was well chuffed,' he said, 'watching you up there on the same stage where all the greats 'ave been – Chuck Berry, Jerry Lee Lewis. 'Course, you lot ain't in the same league yet, but it was an ace show. We was dead proud of you – eh, Carol?'

'Yeah, really proud,' his mum said, smiling at him.

After the final show there was an end-of-tour party in a night club and, when The Bosses arrived, there was a crowd of people outside, hoping to gatecrash their way in. The crush was even worse inside, and the deafening dance music made it almost impossible to talk. Glenn immediately headed to-wards where Sons of Hud were standing, while Olivia grabbed hold of Buddy and started pulling him towards the dance-floor.

'I don't fancy dancing,' he said, holding back.

'Well, I do,' she shouted in his ear. 'There's a photographer from *Sweet 16* – they're doing a photo-spread about the party. We don't want to miss some free publicity.'

Buddy reluctantly moved round the packed dance-floor with her while she tried to get near the cameras. When they finally got their picture taken, she asked Buddy to go and get some drinks while she had a word with the photographer to make sure he used it. There was a huge queue at the bar, and it took Buddy twenty minutes to order the drinks. By the time he got them, Olivia was nowhere to be seen. He pushed here and there through the crowds, looking for her, spilling most of the drinks in the process.

'Have you seen Olivia?' he asked Dave, who was dancing with one of the girls from XS.

'Yeah – she went off with some photographer. She told me to tell you it was business and she'd ring you tomorrow.'

Buddy thought it was a joke, so he laughed; but when Dave shrugged sympathetically he realized it wasn't a joke, it was true. He downed what was left of the two drinks, then went to get another one and just stood, watching the heaving mass of people from the music business. He found himself despising their trendy clothes and their phoney smiles. All they wanted to do was drink the free booze and prance around showing off to each other. They didn't care about music, all they thought about was image and making money.

Suddenly there was a roar of laughter from the other side of the room and Buddy saw people scatter as the members of Sons of Hud ran around, throwing bits of food and drink at each other. And there was Glenn, reeling around with them, grinning stupidly and hurling sausage-rolls at Tyrone.

Buddy grabbed his jacket from a chair and left.

At least outside it was cool and he could breathe. He walked quickly along the night streets until he came to the Thames. The river was high and running fast towards the sea. He stood, staring at the lights sliding on the racing water, feeling empty. Why? He was starting to get everything he'd ever dreamed of and it felt like nothing. Playing music, yes, that was great, but all the rest of the stuff – the interviews,

41

the photos, the stupid image – was almost the opposite of what he found in the music.

So, what did he find in the music? Well, when it really took off it was like almost being in touch with something special. Something lost. Like a memory he couldn't quite remember. Like now – gazing at the flickering lights on the oily water. If he could only concentrate, it would take shape and it would be perfect. He would no longer be lost in this strange world where things didn't make sense. He would understand and he would be free.

A police car raced by on the other side of the river, its siren howling across the river, and the almost-memory melted away again.

In its place were two other problems that had to be sorted out: Glenn and Olivia.

All next day he tried ringing Olivia but he kept getting her answer-phone. He couldn't get hold of Glenn either. They had planned to listen to the *Chart Show* together so, early in the afternoon, he went round to pick him up at his mother's house. He wasn't there.

'Who knows where he goes to commit his sins,' his mother said bitterly, standing at the front door with her Bible in her hand. 'Round with his cheap girlfriend, probably. On the Lord's Day, too.'

Buddy knew it would be a waste of breath to argue, so he just thanked her politely and left. On top of everything, she was wrong – Glenn wasn't with his girlfriend.

Tears filled Alice's eyes when she opened the door and saw Buddy. She asked him in and started to tell him how worried she was about Glenn.

'He's so moody, Buddy. One minute he goes on about how much he loves me, and the next he doesn't even bother to turn up. He says it's 'cos he's busy with the band but . . . Is he seeing someone else, Buddy? Groupies or something?'

'Groupies? No – we haven't got any. I swear. Listen, Alice, don't worry – I'm sure he's not seeing anyone else.'

He stayed to listen to the *Chart Show*, and when the DJ announced that 'She Got' had moved up to number 17 Alice gave him a little kiss of congratulation on his cheek.

'It means you'll be on *Top of the Pops*, doesn't it?' He nodded, and her large brown eyes shone with genuine pleasure. 'I'm so happy for you, Buddy.'

He put his arms round her and gave her a hug. She was so warm and gentle and uncomplicated compared to Olivia. She was pleased about the song for his sake, not because it would mean more publicity for the record company. Alice turned her face and pressed it against his chest, and he wondered if she could hear the thumping of his heart. He closed his eyes and rested his cheek on the top of her head as she held on to him.

For a moment they stood like that, and it could have ended there – a warm hug between two friends – but the scent of perfume from her hair was making his blood race. When she raised her pretty, round face to look at him, Buddy bent down and kissed her lips. There was a second's hesitation, then her mouth opened and her arms tightened round his back.

Still kissing her, Buddy moved the few steps to the sofa and pulled her down on top of him.

Chapter Seven

Each time Buddy rang Olivia at XS on Monday he was told she was in a meeting and couldn't come to the phone. He left a message, but she didn't call back, and when he rang her flat in the evening there was no reply. He thought she might turn up at the TV studios on Tuesday for the *Top of the Pops* rehearsal, but she didn't.

The rehearsal was terrible. Glenn arrived late, looking pale and tired, and his drumming was so sloppy that a couple of times they had to stop the song and start again. Luckily it was mainly a technical rehearsal for the camera moves, but it was embarrassing to play so badly. On top of everything, Buddy was worried that Glenn's poor drumming was connected with Alice. Perhaps she had broken her promise and told him what had happened.

The others were furious afterwards and they yelled at Glenn in the dressing-room, but he just sat, head down, and refused to speak. Mike got so angry that he hurled a guitar case at him. It hit him on the shoulder, but he still didn't move or say anything.

Eventually Buddy persuaded the others to leave while he tried to sort it out.

'What's up, mate?' Buddy asked.

'Nothing,' Glenn mumbled.

'Come on, Glenn, you turn up late, looking like a corpse, then you drum like a total plonker. What is it?'

'Nothing. I haven't had any kip, that's all.'

Buddy took a deep breath and said, 'Look, is something worrying you?'

'No. I've just been with the lads from Hud, and we went clubbing . . . stayed up and all that . . . you know. Anyway, they've gone back to the States now. So, I'll get some kip tonight and everything'll be fine, OK?'

Buddy was so relieved that it wasn't anything to do with Alice that he put his arm round Glenn's shoulder and said, 'Yeah, sure. Come on, let's go home.'

Glenn was very quiet again during the drive. When they stopped outside his house, Buddy told him the travel arrangements for the next day. Glenn nodded, then suddenly his eyes filled with tears.

'Buddy,' he said, his voice breaking as the tears began to run down his face. 'I'm cracking up, man. I'm cracking up. My mum . . . the band . . . everything. You gotta stick by me, man.'

'Yeah, course I will. Hey, you're just tired. You've got to go and get some sleep.'

Glenn sniffed and wiped the tears away with his sleeve. 'Yeah. You're my only friend.'

Glenn's words kept running round Buddy's head; late that evening, he decided he had to talk to Alice. He didn't want his mother to overhear, so he went to the nearest phone-box and kept pumping coins in while he described what had happened with Glenn.

'We're going to have to tell him,' Alice said.

'Alice, he's in a terrible state – it'll do his head in.'

'We can tell him we didn't . . . go the whole way.'

'Oh yeah, that'll cheer him up. "Things are pretty heavy, Glenn, but we haven't gone all the way yet".'

'There's no "yet". If I'm still going out with Glenn, and you're still going out with Olivia . . .'

'So what does that mean – we just forget Sunday? Alice, is that what you want?'

'I don't know. I feel all mixed up.'

'Me, too.'

Olivia turned up at the TV studios a couple of hours before the recording of *Top of the Pops*, but the band was so busy that Buddy didn't get a chance to talk to her. They were all very nervous and Buddy had to keep drinking water to stop his mouth drying up with fear. Once they were on stage, though, with the laser lights flashing round him and the audience clapping and cheering, he got caught up in the atmosphere and enjoyed himself. Afterwards, the producer came up and told them that it was one of the best live performances they'd had on the programme for ages, and he hinted that they'd be invited back if the record got into the Top Ten.

Buddy found Olivia talking to some TV people in the studio bar and he had to spend half an hour smiling and being polite before he could get her to leave.

As they crossed the car-park he let her chatter on about the show, but as soon as they were in the car he turned on her and bombarded her with questions. For a moment there was a flash of anger in her eyes, but she kept her temper and answered his questions quietly and coolly: she'd left the party to give the photographer a lift because she thought he'd be grateful and would publish the photos; she hadn't rung from XS because she was busy.

'Too busy just to pick up the phone? I don't believe you,' he snapped.

'Oh – and what do you believe? That I went off because I fancied him?' Olivia asked fiercely.

'Yes – that's exactly what I think.'

'Well, you can think what you like. I'm not going to stop doing what I want just because you're jealous. That's what my father did to my mother – stopped her working, stopped her doing anything. And then one day he just walked out. Well, that's not going to happen to me.'

Olivia got out of the car, slammed the door and walked away across the car-park. Buddy watched as she disappeared round the corner. He waited for a few minutes, hoping she might come back, then he drove after her. He sped along the road to the Tube station, but she had already gone.

Later, as he lay in bed, he made up his mind: he would stop seeing Olivia. It was over. She'd treated him badly. She couldn't love him if she treated him like that. Whatever she said, there was something strange going on with the photographer. Nobody could be too busy to pick up the phone and ring to say hello. No. It was stupid to go on. It was over.

It felt better to have made up his mind. He turned over and fell asleep.

The next morning he woke early and his first thought was about Olivia.

What a nerve he had, accusing her of being un-faithful when he had no proof . . . and when he knew full well what he'd done with Alice. *He* was the cheat.

And it was probably true that she'd been too busy to call him. Look how many times he'd popped into her office and the phone had rung non-stop. And that stuff about her father stopping her mother from doing what she wanted. No wonder she was scared of someone doing the same thing to her. He should have learned from his own parents. His dad had got used to it now, but Buddy could remember all the rows there'd been when his mum started being successful at work.

Perhaps he was like his dad. People said you couldn't escape the influence of your genes. Perhaps deep down he'd inherited his dad's attitudes, and he couldn't cope with Olivia's success.

At nine-thirty he rang XS and got straight through to her. He told her he was sorry. He'd been wrong to accuse her. He had been jealous, but it was only because he loved her so much. It wouldn't happen again. He promised.

There was a long pause. His heart felt as if it was beginning to split open. It was too late. She was going to say no. She was going to leave him. It was all over.

'Buddy, listen,' she said at last. 'I think we ought to let things cool off a bit. We're both a bit stressed. Let's have a break and see how things are. Meet up again in September. What do you say?'

'Yeah, sure – good idea.'

September. Over four months. He could stand that. It would hurt, but he could stand it. And at the end of that time he'd prove how much he loved her. And he wouldn't ever hold her back. He had to learn from his dad's mistakes.

Four months wasn't long. He could find a flat so that he'd have somewhere to take her and she would think he was more grown-up. Maybe that was his problem. Maybe he wasn't grown-up enough. He was nineteen and yet he still felt the same way he had when he was eleven or twelve. The same emotions, the same thoughts, the same fears, the same stupid games in his head, the same confusion. He'd always imagined that by the end of his teens he would be different. Not old and wise, exactly, but that things would make sense. And yet here he was, still bobbing around like a little cork lost in a huge ocean.

Well, it was time to grow up. Perhaps leaving home and living on his own would be the start.

'She Got' went up to number 12 in the next chart, climbed one place the following week, and then entered the Top Ten at number 9. As promised, The Bosses were invited back onto *Top of the Pops* and they performed the song live again. A week later it went up to number 7.

Apart from that one TV performance, things were very quiet for the band. The publicity department at XS decided not to push them any more for a while in case people got fed up with hearing about them and seeing their photos in the teen magazines. So, strangely, at the moment of their greatest success so far, they found themselves with nothing to do.

The twins and Dave went off on holiday to Spain for a couple of weeks, but Buddy decided to stay at home and look for a flat. He called round at Glenn's house once, but he wasn't there and Buddy hoped that he was with Alice.

Buddy had rung Alice as soon as he'd decided to stay with Olivia. He wanted to tell her straight out that it was all over, but instead he just rambled on about how he didn't want to hurt anybody and how maybe she ought to patch things up with Glenn. In the end Alice had agreed, but he knew he'd handled it all wrong.

Meanwhile he started looking for a flat. It had to be quite cheap because, even though he had a hit record, he was almost broke. XS had warned them that they wouldn't start getting money from the record for over six months, and even then most of it would go towards paying for the cost of making the album. They'd made some money from the tour, of course, but a lot of Buddy's share had gone towards repaying the bank loan he'd taken to buy and insure the car.

He got a list of cheap flats and went around to look at them. Some were dirty, some were damp, and all of them were depressing. He visited the first ten, then gave up.

His mum was dead against the whole idea. She said it was a waste of money to pay for something that couldn't possibly be as nice as their house and anyway she liked having him at home. And yet in the end she was the one who found the flat. One of the secretaries at her office was getting married and was giving up her flat, so Buddy went round to see it and fell in love with it at once.

It was at the top of an old house overlooking a park, and the large living-room, bedroom, kitchen and bathroom all had views of the trees below. Best of all, the rent was cheaper than some of the one-room places he'd seen. The only drawback was that the girl wasn't leaving for another four months. It was a long time to wait, but Buddy knew he'd never find anything as good, so he accepted.

'She Got' stayed at number 7 for three weeks, then

dropped two places. The day after it started to go down, the band got an urgent phone-call from Bobby Rosen. He wanted a meeting with them at once.

Chapter Eight

Rosen was sitting on the sofa with Sharkey stretched across his lap when The Bosses went into the office. He tried to ease himself out from under the huge dog, but it whined and refused to get up.

'Oh you're such a baby, Sharkey. Come on, let daddy get up and do his work,' he grunted, finally pushing the dog off and walking to his desk. 'Well, boys, "She Got" has peaked and we need a follow-up. If we can come up with another smash, we can release the album and it'll go monster. But we need a hit song fast.'

The others looked at Buddy, and a tremor of panic ran through him. He hadn't really written anything for nearly a year and he'd begun to worry that his first songs had been a fluke and that he couldn't write any more.

'Well?' Rosen asked. 'I can always pull some other writers in if you don't feel up to it . . .'

'No,' Buddy said. 'Give us a month – we'll do it.'

That evening Buddy sat down with his guitar and tried to write. He strummed various chord-sequences, humming tunes and trying to think of words and phrases to start off a song.

What could he write about? Love, of course – ninety per cent of songs were about love. But what could he say about it? I love you, You love me, Oh how happy we will be.

Stupid things that people had said a million times. And anyway, love wasn't like that. It was difficult and painful. He wasn't even sure what the word meant. Fancying someone? Caring? He cared about lots of people. Needing someone? He needed Olivia. And Alice? No, forget love. It was too confusing. Think of something else.

He looked through the newspaper. A rail crash. A murder. TV Star On Drink Driving Charge. Nothing there to write a song about. Or maybe there was, if you were inspired. He just wasn't inspired, and maybe never would be again.

A spiral of doubt began to nag away inside him. He kept strumming the guitar but his brain kept telling him he couldn't write. His own brain was trying to defeat him.

He forced himself to stay in his room all evening, but he got nothing done. Then, just before midnight, the phone rang. It was Alice.

'Buddy, I've got to see you.'

'Alice, listen, we agreed . . .'

'It's important. I've got to see you – now.'

Alice was waiting outside her house when he arrived, and he knew as soon as he saw her that he should never have agreed to meet her. She looked worried and she looked beautiful.

They drove out of town and parked on the clifftop, overlooking the sea. As soon as they arrived, Alice began to cry and Buddy just sat there, looking at the huge ribbon of moonlight shaking on the water. He mustn't get involved. But when she started to sob, he put his arm round her shoulder to comfort her. She turned to him, slipped her arms round him and pressed her tearful face against his neck.

Gradually her sobbing subsided and she started to talk. She'd tried to sort things out with Glenn but it was impossible. He hadn't even bothered to come and see her for two weeks, and then he'd suddenly arrived and he was like the old Glenn: sweet and kind and funny. For a couple of days everything had been fine. Then, tonight, he'd come round to see her and he'd been jumpy and bad-tempered. He'd started to accuse her of saying things behind his back, and telling lies about him to his mother.

'Then he asked me if there was someone else,' Alice went on, tears welling up in her eyes again. 'I didn't know what to say ... I sort of said no, but I know he didn't believe me. And I felt so awful lying to him.'

'Alice, it's not a lie. What happened between us was just ...'

'Just what?' she cried, her voice cracking with unhappiness. 'Just a bit of fun for you because you couldn't have Olivia? Is that it?'

'No!'

'You were just using me, weren't you? You don't care about me.'

'I do. I do care about you.'

She looked at him with tear-filled eyes, and a rush of emotions swept through him. Nothing else mattered but pulling her close and kissing her. Nothing else but her lips. And the warmth of her. And the smell of her. And the softness of her.

When he got home, he found himself saying to himself, 'Crazy. You're just crazy.' And that's what it felt like. When that surge of desire hit, it was like going mad. Like being swept away on a flood. Losing control. Forgetting everything. Until later. Until now, when he was alone again and he wished it hadn't happened.

He lay awake for ages, trying to think what to do, but there seemed no way out.

He woke up late, with the words 'no way out' in his head. He made a quick cup of coffee, then sat in the kitchen with his guitar, strumming chords in a slow blues riff. C7-B7-Em. No-Way-Out. The words fitted.

An hour later the song was finished, and it was good. Already he could hear in his head how it should sound. It would be completely unlike anything The Bosses had ever done.

The excitement of music lifted him, and he played the guitar all day, while words and phrases tumbled around in his head. He wrote another song that evening: a long, angry song called 'Shape of my Heart'. And by the end of a week he had five new songs.

The songs seemed so full of the pain and confusion of what he'd been going through that when he played them to the band he felt as if he was screaming out a confession. If Glenn already had suspicions about Alice, surely he would realize what the songs were about. But he didn't. None of them did.

They decided to rehearse all the songs and let Kris Dox decide which ones to record. The first rehearsal went well and the band learned the songs quickly. At the end of the session Buddy stayed behind to help Glenn put away his drum kit. He looked thin and pale, but he was charged up and excited.

'Wow, what a buzz. Some of those songs, man – they're the best you've ever done. I love that one, "Midnight Call", but my favourite is "Best of Friends": "We're not lovers, just the best of friends". It's ace stuff.'

'Thanks,' Buddy said, not daring to look Glenn in the eyes. 'Hey, what you been doing? You haven't been around.'

'Nothing much.'

'Seen much of Alice?' Buddy asked casually, bending down to pick up the bass drum.

'A bit, yeah. Hey listen, Buddy, I wanted to ask . . .'

A wave of hot shame rose into Buddy's face. This was it. He lifted the drum and looked directly at Glenn, 'Yeah?'

'Well . . . I've . . . written this song, and I wondered if . . . you know . . . we could maybe, like, learn it with yours. Just to see what it sounds like.'

'Yeah, of course we can, mate. That's great. We'll do it tomorrow.'

The relief made it easy to be enthusiastic, and Glenn's thin face lit up with pleasure. It seemed ages since he'd seen his friend smile like that, and he made up his mind to encourage him. Glenn's confidence needed boosting.

The song was called 'Driving'. It had a very simple tune and the words were a bit stupid; but Buddy kept telling Glenn how good it was, and he worked hard on a guitar riff to make it sound more interesting. Then he had a quiet word with the rest of the band and told them to go along with it in order to encourage Glenn.

They played all the songs to Kris Dox at the end of the week, and Buddy was shocked when he chose

'Best of Friends' and 'Driving' as the two they should record. Mike opened his mouth to say something, but Buddy sent a warning glance to stop him. Glenn was thrilled, of course, and while he talked to Kris about how he wanted the song to sound, Buddy went out into the corridor with the others.

'This has got to stop right here,' Mike exploded. 'I know we're supposed to be cheering Glenn up, but I'm not recording something that sounds like the bloody Eurovision Song Contest. It's crap.'

'Look,' Buddy reassured him, 'Rosen's going to hate it. Let him be the bad guy who turns it down. That way, Glenn thinks we're on his side and stops being paranoid.'

In the end they actually spent more time recording 'Driving' than they did 'Best of Friends', mainly because Buddy just couldn't sing the words as if he believed in them. They did over thirty takes of his vocal, and even then he knew that Kris Dox would have to edit bits from various takes – something that Buddy hated because it lost the 'live' feel.

Two weeks later, Kris played them the final mix of the tapes. 'Best of Friends' sounded good and it was a much better song, but Kris had given 'Driving' a huge sound production. He'd used a drum machine to add a pounding dance-beat, and there were so many overdubs on the vocal that Buddy hardly recognized his own voice.

It was exactly the kind of music that Buddy hated – soulless, machine music that meant nothing. He felt sure that Rosen would feel the same way when he heard it the next day, but he couldn't help worrying.

*

That evening, when Buddy got back home, there was a letter waiting for him and he recognized the writing at once. Charmian Rybeero. He hadn't heard from her or her twin brother, Julius, for over two years and he ripped open the envelope in excitement. Even though it was four years since they'd moved away, they had been his best friends during the worst time in his life and he still felt close to them.

Dear Buddy,

Remember me? I hope so. Perhaps you're living in some big Rock Star mansion now and this letter won't reach you. As you'll guess, I've heard your record and seen you on TV. It's a lovely song and you sing it brilliantly – it makes me cry. Really. I always thought you were a star!

You don't half look different, all grown up! I almost didn't recognize you on *Top Of The Pops*. That didn't stop me rushing round telling everyone that I knew you. Honestly I felt dead proud – talk about reflected glory. Of course I'm happy for you but it's sad to think we've drifted apart. I often think about the good times we had when we were young. Do you?

When we were young – makes us sound like old codgers, doesn't it? Nearly twenty, though. Gulp! Time goes by.

What about me? I was planning to go to University but Dad had a heart attack in my last year at school and he had to give up the taxi business. My uncle took it over and Mum still works there – on the radio as usual (do you remember?) – but Dad can't do much because he gets very tired. There's not much money coming in and I couldn't expect them to pay out for my studies so ... Maybe one day. Meanwhile I'm working in a department store. They call it 'trainee manager', I call it 'shop assistant'. It's not bad and we have some laughs but ...

I suppose I'm still the old Char you remember (if you do, of course) but you wouldn't recognize Julius. Can you imagine dreadlocks, the whole Rasta bit? It's true. Mum and Dad keep hoping it's only a phase but I'm not so sure – I know how ANGRY he is. Yes, jolly old Jules who never cared about anything. Sometimes even I can't understand him and you know how close we are (were?). He's crazy about music, though, and he plays drums in a small band that do a kind of rap/reggae fusion. The raps are all black power stuff – really heavy.

Well, I think that's all my news. Actually there's loads more – I haven't told you about the books I've been reading or things I think about or ... but maybe you're too busy now you're a STAR. If you get any time, write back – eh? Don't let's lose touch. You know you were always special to me.

Love,
Char.

PS. Jules says 'Hi!' (You're lucky, he doesn't usually talk to white guys.)

Buddy felt so happy to hear from his old friend that he read the letter four times, then sat down and wrote a reply. Telling Charmian all the things that were on his mind – without going into details about

Alice – seemed to make the problems less important. Even the problem of 'Driving'.

Rosen was smiling as they filed into his office and sat down on the sofa.

'"Best of Friends" – what a song!' he began, and Buddy relaxed. 'Terrific stuff. And Kris says there are some other crackers for the next album, too. Great. But, I hear that it's Glenn we have to thank for the next single.'

There was a stunned silence, then Mike leaned forward and said, 'You want "Driving" to be the single?'

'Hole in one,' Rosen beamed.

'You can't,' Mike gasped. 'It's a joke song. People'll laugh at us.'

'We're the ones who'll be laughing,' Rosen chuckled. 'All the way to the bank. I've got a hunch that it's going to be a huge hit.'

'No!' Dave shouted, standing up and taking a couple of steps towards Rosen's desk.

Sharkey raised his head and sat up, growling softly. Dave stopped and turned to the rest of the band for support.

'Tell him, someone,' he pleaded. 'Buddy, tell him.'

Buddy saw Glenn looking at him, but he stood up all the same. He might be letting his friend down, but this had to be stopped.

'Look, Bobby,' Buddy said, trying to stay calm and reasonable. 'We're all pleased that Glenn's started writing, but there's no way we can release that song.'

A look of shock and pain crossed Glenn's face and Buddy knew how much he was hurting him.

'I hear what you're saying,' Rosen said, leaning back in his chair, 'but I'm afraid it's out of your hands.'

'What's that supposed to mean?' Buddy cut in, his voice rising with anger. 'It's our record. We can do what we want. And we don't want "Driving".'

'Is that right? Check your contract, laddie. XS owns you.' Rosen spoke quietly but there was no missing the cold steel behind the words. 'You make the product, but we make the decisions. We decide whether to sell things or to shelve them. Now, which of those do you want to happen to your album? Hm?'

He looked at each of them in turn, his eyes hidden by the glare of light on his glasses. No one spoke or moved.

'Good,' he said. 'We're all agreed. "Driving" will be the next single.'

CHAPTER NINE

Glenn disappeared.

He stormed out after the meeting and went into hiding. Buddy kept ringing his home, but his mother said he was probably staying with friends in London.

He was still missing when Olivia rang, two weeks later, and gave Buddy the details of interviews that had been set up to promote 'Driving'. He scribbled down all the details and then, before there was a chance to chat, she said goodbye and put the phone down. No chance to tell her how wonderful it was to hear her voice. And how he couldn't wait to see her again. And how he was getting a flat. And . . . But she was gone, and his heart was being squeezed with pain.

The first interview and photo session was at *Teen Beat*, and when the band met up in a coffee bar opposite the magazine's offices they were all feeling edgy.

'You realize they've probably had an advance copy of "Driving",' Jason said. 'They'll know it stinks.'

'Trust Jet not to be here when we need him,' Mike grumbled. 'Now we've got no one to blame.'

'Nobody's heard from him?' Buddy asked.

'Apparently he dropped into XS yesterday,' Dave said, and they all looked at him in surprise. 'Yeah, Anita from Reception said he called in, went up to see Paul Maxton, the sound engineer, for about ten minutes, then left.'

'Paul Maxton?' Buddy asked. 'What for?'

'Well, that's what I've been wondering,' Dave said. 'Either he wanted to ask him some technical questions about recording, or he was after some of Paul's other speciality.'

'What's that?' Jason asked.

'Well, rumour has it that if you're looking to twist your head, Paul's your man.'

'Drugs? Glenn?' Buddy said slowly, letting it sink in.

'Think about it,' Dave said.

It didn't need much thinking about. It was so obvious that none of them could believe they hadn't seen it before. Everything fell into place: the mood changes, the paranoia, the energy bursts and the slumps. All the signs.

'What kind of stuff do you reckon he's doing?' Buddy asked.

'Dunno. Speed, probably,' Dave said.

'I don't care if he's mainlining toilet cleaner,' Jason said. 'He's a big boy and it's up to him if he wants to ruin his life. But I don't want him screwing up things for us.'

The photo session took place in the courtyard behind the *Teen Beat* offices and consisted of shots of the band sitting on an old sports car.

'Who thought this up?' Mike complained to the photographer. 'Driving. Sports car. It's a bit obvious, isn't it?'

'Naff idea for a naff song,' the photographer snapped back, and they all winced.

It was hard to keep smiling and posing for the photos after that and they all had a feeling of doom. 'Driving' was going to be a disaster and there was nothing they could do about it.

Buddy's brain was racing on the way back and he needed someone to talk to, but when he got home his mum was working late. He drove around to the breaker's yard, but the caravan was locked and his dad wasn't even in his usual pub, down the road.

A voice inside him kept whispering about going to see Alice. He knew that if he went it would be too much of a temptation, and he started to drive home. Then, at the roundabout, he found himself swinging the car all the way round and heading back towards her house. As she opened the door and smiled and invited him in, he knew he should leave.

They went into the sitting-room and watched TV

with her parents, and he deliberately sat on a chair rather than next to her on the sofa. Yet as soon as her parents went up to bed he found his desire starting to stir. He wanted to be near her. No, stay away from her. Think about Olivia. Think about Glenn. He couldn't cheat on them.

Just a little closer – nothing would happen.

He went and sat on the floor next to her. Not touching. Just near. And he wasn't going to make a move. If she didn't react, he wouldn't do anything. It would be better like that.

He sat there, torn in half. Part of him wanted to get up and leave. Now. Before anything happened. It would be so good to go home without betraying anyone. But another part of him was willing her to make the first move. Her knee was only an inch away from his shoulder. Just a slight shift and she would be touching him. Come on, Alice, move.

When her hand began gently brushing the top of his head, the pounding of his heart rocked his chest and he turned round and pulled her down on to the floor next to him. He kissed her, crushing his mouth against her until they were both straining against each other.

Here. Tonight. Now. Yes.

'Buddy, no,' she whispered urgently and pulled away from him.

The blood was pulsing so fast in his body that, as he sat up, he felt for a moment as if he was going to faint. His lips were thick from kissing, and a sharp ache started to knife up into his belly.

'God, Alice, we've got to stop this,' he mumbled.

'It's my parents. I'm scared they might come down.'

'I don't mean that. I mean everything. Seeing each other. Listen, I'm going.'

He staggered to his feet, the pain piercing right through his guts.

'We mustn't see each other any more, Alice.' He tried to say it gently, but the pain was making him clench his teeth and the words came out cold.

'It's Olivia, isn't it?' she said. There were tears in her eyes and he wanted to get hold of her and comfort her.

'Olivia. Glenn. It's not right. Look, I really like you but ... Maybe we can just be friends, like before.'

He wanted to say more, but the sharp stabbing was getting worse so he grabbed his jacket and left.

Bit by bit the ache faded away as he drove home. It was over. He mustn't see her again like tonight. He had to stop thinking about Alice. He had to.

CHAPTER TEN

His dad called round early next morning and Buddy played 'Driving' to him.

'Blimey, what a load of manure, Buddy. You can't 'ave that as your next single.'

'We've got no choice. XS say they own us and that we're just a product to sell.'

'Yeah, well that's what 'appens when big business gets you by the short and curlies. You'll just 'ave to write a fantastic new song for the next single when this one bombs.'

He was right, and Buddy spent the rest of the morning playing his guitar and trying to write. Just after midday the phone rang but he didn't answer it. It was Alice's lunch break and he didn't want to risk a painful phone-call with her.

What would she be feeling?

He didn't know. In fact, when he thought about it, he realized he didn't know very much about her at all. She was pretty. She didn't talk much. She was gentle. That was about it. The rest was just about wanting to make love to her. Make love. How could you use that word about someone you didn't even know properly? Make lust.

Could that be true? Was it just sex? No, not just that. When he'd been close to her, mouth on mouth, body against body, there'd been lust of course, but something else as well. Something almost sad. As if the two of them – nearly strangers, really – had been searching. Reaching out. Trying to know someone else. But then sex had taken over. He had stopped thinking about her and had only thought of himself. *His* pleasure, *his* need, *his* hunger.

He strummed his guitar, beating out a rhythm on the bass string, a rhythm like the thumping of his blood when he was with Alice. Lines started to come to him.

> Love with a stranger
> Love in the dark
> Lost hearts in danger
> Blinded by sparks
> Love with a stranger
> Love with a shark.

He was still working on the song an hour later when

the front-door bell rang. He went downstairs, praying that it wouldn't be Alice. It was Glenn. He was pale and there were dark bags under his eyes, but he grinned cheerfully and invited himself in.

They went into the kitchen and Buddy made some coffee while Glenn bubbled away – joking, telling funny stories about people he'd seen and programmes he'd watched on TV. No explanation of where he'd been. No reference to 'Driving'. Just jabber, jabber. Speed talk. Stoned talk.

Buddy put a mug of coffee down in front of the drummer, waiting for a break in the non-stop chatter.

Finally Glenn took a sip of coffee and Buddy seized the opportunity. 'Listen, Glenn, I know about the drugs. I even know who you get them from – Paul Maxton. Don't tell me it isn't true, 'cos I know it is. And you've got to cut it out, mate, 'cos it's screwing you up. I want to help you. So do the rest of the guys. But you've got to stop.'

It had all burst out of him in a mess, but at least he had said it.

Glenn put down the mug and looked at him with a half-smile and Buddy knew, with a surge of disappointment, what he was going to say.

'Drugs? Get away. Yeah, OK, I've bought a bit of blow from Paul sometimes and I did some "E" once when Hud were over here and we went clubbing, but that's all. It's no big deal.'

He was lying. Buddy could see it in his eyes – those hollow eyes that wouldn't meet his. And he suddenly realized what a huge gap had opened up between them.

'Oh come on, Glenn,' Buddy said, putting his

66

hand on Glenn's arm and shaking it gently. 'Your drumming's been going to pieces, you've drifted away from the band. You haven't even turned up for the publicity of your own song.'

'That's what this is about,' Glenn shouted, standing up. 'You want me out of the band. You all do. I used to think you were my friend . . .'

'I am. I am. I don't want you out of the band. No one does. But you've got to cut out the drugs.'

'I'm not on drugs,' Glenn yelled.

'You are. It's obvious. I even reckon I know what it is – Speed.'

'Oh yeah, you're a bloody expert, are you?' Glenn sneered.

'Glenn, you've got to believe me. I want to help. I want you in the band, but you've got to straighten up. How can you be in it if you go missing for a couple of weeks? There are loads of publicity things going on, and we don't even know if you'll be there.'

Glenn walked to the door, then stopped. 'Don't worry, I'll be there. Just don't try and tell me it's got anything to do with friendship, right?'

He crashed the front door behind him, and Buddy sat down at the table and reached for his mug. His hands were shaking.

From then on Glenn turned up at all the publicity meetings that XS arranged to promote the single. He was always talkative and funny with the journalists and photographers but said hardly anything to the members of the band.

Then the reviews started to appear, and they were terrible. The *Melody Maker* called the record 'mindless trash' and the *NME* said it was 'an instant candidate for a place in the Top Ten Worst Records of All Time'.

Even the teeny magazines which carried pin-up photos of the band managed to get digs in about the record. One had the headline 'Are The Bosses One Hit Wonders?' over the photo.

The record was released, and for about a week Buddy seemed to hear it every time he turned on the radio, usually followed by some snide remark by the DJ. Then, suddenly, silence. Total silence. No airplay. No more articles. No chart entry.

Diana Armstrong in the Publicity Department told them that sales were 'very poor' and that XS had decided to drop any further promotion. She made a few reassuring noises about a poster campaign for the album, but they all sensed that the record company had lost confidence in them. They kept trying to call Rosen, but the message from his secretary was always the same: 'Sorry, he's in a meeting and he'll be tied up all day.'

As Jason said in his usual bitter way, 'From Flavour of the Month to Stink of the Year in one easy step.'

The one who was hardest hit, of course, was Glenn. His speedy, fast-talking, fast-joking front split apart and was replaced by a haunted, downcast silence. Buddy kept trying to cheer him up but every time he was met with a hate-filled look and a snarled 'Get lost!'

Even the release of the album didn't help. The reviews were nearly all positive and some were very enthusiastic, but they all brought up 'Driving' again. The comments in the *Music Mirror* summed up the way everyone managed to hide their praise for the album behind cruel references to the single:

68

The first album by recent chart-floppers, The Bosses, is called *In Business* and they've wisely left off their monster miss, the dismal 'Driving'. They write their own material and there are some songs with tasty tunes and stand-out lyrics, including their hit 'She Got'. Will the album put them in business or has the single put them on the dole queue?

Buddy tried to concentrate on the positive things, but he had a horrible feeling that most people would remember comments like 'chart-floppers' and 'monster miss'.

The album came into the chart at number 52 – then, to his surprise, it shot up to 32. Perhaps he'd been wrong; perhaps people would forget 'Driving' and the album would sell on the strength of 'She Got'. Perhaps people would discover what good songs there were on the album, and word would get around. The next week, though, it slipped to 49 and he knew he hadn't been wrong. The following week the album dropped out of the chart completely.

A few days later, Glenn came round to Buddy's house. It was still the summer holiday season but a bitterly cold wind was blowing and the drummer was shivering as he stood on the doorstep. Buddy invited him in, but Glenn shook his head and looked away down the path.

'I've just come round to tell you, I'm out of the band,' he said, then trembled as the wind whipped his flimsy jacket open.

'What do you mean – out?' Buddy asked.

'Out. I've finished. I'm quitting.'

'You can't do that, Glenn. Why?'

'It's what you all want.'

'It's not. Don't be stupid. Glenn – don't go!'

But Glenn hurried away down the path, hunched up against the cold. Buddy closed the front door and started up the stairs to his room then changed his mind and dashed into the kitchen and grabbed his coat and the car keys.

He caught up with Glenn near the park and drew up alongside him.

'Glenn,' he called, leaning across and opening the passenger door. 'Please get in – we've got to talk. Please.'

Glenn was shivering, so Buddy put the heater on full and drove through the town and out along the coast road. He pulled into a car-park near the coastguard station. The wind rocked the car, and iron-grey waves curled and crashed on to the shingle as they sat there with the engine running and the heater blasting away. Fine spray began to mist the windscreen.

Glenn stayed silent, but it wasn't hard to guess all the reasons that had made him decide to quit, so Buddy started to go through them one by one. The jokes about being thick, the nickname, the band's rejection of 'Driving' – Buddy went through it all, saying that he thought they'd behaved badly and that he understood how Glenn must feel.

'But you're wrong, mate, if you think we want you out. You're a great drummer and we need you.'

There was a long silence, then Glenn began to shake again, but this time it wasn't the cold. He slid down in his seat and hid his face as he began to cry.

Buddy put his hand on Glenn's shoulder in a clumsy attempt to comfort him. At that moment another car turned in off the road and stopped at the far end of the car-park and Buddy took his hand away. Stupid. Stupid. To worry about some stranger thinking that they might be gay, but he couldn't help it. He stared out at the blurred coastline and waited for Glenn to stop crying.

'You were right,' Glenn said at last, sniffing and wiping his eyes. 'I've been doing stuff.'

'Speed?' Buddy said after a pause.

Glenn nodded and his face was lined with misery.

'A lot?'

'Yeah. I tried stopping, but it's a bad down, Buddy. A bad down,' he repeated, shaking his head as tears started rolling down his face again. 'And my mum found some of my gear. Now she keeps saying she's gonna throw me out. Oh God, I want to die, man . . .' Glenn sank lower in his seat and crossed his arms over his face while he sobbed.

Buddy just sat there and waited for him to calm down, then he started to talk quietly, telling him everything would be OK. He could get help to quit the drugs; the band would stick by him; his mum would change her mind when she knew he was off the drugs; he could sort things out with Alice. He even told Glenn about the flat, and he promised to let him have a key so that he could use it whenever he wanted.

And bit by bit, Glenn responded. He stopped crying and began to talk about the drugs. And once he started he couldn't stop, pouring out the details that he'd hidden for so long.

By the time he had finished it was dark, and all that could be seen of the sea was an occasional line of white breaker when the moon burst briefly from behind the scudding clouds. The engine was still running and the heater was pumping out warm air, but Buddy felt chilled.

As they drove back into town, Glenn promised that he would see a counsellor at the Drug Centre if Buddy fixed an appointment for him.

'And you're not kidding . . . you know, about the band?' Glenn asked as they sat in the car outside his house.

'It's the truth. We all want you to be the drummer. So bloody get this stuff out of your life, right? OK, go and get some sleep. I'll call you tomorrow evening.'

Buddy felt drained on the way home. 'Driving'; the failure of the album; an uncertain future for the band. And now, on top of all that, he had to cope with Glenn's damn drug problem. A moment of anger at Glenn's stupidity came and went.

Stupid or not, Glenn was his friend. It was going to be a struggle, and he didn't need the extra hassle; but he owed it to him. He'd let him down so badly with Alice – he couldn't let him down again.

Still, autumn was coming. Soon he would have his flat. Soon he'd start seeing Olivia again. A few more weeks, and life would be great again.

CHAPTER ELEVEN

Buddy made an appointment for Glenn at the Drug Centre, but a couple of days later they rang and said he hadn't turned up. Buddy was disappointed and angry, but there was nothing he could do: Glenn had gone missing again.

'Look, he's just a liability,' Jason said when Buddy told them. 'I vote we dump him and get someone else.'

'I agree,' Mike said. 'We know this guy called Rais. Killer drummer. And he's reliable, too.'

Buddy and Dave argued for giving Glenn another chance, but it was Bobby Rosen who really put a stop to the whole idea of changing the drummer.

'Now listen,' Rosen said when they finally got to see him. 'A lot of people here call you "Rosen's Folly" because they think I should never have signed you. But I know that if we can get the strategy right we can turn you into a top band.'

He stopped and looked at them all. Buddy felt like asking how 'Driving' fitted into the strategy, but he kept his mouth shut.

'And whatever you think about him now,' Rosen went on, 'Glenn is part of it. He's a good drummer – but, far more important than that, he's part of the chemistry. Every great band has got it – a sort of magic combination. Lose Glenn, lose any one of you, and the whole thing falls apart. So, no matter how much of a pain in the neck he is, you need him.'

The other thing they needed was a new album, and Rosen said that they should spend the next three months writing new songs and coming into the studio to do quick demo recordings of them. Mike suggested that they also needed more experience playing live, and Rosen promised he'd look into setting up some gigs for them.

A couple of days later Buddy got a phone-call from Glenn to say that he'd been staying in London but that he'd sorted things out with his mum and that he was coming back to live with her.

'And what about the Drug Centre? I set up a meeting and you didn't even bother to go.'

'Yeah, I'm sorry about that. But I don't need it. I can handle it on my own – it's not a problem.'

'You mean you're off the drugs, then?'

'Yeah, of course I am. Listen, I'll come round and see you in your new place when you get settled in.'

Buddy was sure that Glenn hadn't given up drugs, but for the next few days he was too busy with the move to the flat to worry about anything else.

He felt strangely nervous about it all, and when he actually began to pack his things into boxes he couldn't think of one good reason for going. At the last moment he decided not to take his posters as if, by leaving them on his bedroom wall, it would still be his room and he could always come home if he wanted to.

It felt like a big turning-point in his life, and his mum obviously felt the same. She didn't say much, but he knew she was thinking that the house was going to feel empty without him. Of course, it would be the ideal time for her to get back together with his dad, but he didn't say so to her.

He did try to drop a hint to his dad, though, when they were loading his stuff into the van they'd borrowed from Des King's breaker's yard.

'I expect Mum'll find it a bit lonely, living on her own,' he said as he stowed his guitars between some boxes.

'Nah, she'll get used to it. You know what she's like,' his dad said.

End of conversation.

Although it was a furnished flat and he was only moving his personal belongings, it still took him and his dad all afternoon to lug things up the three flights of stairs while his mum went round the flat cleaning everything in sight.

'Don't know why you bother, Carol,' his dad teased. 'You know what kids are – the place'll be a tip after a couple of days.'

'What, like your caravan?' she laughed.

They all sat and had a cup of tea afterwards and Buddy wanted them both to stay. He volunteered to go and get fish and chips or a pizza so they could have a meal together as a sort of flat-warming.

'Nah, some other time, mate – I've gotta go. I've got a date tonight,' his dad said.

'Yes, I've got to go, too,' his mum added.

'You got a date as well?' his dad asked.

'No, just . . . I've just got, you know, things to sort out,' she said.

'Well, don't sit moping at home,' his dad went on. 'Ring up one of your fellas, get him to take you out.'

'Don't be silly, Terry, I haven't got any fellas,' she laughed, then went red.

There was an embarrassed silence, then they both got up and gathered their things together. Buddy went to the front door with them and watched them drive off in different directions.

He spent a lot of time arranging his things and it was fun to feel that he was in charge, but at the end of the evening, when he sat down and opened a bottle of beer, he suddenly felt lonely. It was so quiet that he could hear the branches of the trees creaking as they swayed in the park below. He was just about to put some music on when the phone rang.

'Buddy, hi,' his mum said. 'Just ringing to see if you're OK.'

'Yeah, fine. What about you?'

'Yeah, fine. I'm just going to bed but I thought I'd ring . . . Anyway, 'night.'

''Night,' he said and listened as she put the phone down at the other end. He could picture her so clearly, turning off the light in the hall and beginning to climb the stairs.

He stayed up late, reading, but he still couldn't sleep when he went to bed. The wind was howling outside and something was knocking on the roof. Supposing some tiles came off – would he have to get them fixed? There was a moment of panic as he thought of all the things he'd have to cope with on his own.

Yes, but there was the freedom, too. He was in his own place. He was his own boss. And with any luck, Olivia would soon be coming to stay. The nights wouldn't be so lonely then.

There was a painful tugging in Buddy's heart as he sat in his car outside XS waiting for Olivia. In a couple of minutes he would see her again after twenty weeks. Twenty weeks of missing her. This time he was determined to make it work.

She came out of the building dead on time and waved to him, but then she stood talking to the guy who'd come out with her. It was Paul Maxton. A couple of times Buddy had thought of going to Paul and threatening to tell the cops if he sold any more drugs to Glenn, but it certainly wouldn't be a good time to do it now.

Olivia went on chatting and laughing with Paul

76

for another ten minutes then, when they finally stopped talking, she reached up and kissed him on the cheek. A wave of anger swept through Buddy.

'Hi,' she said as she got in the car. 'Sorry, I got caught up with Paul.'

'Yeah, I noticed,' Buddy said before he could stop himself, then added, 'He's a creep.'

'Oh, don't start all that jealousy stuff,' Olivia sighed. Then she sat back and twisted his rear mirror towards her so that she could check her make-up. 'Anyway, where are you taking me?'

Weeks ago he'd seen an article about what was supposed to be the trendiest restaurant in town. It was at the top of a high building, overlooking the Thames at Chelsea, and he knew it was the kind of place that Olivia would love.

He was right. When they stopped outside she said, 'Clenaghan's? Oh, it's great. I've been here a couple of times and the food's wonderful.'

The river shone orangey-red in the setting sun and they could see all the way downstream to the Houses of Parliament. It was a wonderful view and Olivia was impressed that he'd managed to get a table next to a window. He'd almost forgotten what a non-stop talker she was, and she rattled away about the publicity campaigns she'd been working on, only pausing briefly to look at everyone who came in the door.

A couple of times Buddy tried to steer the conversation away from work, but it was no use. What made it worse, she managed to talk about almost every band and singer on XS Records, but she didn't once mention The Bosses. Perhaps she was one of the people who called them 'Rosen's Folly'.

After the meal, they drank their coffee while Olivia looked around, naming all the celebrities who were there. Buddy had recognized a couple of TV actors, but she knew almost everybody: fashion models, recording executives, a film director, agents.

'Actually,' she said, 'it's a bit light on big names tonight. Usually there are real "faces" here – you know, top movie stars, the lot. Sam often hangs around outside on the off-chance of getting a good shot of someone.'

'Who's Sam?' Buddy asked.

'A photographer I know.'

'The one you met at that party?' he asked, feeling the blood drain from his face.

'Yes, we've become friends,' Olivia said flatly, and her eyes warned him not to go on.

So he didn't go on. He knew what she was thinking – he was as bad as her father, as bad as his own dad, as bad as all men. They wanted to be the boss. That's exactly what she hated. And that's what made her so independent and exciting. It was what made him love her. And she was so beautiful. And he wanted her to love him, and he didn't want her to walk out. So he tried to push the jealousy out of his heart. He smiled and touched her hand and asked if she'd liked the meal.

'Do you still see your parents?' Buddy asked as they drove back to her flat.

She laughed briefly, a sarcastic laugh. But she didn't say anything.

'Do you?' he insisted.

'My mother sometimes. Christmas, birthdays. My father, never. He's in India. He wrote to me once, just after he got there, telling me he'd found peace with some religious group. Great, eh? He wrecks people's lives then goes off and finds peace for himself.'

'How old were you when he went?'

'Twelve.'

'It must have hurt,' Buddy said, remembering the pain he'd felt when his mum had left.

'No, I was glad to see him go. My mother went to pieces, though. She just can't live without some bloke telling her what to do, so she fell for the first pig who came along. A rich pig this time. He couldn't wait to shove me off to a posh boarding school. That's what hurt.'

Olivia stopped talking, and they drove in silence. He glanced at her, worried that the memories might have upset her, but her face showed nothing.

When they got to her flat, she opened the car door and started to get out, but he took hold of her arm.

'Remember I was getting a flat?' he said. 'I've got it. Maybe you could come down there sometime.'

'Maybe,' she said, and got out.

'Olivia . . . I love you.'

She smiled.

'I know.'

She shut the door and walked towards the house.

Chapter Twelve

Buddy got into a routine of writing every day, then meeting up with the band at the end of each week to rehearse and do quick demo recordings of the new songs. Glenn turned up for all the sessions and his drumming was good, but Buddy was sure he was still on drugs. He was pale and thin and his non-stop talking was as speedy as ever. Jason and Mike kept telling him to shut up and, once, there was a near fight when Jason grabbed some of Glenn's drumsticks and threw them at him.

Then Glenn started dropping in to the flat nearly every day. As promised, Buddy had given him a key, and he began to look forward to seeing Glenn's grinning face peering round the door. He often got lonely in the flat on his own and it was good to have someone to talk to – although Glenn did most of the talking. Buddy hoped that they might be able to sort out the drugs problem; but Glenn never mentioned it and, on the one occasion when Buddy tried to bring the subject up, he got angry and left.

Glenn did talk about Alice, though, and it always made Buddy feel strange. Glenn kept saying how much he loved her and how right they were for each other, but Buddy couldn't help noticing how often he also talked about the rows they had.

Late one afternoon Glenn was lying on the sofa with his eyes closed while Buddy was playing some soft, sad chords. He was so still that Buddy thought he was asleep and he almost jumped when Glenn suddenly spoke.

'Do you ever think about dying, Buddy?'

'No, not really,' he lied.

There was a long silence and Buddy felt his heart pumping hard.

'I don't know why,' Glenn went on at last, 'but sometimes I get this feeling that I'm gonna die young.'

Buddy could hardly believe it. He would never have guessed that Glenn worried about things like that. Perhaps everyone did. Perhaps all his own worries about dying young meant nothing. Now was the chance to talk to Glenn about them. Tell him that Buddy Holly's death in a plane crash on a snowy February day in 1959 had haunted him for years because they shared the same name ... Tell him. But he didn't.

'Don't be daft, Glenn,' he said.

Don't be daft. A stupid, meaningless thing to say. But he said it.

Glenn opened his eyes and looked at him, then looked away.

Buddy began playing some fast, loud chords and the moment passed.

Glenn was there the day that Dave rang to say that Rosen had fixed up a short tour of some of the best clubs round the country. There were twenty gigs in all, starting at the end of the month. Buddy had just begun to tell Glenn the good news when the phone rang again.

'Hello,' he said.

'Buddy, it's Alice.'

'Oh, hi,' he said, turning away from Glenn and pressing the phone tighter to his ear.

'I know I shouldn't ring like this,' she said, 'but I want to see you. I've tried to work things out with Glenn but ... Buddy, I miss you.'

'Hey, listen, I've got someone here at the moment. I'll give you a call some other time – OK?' he said quickly and put down the phone before she had a chance to say any more.

He turned around to see Glenn watching him closely, so he put on a big smile and went on telling him details about the tour.

After Glenn had gone, Buddy rang Alice. He wanted to be angry but, when he heard her voice, he couldn't. She apologized immediately and said she'd guessed that Glenn had been there. Could they meet? Just to talk things over?

'Alice, no,' he said gently. 'Look . . . I don't think I can trust myself to see you. Every time I see you I . . . It's just not fair on anybody Glenn, Olivia . . . We just can't.'

There was a silence and he could feel himself weakening. It would be good to see her. He saw so little of Olivia – she was always so busy. And Alice was always so loving and warm. He still thought about her a lot. He'd even dreamed about her a couple of times. Yeah – go on: see her.

'OK, I understand,' Alice said sadly and put the phone down before he had a chance to speak.

He almost rang back, but he didn't.

The band rehearsed hard every day before the tour, working on some of the new songs as well as some of the older material, building up a two-hour show. They were all looking forward to gigging again, although Glenn didn't seem as keen as the others, and Buddy asked him if everything was OK.

'Yeah, sure,' he said. 'Just makes me feel nervous – you know, being out there . . . playing in front of crowds.'

'Don't worry – it'll be great,' Buddy told him.

'Yeah. On the road again, eh? Sex, drugs and rock'n'roll.' Glenn stopped and his eyes flicked away from Buddy's. 'Well, sex and rock'n'roll, anyway.'

The weekend before the tour began, Buddy stayed with the twins and Dave. It meant kipping on their floor, but it gave him the chance to see Olivia. She'd been so busy that they'd hardly been able to see each other, and he knew they wouldn't be able to meet for a month during the tour. He'd arranged to see her for the whole weekend, but at the last minute she'd had to accept another invitation for the Sunday. Buddy didn't ask her what. Instead, he set about trying to make the Saturday a day to remember, choosing things he knew she liked to do.

They spent the morning and most of the afternoon looking round the stalls at Portobello Market. Just to walk by her side made him tingle and, when she grabbed his hand to show him something she'd seen, he couldn't stop himself from grinning with sheer pleasure. He bought her an old Afghan rug that she said would look great in her room, and she was so delighted she threw her arms round his neck and kissed him.

Just before they left the market she saw some antique earrings, gold with small emeralds, and she spent ages trying them on. They suited her perfectly, and the emeralds picked up the colour of her eyes; but in the end she decided she couldn't afford them. When she wandered off to look at another stall, Buddy bought them.

They were terribly expensive but it was worth it to see her eyes light up when he went across and gave them to her. That's all he wanted: to make her happy. If she was happy, she would love him.

In the evening he took her to the theatre, to a big musical show that she'd been wanting to see for ages. He thought the story was boring and none of the songs seemed to have any tunes, but Olivia loved it. In the restaurant afterwards she talked about why the show had been so good, and he didn't want her to think he was stupid so he just kept agreeing with her.

The only slightly bad moment came when they were outside her flat at the end of the evening. She started talking about some publicity she was planning for XS's bands, and Buddy pointed out that she hadn't mentioned The Bosses.

'Well, after "Driving" you're a bit of a publicity nightmare,' she said. 'Nobody wants to know. You lot are going to have to do something to turn your career around, or you're going to be last year's thing.'

It hurt to hear it put so coldly, but he knew she was right. And it was good to know that she could be so honest and truthful with him – it must mean that she respected him.

As he drove home he vowed that he would do all he could on the tour to prove to everyone, but most of all to Olivia, that The Bosses were still on the way to the top.

The tour went even better than he'd hoped. It was hard at first to be playing small venues again after the big places they'd played on the Hud tour, but at least the clubs were packed each night with people who'd only come to see The Bosses.

Best of all, the band was playing better than ever and they were all thrilled by the new style of music they were making. Even the old songs had a harder, bluesier edge to them, and the reaction of the crowds was amazing. By the end of every set the fans were packed tight against the stage, moving and jumping to the driving sound. Buddy was playing harmonica now on some of the songs; his long, wailing riffs always got an incredible reaction, with people punching their fists in the air and whooping with excitement.

Buddy had his twentieth birthday during the tour and it seemed significant that he celebrated it by playing a gig. He had left his teens behind and his music had grown up, too.

Although it was only a small-scale tour, they got quite a bit of publicity in the music papers and there was a great review in *Beating Tracks*:

The Bosses Get Tough

Their record company may want to turn them into wimps with singles like 'Driving' but The Bosses have their roots in Rock, Soul and Blues. They came out snarling and raising hell at Gio's in Nottingham last week. Passion steamed off them. Drums and bass pounding like a hurricane's heartbeat. Guitars riding the blast like streaks of lightning. Harmonica solos stabbing through the storm. It was one glorious, DIRTY noise. Catch them before they self-combust.

'How come no one ever mentions the keyboards?' Dave moaned.

'How come they always mention "Driving"?' Glenn asked.

'Oh, shut up, you two,' Jason said. 'This review's gold-dust. Even XS will sit up and listen after this.'

Jason was right. They got a message that a lot of the people from XS would be coming to their last gig, which was in London, and Bobby Rosen rang to say that he'd make sure all the top Rock press people were there.

The gig was in a converted warehouse near London Bridge. It was the top place to see hot bands, and when The Bosses arrived, a couple of hours early, there was already a long line of people queueing outside. Buddy felt a rush of adrenalin and, from the way they played during the sound-check, the whole band was feeling it, too. There was something in the air. Tonight was going to be special.

They went back to the dressing-room and waited. No one spoke much, as if saving up every bit of energy for the show. Only Glenn moved, pacing round the room, tapping his drumsticks on every surface he could find. The others lay on the floor, eyes closed, breathing deeply.

At ten o'clock they were called, and they filed along the corridor and out on to the darkened stage. They were hit by a wave of heat and noise. Then the lights came up. Buddy plugged in his guitar and walked to the mike. He peered out at the packed audience. He could feel the electric excitement pouring off the crowd, and his heart flipped. This was it. The crowd was ready to go and the band was ready to take them.

He nodded to Glenn, who began beating out the rhythm on the hi-hat cymbal. After a moment the bass drum began to boom. Buddy raised his harmonica to his lips and started to blow one long, wild, silver note before he slid down the mouthpiece and began to whoop the air in and out, faster and faster.

The audience caught it at once, urging him on as

he repeated the notes, bending them, twisting them, whooping them, over and over until his lungs burned. Thirty seconds. A minute. Two minutes. The notes were screaming for release. They wanted to break out of this repetition into the river of the melody, and he started to build to the crescendo. Higher and higher up the scale, stretching the moment longer and longer – until suddenly, with a flick of his head, Buddy brought the whole band in. The tune exploded and the crowd went wild.

It was a sensational start, and it just got better and better. Buddy hardly knew where one song finished and the next began. He hardly knew who he was. He was the music. It was running through him and out of him, linking him to the rest of the band and to the crowd. It was spinning round him, hypnotizing him, hypnotizing them all. Nothing else mattered.

His fingertips were moving, stroking sounds out of the guitar strings. It was magic. He was making dead steel come alive and sing. He was breathing, and his breath was being turned into music. His voice was making sounds that were perfect for every word he sang. He didn't have to think. It was too fast for thought. The emotions passed straight into his breath and out in his voice.

At the end, it was the voice of the audience that took over. The cries of 'More! More! More!' rolled over the band as they left the stage and staggered along the corridor, back to the dressing-room. For ten minutes they sat, slumped on chairs, too exhausted to drink or even wipe the sweat from themselves. Then Dave reached for a towel and began to mop his face. The mood broke.

The crowd was still yelling for more, but it was too late. There was no more to give. For two hours they had given everything.

Slowly they all got up and began to do the ordinary, everyday things again. Drink water. Change clothes. Check their instruments. They were back on earth.

Buddy looked at the others, and they all had a faint smile on their lips. They felt it, too. They had created something wonderful. Live on stage, they had faced all the dangers. Nothing had been safe. The music had been daring. They had taken risks. They could have made fools of themselves. Like tightrope walkers, they could have fallen off. But they hadn't. They had walked the high wire.

It was the hour of their greatest triumph.

It was the last gig The Bosses ever played.

Chapter Thirteen

The door to the dressing-room burst open and people poured in. Buddy was still high from the music and he wanted to be alone with the band, but there was no stopping the endless line of people who came to shake his hand or pat him on the back and tell him what a great gig it had been.

Some journalists wanted to interview him, and he found himself stuck in a corner for nearly half an hour, trying to answer their questions. He kept looking around to see if Olivia had come, but there was no sign of her.

He did see Paul Maxton talking to Glenn, though, and when the questions finally stopped, Buddy started to push his way through the crowd towards them. A hand grabbed his elbow. He turned, and Olivia threw her arms round his neck and kissed him. A flashbulb exploded.

'Buddy, you were wonderful,' Olivia said, pulling her hair away from her face and smiling a smile that squeezed the breath out of him. 'The reviews are going to be out of this world and the press are going to be begging me for stuff about you!'

She put her hands round the back of his head and pulled him on to her lips.

Another flashbulb exploded.

'You were so sexy,' she whispered between her teeth. 'You had everybody looking at you, listening to you. All that power. What a turn-on. It was incredible. I wanted you.'

She twisted his hair round her fingers until it hurt, then she reached up and kissed him again, biting his lips.

The flashbulb exploded.

'We must celebrate,' she said, darting away.

Out of the corner of his eye he saw Paul Maxton and Glenn going out through the door.

Olivia was back with a bottle of champagne. She took a swig from the bottle then held it up and began to pour it over his head.

'To Fame!' she shouted, and people began to laugh and cheer as the champagne glugged out, soaking him.

The flashbulb exploded.

As the rain of champagne stopped, Buddy wiped his eyes and looked to where the light had flashed.

He knew who he would see. The photographer took the camera away from his face. It was Sam.

Olivia leaned towards him, her tongue out to lick the champagne from his face, and Sam raised his camera again, ready to catch the moment on film. Buddy jerked his arm out of Olivia's grasp and he made for the door, shouldering Sam out of the way.

The corridor was crowded with people. A couple of them slapped him on the back. Faces, faces. Smiles. Eyes looking at him. He was famous. Someone tried to ask for an autograph but he kept going. End of the corridor. Down the stairs. He crashed the bar on the exit door and stepped out into the night.

The chill clamped down on to his wet hair and his soaked shirt. The door opened behind him and Olivia stepped out and put her arm round his shoulder. He shrugged it off.

'Buddy, don't be like that,' she said, pulling him round to face her.

'How could you do it?' he shouted. 'Set it all up like that?'

She looked away down the street, avoiding his eyes. Good, he had shamed her.

But her profile was proud, and a moment later she looked back, straight into his eyes. 'It's my job,' she said. Her voice was cool and steady. 'You want to be a star. I'm here to get you seen. Tomorrow, next week, people are going to read about how great you were tonight and they're going to see photos of you. It's what you want. Fame.'

He shook his head. 'No, not like that,' he said. 'Through the music, yes. But not . . . selling you and me like that.'

'It's only a photograph.'

'Yeah, like it's only a kiss, I suppose? What's a kiss? Nothing real. Just a photo opportunity.'

She grabbed hold of his arms and stepped close. 'The kisses were real,' she said urgently. 'You know they were. What I said was real. I want you.'

'Oh yeah? And what about Sam? Is it real with him, too?'

'Sam's a friend. I use him to take photos.'

'And what do you use me for?' he asked. He'd wanted to make it a challenge, but it came out self-pitying.

'I don't use you. I want you. The Christmas holiday. I want to stay at your flat.'

Buddy was sure she would see the juddering of his heart through the shirt that clung, wet and cold, against him. He shivered.

'Come on, Buddy, let's go in. You'll catch cold.'

'No, I've got to find Glenn.'

'Forget him – he's a loser. You're the only one that counts. You and me. Come on, come back inside – there are people you've got to meet. And we can talk about Christmas. Buddy?'

She kissed him gently, and his heart gave in. She took his hand and he let her lead him inside.

Chapter Fourteen

Kris Dox decided they had enough material to start recording the new album. For the two weeks before Christmas Buddy arranged to stay with Dave and the twins in order to be near the studio. They invited Glenn, but he said he'd made other arrangements.

'Where are you staying?' Buddy asked him.

'With friends.'

'Paul Maxton? Listen, Glenn if you . . .'

'Look, you're not my keeper, right?' Glenn snapped. 'Just leave off me.'

Buddy looked into the dark, glassy pupils of those hollow eyes. This wasn't his friend. Behind the speedy front, Glenn was empty.

He wasn't the drummer he had been either. The rhythm tracks – bass and drums – were the first to be laid down for each song, and Glenn kept getting things wrong. Even when he managed to get the tempo right, it didn't have the swing and drive that he'd always had before. There were constant rows between him and Jason, and even Kris Dox lost his temper with him.

When Glenn failed to turn up one day, Kris used a drum machine instead, and the twins again brought up the idea of getting rid of Glenn and bringing their friend, Rais, down from Birmingham. Buddy and Dave were forced to agree that they ought at least to discuss the possibility with Rosen.

In the end they didn't get the chance because Rosen had news of his own. He and Kris Dox came into one of the recording sessions and announced that XS was being taken over by the Japanese company, Takeena.

'It came out of the blue yesterday morning,' Rosen said. 'Well, Kris and I don't fancy working for some huge faceless conglomerate, so I've been in touch with some contacts at Saroudan Records and we're both moving over there.'

'What about us?' Jason asked.

'You've got no choice; you're on contract here for another two albums. But if things don't work out after that, Kris and I would be more than happy to see you at Saroudan. I start the new job in January, but Kris is staying here until March, so I suggest you get a move on and finish your new album while he's still around. Anyway, I'll keep in touch – don't worry.'

The new sense of urgency kept them working hard in the studio until just before Christmas. Glenn didn't turn up for any of the sessions, and they ended up completing three songs without him, all using a drum machine instead.

'I don't know about you, but I'm not having some speed-freak screw things up for us any more,' Mike said as they packed up for the holidays. 'How about if I ask Rais to come down and sit in?'

The idea of being free of all the problems was very tempting. Glenn had been nothing but a pain, and now there was the need to get the new album made fast. Buddy felt awful about it, but he voted with the others to give Rais a chance. He knew it was the sensible and logical thing to do, but he couldn't help feeling that he was letting his friend down. Especially after Alice. He tried to push it to the back of his mind. Think about it next year.

In the meantime there was something more important to think about. Olivia was coming to stay with him on Boxing Day.

He usually spent Christmas Day with his mum and Boxing Day with his dad, so he'd rung his dad and explained the situation, asking if they could spend Christmas Eve together instead.

'What, you mean you'd rather spend your time with some bird than your poor old dad?' he teased. 'Yeah, OK, Casanova. We'll 'ave a knees-up on Christmas Eve – go down the boozer for a laugh.'

Buddy spent a whole day getting the flat tidy, and then he decided it looked too bare for Christmas. The next day he rushed out and bought holly and mistletoe and a tree and decorations and had a great time putting it all up. It took him ages to decide on a present for Olivia, but he eventually chose a beautiful black dress that he wrapped and put under the tree.

He couldn't think about anything else except Boxing Day and he wanted to get the rest of Christmas over as fast as possible. He went to a pub with his dad on Christmas Eve, but he wasn't really in the mood for a booze-up. He drank a couple of beers then went on to soft drinks, and his dad got a bit irritated and called him a wet blanket. Then his dad's friends started nagging him to get up and sing in the karaoke.

'Go on, you're supposed to be a star, ain't you?' a woman called Cheryl said.

She was about thirty-five, wearing a silvery jump-suit and pink lipstick that clashed with her straggly red hair. She obviously fancied his dad, and she kept draping her arm round his shoulder and putting her face close to his when she talked to him. Buddy just smiled and shook his head, and he was grateful when his dad chipped in and rescued him.

'Don't be daft, Cheryl. He doesn't wanna make everyone else look like berks, does 'e?'

His dad was a bit drunk by the end of the evening, and Buddy drove him back to the breaker's yard. He got out slowly, then walked round the car and rapped on the window. Buddy knew he was going to say something about his mum. He wound the window down and waited, determined that he wouldn't feel sad.

'Oh well,' his dad said, putting his hands on the roof of the car and leaning in through the window, ''ave a nice day round your mum's tomorrow. Give 'er a Christmas kiss from me. Pity it all went wrong, eh? Still . . .'

He sighed and his eyes brimmed with tears as he reached in and gave Buddy the old, old sign of his love – a pull of the nose, a tap under the chin and a quick ruffle of the hair.

''Night, son,' he said then swayed over to the caravan. He stumbled up the three steps and went inside.

Buddy couldn't help it. He'd known it would happen because his dad always got sentimental when he had too much to drink, but he still had a lump in his throat as he drove home.

Christmas Day at his mum's was the same as ever. Her friend Joyce came round for lunch. They all ate too much, as usual, and then sat around talking – which mostly meant listening to Joyce. At one time Buddy had almost hated her because she had encouraged his mum in all the changes that led to the break-up with his dad, but nowadays he agreed with nearly everything she said. He still didn't like her much, but at least he didn't sit there, seething with fury, like in the old days.

As soon as he woke next morning, Buddy's heart started to race. He wanted to be on the move. He wanted it to be five o'clock. His mum was in a relaxed, holiday mood, simply wanting to sit around and chat, and it was hard not to let his restless excitement show. Usually he loved the cold lunch of leftovers on Boxing Day, but today he could barely eat two slices of turkey, and he refused all the salads and trimmings. He was already worried whether his breath was OK, and he certainly didn't want it smelling of garlicky dressing or pickled onions.

After the meal, he washed up quickly then said he had to go.

'OK, love. Are you going round to your dad's?'

'No, I've got a date.'

'Oh,' she said, tactfully not asking any more.

At the front door he kissed her goodbye and was suddenly seized with the urge to say, 'Mum, I'm going to sleep with a girl tonight. Next time you see me I won't be a virgin.'

He didn't say it, of course. Merely got in the car, waved, blew a kiss, and drove away. In the rear-view mirror he saw her standing at the gate watching him. Did she know? Could mothers tell about things like that?

When he got back to the flat, he turned all the heaters on and put clean sheets on the bed. Then he ran the bath and poured lots of bath oil in. The oil was Joyce's Christmas present to him.

'Sexual equality,' she'd said, half jokingly. 'Men should smell as nice as women.'

Trust Joyce to make political points even when she was giving presents. It smelled great, though, and he soaked himself in the bath for nearly an hour. When he got out, he wiped the steam from the mirror and looked at his body. Was it all right? Would Olivia like it? Not at the moment – he was as pink as a lobster. He put on loads of deodorant and then took ages trying to decide which underpants to wear. He finally chose the dark-blue briefs and he sprinkled aftershave over them before putting them on.

The steam had done something funny to his hair, and he spent ten minutes brushing and running his fingers through it, trying to make it look right. He glanced at his watch. Four-thirty. He had to get a move on if he was going to meet her train at five.

He finished dressing quickly then dashed into the bedroom to turn the edge of the covers down on the bed to make it look inviting; then he sprinkled some aftershave on to the pillows. Big mistake: it left nasty little stains on the pillowcases. He turned the pillows over and hoped Olivia wouldn't notice. He also hoped that the aftershave hadn't made nasty little stains on his briefs. Would they show on dark blue?

Four-forty. He was going to be late.

There was an amazing amount of traffic blocking the centre of town – people out visiting families, probably – and by the time he got to the station it was ten past five. He skidded into a parking space and ran into the station. The booking hall was empty. He dashed on to the platform. There were a couple of people sitting on a bench, but no sign of Olivia. He looked across the lines to the other two platforms. She wasn't there.

What a fool! He'd missed her. He couldn't believe it. His mind scrambled in panic through the possibilities. Perhaps she'd caught a taxi to his place. Did she know the address? Perhaps she'd gone straight back to London.

At that moment a voice came over the loudspeaker

announcing that the 17.00 from London was running fifteen minutes late.

The two people on the bench jumped in fright when he punched the air, yelling 'Yeah!'

'What a nightmare journey,' Olivia said as she stepped off the train, five minutes later. She handed him her bag and went on about the terrible journey.

'I'm absolutely starving,' she said as they got in the car.

His brain went into another scramble of panic. He'd assumed that she would have eaten lunch at her mother's house, so he'd only bought a few snacks to have with drinks.

'I thought we could send out for pizza,' he said, feeling certain she would sneer at the idea. The whole evening would start badly.

'Brilliant,' she said. 'I could murder one.'

He took hold of her hand and kissed the tips of her fingers. Everything was going to be wonderful.

When they got to the flat, she had a bath to relax after the journey; he rang for the pizzas. She'd chosen American Hot with extra onions and couldn't understand why he found it so funny.

She came out of the bathroom wearing jeans and a white T-shirt. She looked so at ease walking around barefoot, gently rubbing the damp ends of her hair with a towel while she inspected the room. She pointed to the holly on the wall and smiled.

'A joke, right?' she laughed. 'You and it – a fifties rock star.'

'Oh yeah,' he laughed. 'I hadn't thought of it.'

'Where's the bedroom?' she asked.

He pointed to the closed door, and a ridiculous wave of heat swept up his neck to his face.

She nodded. 'It's a great flat,' she said, continuing to prowl around, examining his books and albums.

Buddy poured some wine, and they clinked glasses. She took a huge swig of hers and her eyes danced with sexy laughter as she looked at him.

The pizzas arrived and they sat together on the floor, eating them out of the boxes and drinking wine. Then Olivia pulled out a sheaf of reviews and newspaper-cuttings about The Bosses' gig in London and sat next to him to show them to him. She seemed to be more impressed by them than he was, but he used it as an excuse to put his arm round her shoulder and be close to her.

'Now all you've got to do is follow it up with a great record,' she said as they reached the end of the pile.

'We're working on it,' he said. 'Do you want me to play some of the songs?'

'Yeah, great.'

He got his guitar, and she lay on her back on the sofa while he played. He loved singing them for her and he thought he'd sung them well, so he was disappointed by her reaction at the end.

'They're good,' she said but there was no enthusiasm in her voice.

'Don't you like them?'

'Yes, I do. I'm not sure how commercial they are, though.'

'Yeah, but you can't worry about stuff like that. You just have to do what you want to do.'

'A man's gotta do what a man's gotta do,' she laughed.

'No, not like that. I mean . . .'

But she cut him off by turning on her side and

beckoning him over. He put down the guitar and went and knelt by the sofa. She reached up, pulled his head down towards her and kissed him, then looked straight in his eyes.

'I want you to be a star. There's no point in doing anything unless you get to the top. But you have to make the right moves.'

She pulled his mouth down on to hers again, and he slid on to the sofa with her. She undid the buttons of his shirt and slipped her hand against his skin. He shivered with excitement as her teeth started to nip his lower lip, then she twisted his head and began to kiss his ear.

'Let's go in the other room,' she whispered.

He rolled off the sofa and stood up. He took her hand and led her across to the bedroom door. He turned the handle and stood aside so that she could go in first. She walked past him, then stopped suddenly and turned with a look of shock on her face. He glanced past her. The bedside light was on.

Glenn was lying, face down, on the bed.

CHAPTER FIFTEEN

Nothing he tried to say to Olivia could make her change her mind: she wanted to be driven back to London. Now.

While she packed her things into her bag, Buddy managed to get Glenn into a sitting position and half open his eyes. It was obvious that he'd been taking drugs and hardly knew where he was.

'Let me sleep, man,' he mumbled. 'Gotta sleep.'

Buddy kept shaking him. 'Come on Glenn, you've got to go,' he said as Olivia came into the room, holding her bag. Perhaps even now she might change her mind if he could just get rid of Glenn.

'Can't. Mum ... Mum kicked me out,' Glenn said, his head rolling as he tried to sag back into sleep.

Buddy let go of him, and Glenn slumped down on the bed.

'I'm waiting,' Olivia said.

Neither of them spoke during the journey back to London. When they got to her flat, he tried to lift her bag out for her but she grabbed it off the back seat. He stood awkwardly as she slammed the door and turned around.

'Olivia . . .' he began.

'What?'

'I'm sorry.'

She nodded and walked past him up the steps and into the house. He felt his chest dissolve in pain and he wanted to run after her, but he forced himself not to. Better to let her go now, and try to sort it out later. There was still hope.

Glenn was fast asleep on the bed when he got back, so Buddy crashed out on the sofa.

He woke at about eight, cold and uncomfortable, and lay for nearly an hour, numbly watching the lights on the Christmas tree flick on and off. Then he got up and went round the flat, tearing down all the decorations and getting rid of them.

Glenn finally woke up just after noon and shuffled out into the living-room and said he was starving hungry. Buddy didn't say anything while Glenn raided the kitchen and made himself a huge pile of toast and a pot of tea. Then, while he was gulping the food down as if he hadn't eaten for days, Buddy told him what he'd done.

He wanted to hurt him, wanted him to feel guilty. By halfway through the story, Glenn looked beaten and helpless. Tears began to slide down his face and he started to apologize, and he went on apologizing until Buddy told him to stop. He'd wanted Glenn to be sorry; but he didn't want this, didn't want to hear his friend say such terrible things about himself.

When Glenn finally stopped crying, he fell asleep in the chair. As the afternoon light grew thick and grey, Buddy sat and looked at him lying there with his mouth open. He wanted to hate him. He wanted to kick him out of his flat and kick him out of the band, but he couldn't. His open mouth and the line of dried white spittle on his lips were repulsive. He was sad and weak and annoying and unreliable. But Buddy couldn't hate him.

Snow started to fall. The fat flakes swirled and settled. By the time Glenn woke again at nine that evening, the snow was too thick for cars to move in the street below. Buddy wished he could get rid of him, but he told him he could stay.

It was so cold that the snow didn't show any sign of melting. There was hardly any movement on the streets, and for three days they didn't go out. Buddy stayed in his bedroom most of the time, playing his guitar and writing songs, while Glenn dozed in the front room. Sometimes Buddy stood at the window, watching groups of kids sledging down the big hill in the park. He felt empty and drained, as if the world was a long way away from him.

On the Sunday morning there was a phone-call from Jason.

'Have you seen the *Sunday Herald*?' Jason asked.

'No. Why?'

'Buy it and see,' he said, and rang off.

Glenn wanted to come with him, so they tramped together through the snow to the nearest newsagent's and bought the paper. They stood outside, turning the pages quickly. When they got to page ten, Glenn grabbed the paper.

There was a photograph of him and his mother. Next to it, the headline read: 'Mum Boots Out Drug Star'.

Dave and the twins came down for a meeting. Glenn said he'd go out because they obviously wanted to talk about him, but Buddy insisted that he stayed.

'We've all got to say what we want to say, and you've got to hear it. Get it out in the open.'

And they did. All the complaints about Glenn came out and he sat there, nodding. He didn't even look surprised when Jason said that they were thinking of getting Rais to replace him as drummer.

'So, is that it, then?' he asked 'Am I out?'

There was a long silence.

'Well, I'll tell you the truth, Jet,' Mike finally said. 'If it wasn't for this newspaper thing I'd say yes, get lost. But I hate it when papers do stuff like this. It stinks. And I want to stick one on them. But you've got to cut out the drugs and start drumming like you really can. You put one foot wrong and you're out.'

They took a vote. It was unanimous: Glenn had one more chance.

Buddy had been worried that the newspaper story would make Glenn depressed but it had a totally different effect. He became angry. And his anger seemed to fuel him through the next couple of months.

The first thing he did was go round and see his mother. She was already regretting talking to the paper, but Glenn was too angry to listen. He took all his belongings out of the house and brought them back to Buddy's flat. His mum wrote to him every week, but he tore up the letters without reading them.

His anger also gave him the strength to deal with the Press. While the band was recording the album, a number of music journalists came to interview them. All of them wanted to know about Glenn's problems with drugs and with his mother. Whenever the question was asked, his face would harden into a silent glare that was so menacing that the journalist would immediately change the subject.

It was never funny at the time, but they always laughed afterwards when Jason did an impression of how Glenn looked. 'Give him The Glare' became one of the band's private catch-phrases.

The anger and tension also seemed to drive his drumming and, as usual, when Glenn drummed well, the band played well. They laid down track after track and everyone began to be excited about what was happening. Even while they were recording, Buddy was still coming up with new songs and he felt that some of them, especially 'High Speed Crash' and 'Dying Is Easy (If You Want To)', were as good as anything he'd ever written.

He felt optimistic about The Bosses again. The only shadow hanging over him was the unfinished business with Olivia. He put it off for nearly a month, but the time came when he knew he had to confront her.

As he went to her office, he thought that perhaps the best thing to do was follow Jason's advice: give her The Glare and then leave. What astonished him was the way his heart still flipped when she looked up and smiled at him.

'Buddy, hi!' she said, as if nothing had changed. It threw him. Perhaps there was still a chance . . .

'Why did you tell the *Herald* about Glenn?' he asked straight out, before he could get side-tracked.

'I didn't tell the *Herald*.'

'Well, Sam or whoever it was you tipped off.'

'Buddy, I didn't tell anyone.'

If she'd said anything else, he might have forgiven her. But suddenly he saw how easily she lied to him and how often she must have lied in the past. Her big, innocent eyes gazed at him, certain that he would believe her. He just looked at her. It wasn't The Glare, but it must have had its own power because she lowered her eyes.

He turned towards the door.

'Buddy, don't go,' she said. 'All right, I told the *Herald*, but I did it for you and the band. Give Glenn a bit of a shock, make him realize. And from what I've heard it's worked – he's off drugs and drumming like a dream. Yes or no?'

He looked at her, and again she couldn't hold his gaze.

'And it's toughened up the band's image,' she

went on. 'Made it more dangerous, more rock'n'roll. That new sound of yours needs a new image.'

Buddy opened the door.

'You know what?' he said. 'I pity you. You don't even know when you're lying any more.'

He started to close the door, then stopped. It hadn't actually been said yet. All those months he had lived in fear that she would say it, but in the end it was going to be his decision.

'It's over, Olivia. I don't want to see you again.'

CHAPTER SIXTEEN

By mid-February they had recorded twenty-five songs, and Kris Dox called a halt. It was less than a month before he was due to move to Saroudan and he would need all that time to do the final mixes for the album. They chose the twelve best songs and left him to get on with it.

The work on the album had kept Glenn going but, now that it was finished and they were back in the flat, Buddy often found him alone, staring at nothing. His anger was fading and, as the pain came through, the temptation of drugs would grow.

'You ought to get out and see people,' Buddy said when he found him slumped in a chair one day, looking miserable.

'No one to see,' Glenn mumbled.

'What about Alice?'

'Rang her the other day and asked her round here,

but she said she didn't want to. What's up between you two?'

'Nothing. Why?'

'Well, she went all weird when I said I was staying with you.'

'Rubbish,' Buddy said, sure that his blush was showing. 'She was probably just weird 'cos you haven't bothered to see her for so long. Take her out for a meal or something.'

Glenn just shrugged, but a couple of days later Buddy got back from visiting his dad and found Alice there.

'We went out for a nosh-up and then I asked Alice back,' Glenn explained.

'Great! Hi, Alice. How are you?'

'Fine. You?'

'Yeah, great. Apart from having this berk living with me.'

Alice smiled, and their eyes met. His heart skipped. She still cared. And so did he. They both felt the force of the look between them, and they had to lower their eyes before Glenn noticed.

'Well, I'll leave you two alone,' Buddy said.

He went into his room and picked up his guitar. He kept playing for over an hour. He didn't want to hear them talking – but, even more than that, he dreaded hearing silence or the creak of the sofa. When they left, Buddy went out into the living-room. The smell of her perfume still lingered in the air, and especially on the back of the chair where she'd been sitting.

Thank God she hadn't stayed the night. It would have been torture to be in his room knowing that she was next door with Glenn.

From then on, he made a point of being out every time Glenn asked Alice round. A couple of times he rang to say that he'd decided to sleep at his mum's for the night. He never asked Glenn whether Alice stayed on such occasions. It would hurt too much if the answer was Yes.

On Kris Dox's last day, the whole band assembled at XS to hear the finished album, and it sounded great.

'It's a wonderful album,' Kris agreed. 'And I think "Dying Is Easy" is the best thing you've ever done. Let's just hope that the new people at XS see it that way, too. Anyway, good luck.'

The new managing director at XS, Alec Miller, had already been in charge for over a month, but they still hadn't met him. They'd heard about some of the changes he was making, though. Many of the people in the company had been pushed out and were being replaced by Miller's own people. One of the big changes was that Olivia had been promoted to second in charge of publicity. The other thing they heard was that Miller wanted the label to release more dance music.

Finally they got the call to meet him.

He was a tall man, much younger than Rosen, and he smelled strongly of aftershave. He was dressed in an expensive casual suit and his broad face was tanned, showing up his white teeth as he smiled briefly at them.

'The Bosses,' he said, consulting a file in front of him. He leafed through the pages. 'One hit record, "She Got". One flop, "Driving". One album, poor sales. Money from the single not enough to cover the costs of the album. Some successful gigs, mostly as support band.'

Miller turned the page.

'I see there's been some negative publicity concerning drugs . . .'

Miller looked up, singled Glenn out with his pale-blue eyes, then went back to the report.

Glenn blushed crimson.

'The word from the people in Publicity and Sales is that you haven't established a solid market,' Miller went on, 'and that you've been ignoring advice about the proper direction to take.'

Buddy felt his stomach sink. That must have come from Olivia.

'Well,' Miller said, closing the file, 'I've listened to the album and I have to agree with Publicity — it's too bluesy and off the wall to do much in the marketplace. But it's classy and unusual. Sometimes odd stuff like this finds a cult audience, so I'm prepared to run with it and see. I can't promise much promotion, but I'll mark it down for an April release. All right with you?'

He didn't expect an answer, and nobody volunteered one. He held out his hand and one by one the band shook it. Nobody spoke and they filed out of the office while he sat down and picked up another report.

The record came out at the end of April and it got terrific reviews in the music press. *Beating Tracks* made it their album of the month; *Vox* gave it a 9-out-of-10 rating; *Q Magazine* said it was 'essential listening'; and *Melody Maker* called it 'powerful and important'.

But, despite the reviews, the album disappeared.

There was no air-play, no interviews, no adverts, and the record wasn't even available in most shops they went into. They were all so disappointed that Buddy agreed to go up to XS to talk to Diana Armstrong in the Publicity Department.

'I'm sorry, Buddy,' she said, 'but under the new arrangements The Bosses are being handled by Olivia. You'll have to go and see her.'

For ten minutes he wandered the corridors, wondering whether to leave it and get one of the others to see Olivia instead, but in the end he knocked on her office door and went in.

She was cool and formal, and he found himself stumbling through the list of complaints, feeling that he must sound like a whining kid asking for sweeties.

'Well, I hear what you're saying,' she said flatly, 'but obviously XS can't spend a fortune on an album that isn't commercial. Frankly we thought we did rather well to get the kind of reviews we did.'

'Hold on,' Buddy cut in. 'The album got the good reviews on its merits, not because of anything you did. And now you're not doing anything to cash in on the reviews.'

'We can't force shops to order it. The problem is that they got burned by your last album and they don't want to end up with another lot of unsold stock. They think you're last year's thing.'

It was a vicious circle. The shops wouldn't stock the record unless it sold, but it couldn't sell unless it was in the shops. XS wouldn't promote it unless it sold, and it wouldn't sell unless they promoted it. And here was Olivia, loving every minute of his hopeless position.

'Well, thanks for your help,' he said, getting up and looking her straight in the eyes.

She smiled, and he remembered what she had said about how exciting it was to have power. Now she had power over his career.

'By the way,' she said as he opened the door, 'next time you want a meeting, can you make an appointment? I get awfully busy.'

He went straight round to Walter Shielby's office and asked to see him.

'I agree; it's most unfortunate that Bobby's gone from XS,' Shielby said. 'I suggest that the best course is to fulfil your contract by making another album as quickly as possible, and then we can follow him to Saroudan.'

'What about this album, Walter? You've heard it, you've seen the reviews. It's too damn good just to let it disappear.'

'Well, I agree. Things like "Dying Is Easy" are marvellous, but what can I do?'

'You're our bloody manager, it's your job to know what to do,' Buddy shouted, not caring if Shielby took offence. Things could hardly get worse.

'Yes, well, look, I tell you what. I'm off to Japan tomorrow for a week; but the minute I get back, I'll set up a tour for you, something that'll give you a chance to showcase the new material. What do you say?'

Buddy felt like saying it was about time, but he didn't.

And Shielby kept his word. By the end of May he'd fixed up a tour of thirty-six clubs, starting in July, and he'd secured a couple of TV bookings for the autumn.

*

During the last week of June they rehearsed every day in a hall that Walter Shielby had booked for them in London. They usually finished late, so Buddy and Glenn kipped down on the floor of the others' flat. It was good to be back together as a band, sharing things and getting into the music again. They laughed and mucked about a lot, but they worked hard at the rehearsals and they knew they were playing well.

Jason summed up the general feeling of optimism as they packed up after the last rehearsal: 'It's only a question of time, you know.'

'What's that?' Mike asked.

'Before we make the breakthrough. I mean, if we keep on playing as good as this, it's got to happen. I know it.'

They all laughed and called him bighead, but they knew it, too. They were good, really good. Something special. And the world was going to realize it. Soon.

The first gig was going to be in Swindon, so Buddy decided to go home and get a proper night's rest in his own bed rather than spend another night on the floor. He'd expected Glenn to come with him, and he was surprised when he said he was staying in London.

'Yeah, I've asked Alice up,' he said. 'So I'm off. See you all at the club tomorrow.'

Buddy drove home and called in to see his mum. They chatted for a while, then he drove round to the breaker's yard and asked his dad out for a drink. When he got home at about ten-thirty, the phone was ringing. It was Alice.

'Hello, Buddy,' she said. 'Can I speak to Glenn?'

'I thought you were meeting him in London.'

'No.'

'Oh, must be some mistake. Listen, Alice, I don't know where he is. I'll get him to call you if I contact him.'

As soon as she had rung off, Buddy called directory enquiries and got Paul Maxton's number. He rang the number, but there was no answer.

He kept telling himself that perhaps there was some perfectly innocent explanation, but he didn't believe it. There was only one reason why Glenn would lie about where he was going.

The following morning, he rang Paul Maxton again. No answer. He rang Alice. She still hadn't heard from Glenn. He rang the London flat and spoke to Jason.

'Oh no,' Jason groaned when Buddy explained why he was ringing. 'If he's stoned tonight, I'll break his neck.'

Buddy left early and drove up to Swindon in the hope that Glenn might already be at the club. The van was there and their two roadies had set up all the equipment, but there was no sign of Glenn.

The other three arrived on time for the sound-check. They waited for a while, but, when Glenn still hadn't turned up, they checked the sound with one of the roadies sitting in on the drums. Then they went back to the dressing-room.

The gig was due to begin at nine, and by eight they were starting to get worried. The doors were already open, people were coming into the club, but there was still no Glenn.

At nine-thirty Buddy went on stage and apologized to the crowd – the gig was cancelled. He had just got back to the dressing-room, the boos of disappointment still ringing in his ears, when the manager of the club called him to the phone.

He picked the phone up, ready to bawl Glenn out and tell him that he'd let them down one time too many. Tell him that he was out of the band. But it wasn't Glenn.

It was Alec Miller. He had just had a phone-call from Paul Maxton. Paul was at the hospital. He'd been there all afternoon.

There had been an accident. Glenn had fallen from a second-storey window at Paul's flat. He had dropped twenty-five feet on to concrete.

He was alive but unconscious. There was damage to his skull and the doctors feared that his back might be broken.

CHAPTER SEVENTEEN

Glenn's mother was by his bedside every time Buddy went to visit him. Glenn was unconscious, and it was frightening to see him lying there, so still and white, with a respirator keeping him breathing. His mother sat there and held on to his hand while she prayed and read the Bible. Buddy always felt awkward; he hated the idea that she might ask him to join in, so he never stayed long.

'It's God's will,' she said to Buddy one day just as he was going.

'Sorry?' Buddy said.

'God's will. God is punishing my Glenn and telling him to change his ways.'

Buddy smiled and left, but he couldn't stop thinking about what she'd said. Surely it couldn't be true
that God had deliberately made Glenn fall out of a
window to teach him a lesson. Could it? Glenn had
been stupid, getting mixed up with drugs, but he
didn't deserve to be lying in a coma, perhaps dying.
Anyway, people didn't get what they deserved. Some
good people had terrible things happen to them, and
some terrible people had good things happen to
them. It just didn't work like that.

So, how did it work? Why did things happen? The
question haunted him.

'Do you think something like that is meant to
happen?' he asked his dad. 'You know, it's Fate or
something?'

'Search me, mate. Things just 'appen, don't they.'

'Yeah, but why? Like, a bomb explodes, right?
One person gets killed and the person standing next
to them doesn't. Why?'

'Luck.'

'Yeah, but what does that mean?'

'It means luck. Luck is luck, that's it. 'Ere, fancy
going down the boozer?'

And that was most people's reaction: luck, chance,
things just happen. But if good things or terrible
things just happened by chance, it meant that life
was cruel and pointless. If the things that happened
in life were just random, that would mean that
nothing mattered, nothing meant anything. But the
alternative didn't make any sense either: a God sitting
up in the sky controlling everything. What kind of
God could decide to let this person get blown up by
a bomb or this baby starve to death, and the next
minute decide who would win the lottery?

If Glenn had come home with him that night and not gone to Paul Maxton's, everything would have been different. One little decision had changed all their lives. Not just Glenn's or the band's lives, but even the lives of the audience. People who had been planning to see their gigs had done something else instead. Perhaps some bloke had gone out driving instead and had an accident. Or perhaps some girl had gone to a pub instead and met the person she would end up marrying. If Glenn hadn't fallen out of the window, she would have gone to the gig and she would never have met that person, and their child or children would never have been born.

That night Glenn had had two choices, like two doors in front of him: go home to Buddy's flat or go round and see Paul Maxton. Behind each door was a string of possibilities, affecting so many people. He chose to open one door and those possibilities happened. And behind the door that he didn't open, all those other possibilities stopped being possible.

But what did it all mean? When you opened one door, rather than another – was it meant to happen? In other words, there might be all these doors, but was there only ever one door you would actually open? Perhaps Glenn could never have chosen to come home that night because he was destined to go to Paul Maxton's and fall out of the window.

The doctors said that Glenn could have died, but he didn't. At the end of two weeks he came out of the coma, and a month later he was transferred to a hospital that specialized in spinal injuries. It would take a long time – perhaps four or five months, the doctors said – but they were confident that he would be able to walk normally. The only doubt was whether he would regain full use of his right arm.

'We can't wait to find out,' Jason said. 'We need to find another drummer, quick, otherwise our career's gonna go down the plughole.'

'We can't just ditch Glenn now,' Buddy argued.

'Buddy, he's never going to change,' Mike said. 'If he gets better and starts to drum again, he'll be back on drugs within a month. We'll be doing him a favour.'

'Doing him a favour!' Dave sneered. 'Don't give me crap. You just want to get this bloke Rais in.'

They ended up having a terrible row and every time they met up to rehearse or discuss the future the row started again. And they didn't just row about Glenn. Suddenly they seemed to be at each other's throats about everything. And increasingly it felt as if the twins were ganging up and trying to run things their way.

Buddy didn't mention any of this whenever he went to visit Glenn, of course. The doctors and the nurses kept saying how pleased they were with his progress, but he still looked terribly thin and helpless. He needed to be lifted in and out of bed and, although he could stand and take a few shaky steps, he needed someone by his side to make sure he didn't fall. Bit by bit, over the weeks, he was able to take more and more steps, but it was a terribly slow process.

Perhaps the twins were right – if they didn't get a new drummer and start work again soon, The Bosses would be forgotten. And perhaps it was true that, even if he got well, Glenn might always have a drug problem.

*

On his twenty-first birthday Buddy went out for a meal with his parents.

His dad went on about how old he felt. 'I'm not kidding,' he said when Buddy and his mum laughed at him. 'I can remember being twenty-one and thinking my old man was clapped out 'cos he was nearly fifty. And now here you are, twenty-one, and me nearly fifty.'

'And clapped out,' Buddy teased.

His dad didn't laugh, and the next day he found out why.

'I didn't want to say nuffin' last night to spoil your day,' his dad said when he dropped into the flat, 'but Arctic are giving me the push at the end of the month, ain't they? They're cutting back on the videos. I've seen it coming for ages, but it don't make it no easier when it 'appens.'

'Oh, Dad, I'm sorry. What you gonna do?'

'Dunno, really. I could try and get another job with some other company, but who's gonna give me a chance? You know, they look at me – an old geezer, no education, dresses funny – and they think, "Do us a favour."'

'You don't have to dress in your Ted stuff.'

'Wouldn't make much difference. Anyway, why shouldn't I? I like Ted gear. Nah, there's all this stuff about equal opportunities but it don't include being old or not talking proper.'

'You're not old,' Buddy said, wishing he'd never called him clapped out, even in fun.

'I know that, you know that – but 'ow many job adverts ask for people nearly fifty? Anyway, Des King says I can always 'ave me old job back at the breaker's. Been dead lucky, really – 'ad a chance to do somefing else for a bit. Made a packet of money and saved most of it, for a change. Can't moan really, eh?'

The twins called a meeting at Walter Shielby's office, and it was obvious that they'd primed him before the meeting because he insisted that the band start to look for other drummers.

'Obviously we all hope that Glenn gets well,' Shielby said, 'but one never knows. I think you should take a look at this chap, Rais, and I've heard about a young lad from Scotland who might be worth checking out.'

After the meeting, Dave took Buddy aside and said that he felt that they were being pressured by Mike and Jason. 'You don't know any drummers, do you?' Dave asked. 'If Rais gets the job, he's going to vote with the twins on everything. They just want to take the whole band over.'

Buddy couldn't think of anybody, and it wasn't until a couple of days later that he suddenly remembered Julius.

He rang Charmian that evening. They'd been writing to each other every couple of months, but they still hadn't managed to meet up, and this was only the second time they'd spoken on the phone. Buddy couldn't get over how much her voice had changed, and he wondered what she looked like nowadays.

'The main reason I'm ringing,' he said after they'd chatted for a while, 'is to ask you how good a drummer Jules is.'

'I don't know, really. He's always getting offers from other bands down here, so I suppose he must be pretty good.'

'Well listen, Char, do you think you can ask him if he'd like to come up and audition for The Bosses next Wednesday?'

'Funny you should say that. He nearly wrote to you a couple of times when he heard your drummer was injured, but he always said he wouldn't have a chance 'cos he's black.'

'That's mad. Brown, yellow, blue – nobody gives a damn in music as long as you can play.'

Two days later, Charmian rang to say that Julius had said Yes: he would be there on Wednesday.

CHAPTER EIGHTEEN

The day before the auditions, Buddy went to the hospital. He'd finally decided that he had to tell Glenn what was going on, but when he walked into the ward he found Alice there. Glenn was proudly showing her how he could walk from his bed to the doorway with only a stick to help him. Buddy stayed for a few minutes, avoiding Alice's eyes, and then left without mentioning anything about the band.

Walter Shielby came to the auditions and he brought Kenny Ross with him. Kenny was from Glasgow and he had a baby face that was half hidden by a mass of red curls which kept swaying across his face. He was quiet and nervous during the interview, but when he started to play he became even more manic than Glenn – bopping around on the stool, his sticks flailing the drums, while his long hair flew all over the place. They played together for over an hour, then it was time to meet Rais. He was very good-looking and he was so funny during the interview that he had them in fits of laughter. There was no doubt that his personality and looks would be a bonus and his drumming was excellent, powerful yet full of subtle rhythm. But even in so short a time, Buddy could see that Dave's fears were right – Rais would take the twins' side in everything and the whole balance of the band would change.

As Rais walked out, Julius walked in. Charmian had warned him, but Buddy was still amazed by the change in him. He had grown really tall and his hair, which had always been short, now hung in shoulder-length dreadlocks. He wore reflective sunglasses, a combat jacket and a black beret, and his whole manner was aggressive. He didn't even smile when he shook hands with Buddy, and he just nodded curtly when he was introduced to the other members of the band.

Dave tried to put him at ease by asking questions about the bands he'd been playing with but his replies were short and unfriendly. And Buddy was really thrown by his voice. When he'd known Julius at school, he had spoken like everybody else, but now he had adopted a very strong Jamaican accent.

They played most of their songs, and Julius drummed well. He picked things up quickly and after a while he relaxed a bit and even grinned a couple of times at Buddy. The main problem was that he had obviously mostly played reggae and he sometimes seemed to be trying to drag the songs into a more Caribbean beat. Jason pointed this out in the middle of one song, saying that it was throwing his bass playing out. Julius immediately corrected the rhythm, but not before he'd thrown an angry look at Jason.

As soon as they stopped playing, Julius retreated into a sullen silence again, and Buddy decided it would be best not to bother with any more chat. He went with him to the foyer and shook his hand.

'Thanks for coming, Jules. It's been great seeing you again. It's always difficult at auditions, but you did really well.'

'Have I got a chance, then?' Julius said, dropping his Jamaican accent almost entirely.

Buddy saw the hope and eagerness in his eyes and he felt a rush of affection for his friend. Somewhere, hidden behind his new image, was the Jules from the old days.

'Listen, Jules, I can't say. We're going to have to discuss it. But you're a terrific drummer. I was impressed.'

Julius nodded. The cool, suspicious, prickly Julius was back. He held his hand up in salute, then left without another word.

Buddy watched him go out through the revolving door. When he got out on to the pavement, he pulled himself up to his full height, straightened his shoulders, and swaggered away down the street, giving all the white people his best gangster stare. The Glenn Glare and the Julius Gangster Stare – they had a lot in common, and they were both a bluff.

When Buddy went back into the rehearsal room the discussion had already started. It was obvious that Mike and Jason had made up their minds against Julius.

'Too damn moody,' Jason said.

'Yeah, and he'd be dragging in that reggae beat all

the time,' Mike added. 'It's got to be Rais – he looks great, and he's the best drummer.'

'No way,' Dave said. 'Kenny was much more powerful.'

'He was just louder,' Mike snapped.

Round and round the discussion went until Walter Shielby called on them to vote. Predictably, the twins voted for Rais. Dave raised his hand for Kenny and, rather than let Rais get in, Buddy voted for the Scot, too.

'Two all,' Buddy said, feeling that it was the best possible result. 'Looks like we'll have to stick with Glenn.'

'I think you're forgetting my casting vote,' Walter Shielby said. 'Check your contract – I have a vote on all changes to the band. And my vote goes to Kenny.'

Buddy decided it would be best to break the news to Julius in person, so he drove down to see him. Mr Rybeero answered the door, looking thin and grey. He stood, panting from the exertion of walking down the corridor, and Buddy was shocked – the last time he'd seen him, he had been so fit and active, now he was like an old man.

'He out,' Mr Rybeero said when Buddy told him he'd come to see Julius. 'Don't ask me where. No one know wid dat boy. Mebbe you go ask Charmian. She at work right now.'

The man at the shop's information desk told him she was working in the Sports Department on the fourth floor. As Buddy stepped off the escalator, he wondered whether he would recognize her – after all, her dad and her brother had changed so much.

In fact he spotted her at once, even though she had her back to him and was half hidden in the crowd of Christmas shoppers. Perhaps all those years of sitting behind her at school had imprinted on his mind the shape of her head and the way she moved her shoulders.

Her hairstyle was different, longer and softer, but her smile was the same. As she turned around and saw him, it burst from her – so wide and genuine that he couldn't help but smile back.

'Buddy!' she said, coming round the counter and throwing her arms round him and hugging him quickly. She stepped back and laughed. 'Oops, I'm not supposed to do that to customers!'

'I'm not a customer. I've come to see you.'

'Great. Listen, I've got my tea-break in ten minutes . . .'

They went up to the top-floor cafeteria and sat by a window overlooking the city centre. Charmian's eyes were still sparkling with pleasure, and he couldn't get over how beautiful she had become. She'd always had a sweet face when she was younger, but now she had lost her puppy fat without losing the curves of her cheeks and lips. Most charming of all, though, was the way her whole face was alive with a kind of cheeky delight. Even when she was talking, her lips seemed just about to curl into a smile.

For a few minutes she chattered about her job and the Christmas rush, then she stopped and looked directly at him. 'You've come to see Jules – and you're going to tell him No, aren't you?'

Buddy nodded.

'Oh, Buddy, he'll be so disappointed.'

'That's why I'm going to tell him face to face.'

'I don't think it'll make much difference. He gets so bitter about things. Still, it's nice of you to bother, and it's given me the chance to see you. You look great.'

'So do you.'

She quickly drew him a map on a paper napkin to show him how to find the hall where Julius was rehearsing, then she gave him a little goodbye kiss on his cheek.

'Stay in touch, yeah?' she asked.

'Yeah,' he said. And he meant it.

He drove to the hall and sat outside for a few minutes, listening to the funky reggae beat that was pounding through the window. Julius's drumming really was good. If only he had fitted in with The Bosses . . .

The music stopped and Buddy took the opportunity to go into the hall. Jules was standing next to his drum kit, talking to the other members of the band, who were all dressed exactly like him. As he looked up and saw Buddy, a smile started to his lips then died. Had he guessed?

Jules said something to the others, then came towards Buddy. He nodded to the door, and Buddy followed him out.

'What you do 'ere, mon?' Jules' Jamaican accent was back.

Buddy took a breath. 'I've come to tell you . . . You didn't get it, Jules. You played well, everybody thought you were a great drummer but . . .'

'But I's not white.'

'No, Jules, that's not why. For God's sake, we're not racist. There were only three of you on the final shortlist and two of you were non-whites, dammit.'

'Who get the job, Buddy? Who get the job?'

Buddy had to look away and when he looked back, Julius was grinning sarcastically.

'OK, the white guy got the job, but not because he was white. Jules, you've got to believe me . . .'

But Julius was already walking back towards the hall. He pushed through the swing door and disappeared without even a wave.

It had been hard telling Jules, but it was even harder telling Glenn. Buddy waited for nearly a week before he summoned up the courage.

As he walked down the ward, Glenn saw him, and his face lit up with delight.

'Buddy, great!' he said. 'Perfect. I've got something to tell you.'

'Yeah? I've got something to tell you first,' Buddy said, determined to get the bad news out while he was still psyched up to do it. 'Listen, Glenn . . .'

But Glenn wasn't listening. He was struggling to his feet and looking down the ward.

'Here she is,' Glenn said. 'Been to get some cokes. Ought to be champagne.'

Buddy turned and saw Alice coming towards them, carrying a couple of cans.

'Here, you can have this one,' Glenn said, handing a can to Buddy. 'Alice and I can share the other one. We didn't know you were coming. But it's great you're here – you can be the first to know. I've just asked Alice to marry me and she said yes.'

Buddy's eyes darted towards her and caught hers before she could look away. They held for an instant and then she turned to Glenn who put his arm round her shoulder and pulled her towards him for a kiss.

'Congratulations,' Buddy said, raising the can and taking a sip. Alice's eyes caught his again, and he felt his heart pump a wave of sadness across his chest.

'So what's your news, then?' Glenn asked.

'Oh nothing,' Buddy said, looking away from Alice.

'Come on, tell me!' Glenn insisted. 'Come on, Buddy!'

So he did. He told him, even though he knew it wasn't the right time to do it. He told him in a rush, not looking at him. He told him, wanting to hurt him – for everything: the drugs, the lies, the whole mess with the band, Alice.

'That's it, then,' Glenn said at the end. 'It's all over.'

'Not forever,' Buddy said, hating himself for his burst of anger and wanting to take it all back. 'Just for now. For the next album. We've got to get an album out fast, otherwise everyone'll forget us. But Kenny's only temporary. Once you're better . . .'

Glenn was slumped in his chair, shaking his head. He looked as if he might cry. Oh God, Glenn, don't cry.

'Look, we'll put it in Kenny's contract if you want,' Buddy promised.

Glenn still sat there, shaking his head.

'Tell him, Alice: it's only temporary,' Buddy said, appealing to her, but she just shrugged and looked down at the floor.

Glenn took hold of his right arm with his left hand and lifted it up. Then he took his left hand away. He gritted his teeth and managed to hold his arm out for a couple of seconds before it flopped down on to his lap.

'It's not temporary,' he said. 'They say it'll get better than that, but I ain't never gonna drum again.'

He looked at Buddy and there were tears in his eyes.

'All the things we've done. Hit record, being on TV – I used to dream about stuff like that when I was on the milk round. We had some great times. But it's all over.'

Chapter Nineteen

Kenny came down from Scotland for a week before Christmas. They rehearsed some new songs and he drummed well but, whenever any of them tried to chat to him, he hid behind his hair, said 'Aye' or 'No', and clammed up. They hoped he would relax when they got down to proper rehearsals after Christmas, but they soon found out there wasn't going to be any rehearsal time. He was going to be thrown straight into recording.

'I hate doing this,' Alec Miller said when they went to tell him that they were planning to record their third album, 'but we live in a tough commercial world. Frankly, the sales of your last album were so poor that I've had to cut the budget on your next one. So, the most that I can give you is four weeks in the studio. There's a slot free on January 3rd. I know it's tight but the next free slot is in July. Take it or leave it.'

They took it.

The tensions started straight after the meeting. The first problem was about the album itself.

'Look,' Mike argued, 'it's obvious XS don't give a damn about us. So let's just give them the songs we recorded but didn't use on the other albums. That way we fulfil our contract, then we can get the hell out to Saroudan.'

'Most of that old stuff isn't good enough,' Buddy said.

'Anything's good enough for a record company that treats you like XS are treating us,' Jason said, siding with his twin. 'Even if it's a brilliant album, they won't promote it. The only way we could get a hit at the moment is if one of us dies and we get a load of free publicity. Any volunteers?'

'Look,' Buddy said, 'I've written a lot of new songs during the last couple of months.'

'We haven't got time to rehearse them, for God's sake,' Jason shouted.

'I'm not putting out a crap album. No way!' Buddy shouted back.

'Oh yeah, right – and we have to do what you want. As usual!' Jason sneered.

'What the hell's that supposed to mean?' Buddy snapped back.

Jason turned away, but Buddy grabbed hold of his shoulder.

Jason swung around and smashed his fist into Buddy's chest. Buddy was so shocked that he swung without thinking and caught Jason a crashing blow on the side of his head. Jason raised his fist again, but Mike grabbed him and Dave got hold of Buddy and pulled him away.

It had all exploded out of nowhere and it calmed

down just as quickly. Jason said that he hadn't meant anything and he apologized for hitting Buddy, and Buddy said he was sorry for reacting. They shook hands, but the tension didn't go away – so it wasn't the best moment for Kenny to announce that he was going back to Scotland for Christmas and wanted to stay until New Year.

'Oh, come off it, Kenny,' Mike snarled. 'That would leave us two days' rehearsal.'

'Aye, but Hogmanay's important in Scotland, see.'

'Tough luck, Jock,' Jason said. 'If you're not back here the day after Boxing Day, I'll ram your drumsticks right up your kilt, OK?'

Kenny shrugged and fell into a moody silence; but he turned up on time after Christmas, and they managed to record an entire song, 'Bad Dreams', in one session. There was still a strange mood in the band, but they all seemed enthusiastic about the song and Buddy began to think that they might be able to make a good album after all.

Then they started work on 'Why Things Happen'. It was a long song and there were complicated time-changes in the rhythm for the drums and the bass. Jason was spot on for every take, but Kenny just couldn't get it right. Suddenly, at the end of the afternoon, Jason exploded and stomped out of the studio, saying he'd had enough. They went on, trying to lay down a proper drum-track, until Buddy saw that Kenny was beginning to panic, so he told him to go home and relax for the evening.

'Happy now?' Mike said to Buddy and Dave as soon as Kenny had left. 'You've landed us with a crap drummer.'

'Come on, Mike, there's no point in blaming each other . . .' Buddy began, but it was no good.

Mike was looking for a row and Dave was ready to take him on. Within seconds they were shouting abuse at each other and it ended with Mike pushing Dave aside and slamming out of the studio.

Buddy couldn't get over the change. For years the band had got on so well, but now it was as if the magic mix, the chemistry that had held them together, had gone. They'd been like a family, but suddenly it was all falling apart.

The next day the twins were late, so Buddy and Dave got on with trying to help Kenny record the drum part. He was much more relaxed and got it right at the second attempt. Then Dave quickly laid down the keyboard track and Buddy began to feel confident – it was going to work. He was just going to have a go at the vocal when the twins came into the studio.

'Hey, you're just in time,' Buddy said. 'The song's really coming together. The rhythm tracks and keyboards sound great. We can do your guitar track now, Mike.'

Mike shook his head.

'What's up?' Buddy asked.

There was a long silence, then Mike shrugged. 'We're jacking it in. We're gonna start a band of our own with Rais. Do our own material, try a different style. Right, Jas?'

Jason nodded.

'Oh come on, guys,' Buddy said. 'This is crazy. We can't break up the band. Let's try and work things out.'

Mike shifted uneasily and looked at his brother.

'We've made up our minds,' Jason said.

'What about the new album? We've got to give XS something,' Dave pointed out.

'Give 'em the old material that's already in the can. Do whatever you want,' Jason said. 'But, as far as we're concerned, we're finished.'

Jason nodded to Mike, and they turned and left the room.

Buddy and Dave looked at each other, but there was nothing they could do or say. They knew the truth. The heart had gone out of the band a long time before and there was no bringing it back. Buddy felt a huge emptiness open up in front of him.

It was the end of The Bosses.

CHAPTER TWENTY

Buddy and Dave spent a couple of weeks in the studio, selecting and mixing the best of the old songs. They added the only new song, 'Bad Dreams', then presented the finished album to Alec Miller.

'Well,' Miller said, 'that ties things up. You've cobbled together an album. Now all that remains is for us to release it and we'll all have done our bit to fulfil the contract.'

And that was that. Something which had been the major part of their lives for five years was over.

'What you going to do, Dave?' Buddy asked.

'Go back to Exeter. Get a job or go to college – I've had it with music for a bit. What about you?'

'Haven't the faintest idea.'

And it was true. He was completely lost and aimless. He spent days trying to think about the future, but he just felt empty and tired.

Finally he went round to see his dad. It was a Saturday and the breaker's yard was full of people scrambling among the piles of old cars, looking for parts. Buddy and his dad sat in the caravan listening to the tape of the new album. Through the window, Buddy watched as two customers struggled to take the rear wheels off a car whose front had been completely smashed in a crash. The windscreen on the driver's side was splintered, and he couldn't imagine wanting the wheels from a car in which someone might have died.

'It's not all that bad, considering,' his dad said, when the tape finished. 'That one, "Bad Dreams" – could be a hit.'

Buddy had to laugh, 'Honest, Dad, you're such an optimist.'

'And what's wrong wiv that? Anyway, what you gonna do now? Form a new band?'

Buddy shrugged. 'I don't know. Maybe I'll pack it in. Do something else.'

'What, come and work 'ere?' His dad chuckled, nodding towards the wrecked cars outside. 'Don't be daft. Music's your life. You can't just chuck away a talent like yours.'

When he went to see his mum, he found himself pouring out all his unhappiness and confusion about the band, the way XS had behaved, and the music business in general.

'Well, I always said you'd be better off playing music as a hobby. Then you can play what you want, without having to please all those awful people.'

'Yeah, but what would I do the rest of the time? I don't want to be stuck in some dead-end job.'

'You don't have to be. A bright boy like you. If you got yourself some more education, you could do anything.'

'Oh yeah, I've heard about all those people who go to University and end up on the dole.'

But the more he thought about it, the more he liked the idea of studying. Perhaps he could learn to write better by reading more, and he liked the idea of learning how the brain works. Perhaps he could do a course in English and Psychology.

He went to the library and read the brochures of various universities, then sent off for application forms. His mum was delighted and when he pointed out that it would cost a lot of money, she said that he ought to give up the flat and go back to live at home.

The band had made very little money from the sales of 'She Got' because it had gone to pay for the making of the albums but, as the writer of the song, he had earned quite a lot for all the times it had been played on the radio. The money was still coming in, and he worked out that it would probably just be enough to support him through a three year course, provided he lived cheaply.

His dad was disappointed, of course.

'You're nuts,' he said when Buddy told him. 'Giving up music and living at home – it's going backwards. You're too old to live in your mum's pocket.'

'I'll only be at home a few months to save money, then I'll be going off to university.'

'Big deal! I wouldn't mind if studying was all you could do – but it's not. Other people'd give an arm and a leg to 'ave the talent you got. It's a crime to waste it like this.'

Buddy moved out of the flat and went back home. It was almost as if he had never been away, and for the first few weeks he was happy to be back in his old room. He was also excited by the things he was reading. The books about psychology, in particular, seemed to explode in his mind and he longed to talk to someone about the ideas. His mum was working long hours, though, and his dad was predictably crushing when he mentioned what he was reading.

'Psychologists,' he sneered. 'They need their brains looking at. By the way, I bumped into Bobby Rosen the other day.'

'What do you mean, "bumped into"? He just happened to come down here looking for spare parts, did he?'

'No, all right, I went up to see him at Saroudan. I just wanted to know if I was the only one who thinks you're off yer rocker, giving it all up. And I'm not. Said 'e'd sign you on the spot. And 'e reckons "Bad Dreams" is gonna be a hit.'

'What's he talking about?'

'Yeah, some Radio One DJ plays it every afternoon on his show and says that XS ought to release it as a single.'

'You're kidding.'

'I'm not. I told you it could be a hit. So, I'm not so stupid after all. That's why you should listen to me now.'

The following afternoon Buddy tuned in to Radio One and, sure enough, the DJ played 'Bad Dreams' and said that he'd had a lot of letters and faxes asking when XS were going to release it. It was good news, of course, but it just had the effect of unsettling Buddy. Maybe it was crazy to give up the music when it meant so much to him.

Then he got a phone-call from Dave saying he'd been in contact with Alec Miller and it looked very likely that XS would release 'Bad Dreams' as a single.

'I think he's having second thoughts about letting us go,' Dave said. 'Maybe we ought to get together again.'

Buddy said no, he was finished with music. He was going to university.

But the truth was that every day he grew less and less sure of himself and he had no one he could talk it over with. His parents were too biased one way or the other. The only person he could think of asking was Charmian, and finally he rang and arranged to go down to see her one Sunday.

Julius answered the door with a wide, wicked grin on his face.

'See what happen when you don't choose me, mon – de whole band fall apart!' Buddy smiled, thinking it was a friendly joke, but Julius went on, 'Gonna be the same for all Babylon. No equality and de whole t'ing fall down.'

Did he mean it? Did he still think that he hadn't got the drumming job because of prejudice? Luckily, at that moment Charmian appeared behind her brother and pushed him aside.

'Don't listen to Mr Angry Rasta,' she said, throwing her arms round Buddy and kissing him on the cheek.

'You don't know you roots,' Julius snapped back.

'At least Ah know dis ain't Kingston, Jamaica, mon!' Charmian laughed, imitating Julius's accent.

She led Buddy inside, and he said hello to her parents. Mr Rybeero seemed even weaker than before but Mrs Rybeero was the same as ever: her large, bustling figure matched by her big, warm personality and welcome. She tried to persuade Buddy to stay to lunch, but Charmian had made up her mind that they were going out.

They drove down to the old dock area and ate in a pub overlooking a wharf that had been turned into a yacht marina. At first the talk was all about the old days. They remembered people and events from school and laughed about things they'd done together; then they began talking about families. Charmian had always been close to her family, so Buddy was surprised when she said that she wanted to get away from home.

'Of course, I still love them,' she said, 'but we're all sort of cut off from each other. Jules is caught up in all that Africa roots stuff and you can't talk to him. Mum's got this big thing about me marrying her best friend's son, a guy called Esmond. I've told her we can't stand each other, but it's like she just doesn't hear me. Then there's poor old dad. Bit by bit his heart is giving out and he spends most of his time thinking about dying, but he keeps it all wrapped up inside himself.'

'What would you say to him, anyway?' Buddy asked. 'Nobody wants to die.'

'That's what he wants to talk about, but he can't. He just sits there, trying to tell himself lies that he doesn't believe.'

'What lies?'

'The things he's been taught in church. You know, that when he dies he's going to wake up in heaven and find all his dead friends and relatives waiting for him. Mum really believes all that stuff but Dad doesn't, not deep down.'

'Do you?'

'What, think that after death it's exactly like being here, only nicer? No. Actually, I couldn't think of anything worse than being me for the rest of eternity. And Dad doesn't believe it, either. He knows that when he dies it's the end of the human being called Malcolm Rybeero, but he can't bring himself to talk about it. And I can't force him.'

'So you think there's no life after death, then?'

'How do you know this isn't it?' she said.

Buddy felt his brain trip over itself, and the surprise must have shown on his face because Charmian laughed.

'You see?' she said. 'Maybe we're living a new life, having lived before. Maybe something goes on when I die. But definitely not my body or my brain – we know what happens to them. People talk about "spirit" but nobody knows what it means. People make guesses, but it's all a mystery.'

'Doesn't it bother you?'

'Not really, no. All the explanations that human beings can come up with are limited by what our brains can imagine, right? Well, we're not nearly as clever as we like to think we are. I hope the answer is something bigger and more complicated than our brains can possibly understand.'

Buddy had never thought about it like that, and it scared and excited him at the same time.

The morning had been dull, but by the time they

came out of the pub the clouds had cleared and it was a beautiful spring day. They walked in the sunshine along the docks and he felt a huge surge of happiness swell inside him.

Charmian was so easy to talk to, and they chatted about all the kinds of things he'd never been able to talk about with other people ... the important things. And it was serious but not gloomy – she made it all seem exciting and fun. And she was so sharp. Time after time she said things that seemed to shake his mind up and change his way of thinking.

Not that she had answers for everything. When he told her about not knowing whether to go to university or back into music, she said it was up to him.

'Personally, I'd love to go to university but I'm not good at music like you, so I just don't know what I'd do.'

He dropped her back home at the end of the afternoon, and they arranged to meet the following Sunday. By the time he'd driven through town and got to the motorway he was already wanting to see her again.

CHAPTER TWENTY-ONE

'Bad Dreams' was released at the beginning of April, and a week later it came into the charts at number 38. XS didn't bother with a video or any publicity, but the next week the record went up to 32. Dave kept ringing to say that the band ought to get together and publicize it, but it was obvious that he couldn't get Jason and Mike to agree so Buddy used that as an excuse not to do anything.

His dad was delighted that his prediction had come true and he increased the pressure on Buddy.

'You can't chuck it up now. You've got a hit, for Gawd's sake. Look, let me do a video. I know Alan and the guys at Arctic would 'elp out wiv the equipment. It could be a break for both of us.'

Buddy was on the point of saying yes, for his dad's sake, when he got a letter inviting him for an interview at Leeds University. It seemed like a sign, and he decided that, if he was offered a place, he would take it.

He got very nervous on the train up to Leeds, but the interview turned out to be very relaxed. The two lecturers, one from the Psychology Department and the other from the English Department, were quite young and they just asked him general questions about why he wanted to do the course. The Psychology lecturer even turned out to be a music fan, and he'd heard of The Bosses.

'I've never taught a rock star before,' he laughed. He wrote something on a form and then looked enquiringly at the other lecturer, who nodded. 'Well, we'll confirm it by letter, but I think I can tell you unofficially that we'll be offering you a place. I look forward to hearing all the inside stories about the Rock world!'

On the train back home Buddy bought an evening paper and saw the mid-week chart. 'Bad Dreams' had moved up to 27. He watched the countryside racing past and tried to hang on to his feeling of exhilaration. He had been offered a place at university. He was going to accept it. But he kept looking back at the chart: 27 ... 'Bad Dreams' ... The Bosses.

His mum was as pleased as his dad was disappointed, and he wondered why he couldn't make them both happy at the same time. She kept saying how proud she was that he would be the first person from her family to go to university, while his dad just watched 'Bad Dreams' slip down and then out of the charts and said that it was a wasted opportunity.

'It could've gone Top Ten, if you'd pushed it.'

'Dad, the band's broken up, XS don't give a damn, there was nothing we could do.'

Buddy filled the weekdays with reading, and on Sundays he went down to see Charmian to talk about the ideas that the books had given him. Somehow, chatting to her while they walked round the docks or out in the country seemed to help him organize his thoughts, and she always managed to say something that turned his ideas upside down or made him think again.

All the reading and thinking seemed to inspire him, and he found himself writing three or four songs a week. He usually took a guitar with him when he went to visit Charmian so that he could play the new songs to her. Julius was as spiky as ever on these visits, but he always came into the room when Buddy began playing. One Sunday he even asked if he could make a recording of one of the songs Buddy had just written so that he could teach it to his band.

The song was called 'Easy Answers', and Buddy saw how it could work with a reggae beat; so when he sang it again into Jules's tape recorder he gave it a chinking rhythm on the guitar and slightly altered the phrasing of his singing.

'Oh yeah, you got soul,' Jules grinned as he switched off the tape. 'Wait 'til you hear my band play it – it'll be monster.'

Jules went off to listen to the tape and Charmian went upstairs to change, so Buddy wandered out into the garden. Mr and Mrs Rybeero were sitting near the garden fence so that they could escape the cool breeze but catch the warmth of the spring sunshine. As soon as she saw him, Mrs Rybeero beckoned him over.

'Buddy, you do me a favour. Talk to Charmian and you tell her she make up her mind and marry Esmond. Him a good boy. She be happy with him.'

'I can't do that,' Buddy said.

'Sure you can. You her best friend, she listen to you.'

'Yeah, but something like that's up to her.'

'She take too long, she go lose him for sure.'

Buddy shrugged, and a moment later Charmian called out that she was ready. They drove out to the coast and, while they were walking along the beach, he told Charmian what her mum had said.

'Honestly, she just won't give up,' she sighed.

'I didn't know what to say.'

'You should have told her you were jealous,' Charmian laughed and her eyes were twinkling, but he didn't know if she was joking or not.

How could he be jealous? Char was great. There was no one in the world he preferred talking to. They had loads in common. They'd been friends for years. But that's all she was: a friend. There was a girl back home called Jenny who was more like a dating girlfriend. He fancied her a lot and they'd been out to the cinema a couple of times. It wasn't like that at all with Charmian. No, Charmian was just a friend. Really important, more important than Jenny, but not someone you got jealous about.

Glenn and Alice got married at the end of May. Buddy was best man, and Glenn said that he had to bring someone to the wedding. He thought of asking Jenny but in the end he knew he'd have more fun with Charmian, so he asked her. She got a day off work and bought a special outfit for the event. She looked lovely and he felt proud to introduce her to all the people he knew.

'Here, that Charmian's a little cracker, isn't she?' Glenn whispered when they got to the church hall after the ceremony. 'Where you been hiding her?'

'Oh, we've been friends for years,' Buddy said.

'Oh yeah, just good friends, eh?'

'Yeah.'

'Not the way she looks at you, you're not. You can't hide things from Uncle Glenn. I reckon you'll be the next one going down the aisle!'

'Don't be daft!' Buddy laughed.

It was great to see Glenn walking so well and looking so happy, and the whole wedding went smoothly. There was only one awkward moment. It came during Buddy's best man speech. He told some funny stories about Glenn, then he mentioned Alice.

'Glenn's dead lucky, because I know what a warm and loving girl Alice is,' Buddy said.

'Oh yeah?' Glenn called out. 'How do you know that?'

It was only a joke and everybody laughed, but

Buddy felt his heart race and he saw Alice's neck blush pink above her white dress.

''Cos you've told me about eight million times, you lovesick little Romeo,' Buddy said quickly.

Everybody laughed again and it was obvious that nobody thought there was anything strange, but it put Buddy off his stride. He cut the speech a bit short and his hand trembled slightly when he held up his glass and asked everybody to toast the bride and groom.

When Buddy took Charmian home after the wedding, Julius casually mentioned that his band had been offered a gig at a small open-air concert in Birmingham in three weeks' time.

'It's nothing, really. We're the first on the bill, and they've only given us twenty-five minutes,' he added.

'Hey, that's great, Jules,' Buddy said. 'We've gotta come and see it!'

'Yeah, if you want,' Julius said coolly, but his eyes lit up and he couldn't hide the smile on his lips.

Buddy and Charmian drove up to Birmingham, following the van that Julius's band had hired. They helped the band set up when they got there, and Jules teased Buddy about being a roadie now instead of a star.

It was a wonderful June day and, when the park gates opened, hundreds of people poured in and began to take their places in front of the stage. Nobody had been expecting so many people, and Julius and the band were nervous as they waited to go on. Buddy caught their excitement and he suddenly realized how much he missed playing gigs.

Buddy and Charmian slipped round to the front to

watch the show and they were both surprised by how good the band was. They only had time for six songs and the sound balance wasn't right; but the crowd loved them and they were up on their feet, dancing and clapping along to the pulsing beat.

'This is our last song,' Julius announced at the end. 'It's called "Easy Answers" and it's written by an old friend of mine who's here today: Buddy Clark of The Bosses.'

Jules pointed to where Buddy was standing, and people immediately turned to look at him. The band played the song well and the audience cheered and were still shouting for more when the second band came on and started to set up.

When they met up backstage, Julius was jumping around with excitement like the Jules of the old days: alive and enthusiastic and brimming with energy.

'Did you hear that?' he shouted. 'They loved us.'

'That's 'cos you were terrific,' Buddy said. 'Really. You've got to keep playing, Jules – you've got an ace band there.'

'Thanks,' Jules beamed. 'The bloke who organized the concert wants us to go on at the end with the main band for a sort of big finale. Can you stay? It'll be monster.'

'No,' Charmian said, before Buddy could reply. 'Now you've told them that Buddy's here, he'll only get pestered if we hang around. So we'll push off.'

Buddy was surprised at her hurry, and on the way to the car he told her that they didn't have to rush away.

'I know, but I just fancy being on our own a bit. Drive back slowly, see a bit of the countryside, maybe stop and have a meal. It's such a lovely day. What d'you think?'

'Yeah, great.'

They drove south out of Birmingham and took some small roads across the Vale of Evesham and into the Cotswold Hills. The weather was perfect and they drove through the rolling countryside, chatting and listening to music. Buddy had caught the sun earlier, and the warm rays shining through the windscreen made his face glow. He felt relaxed and happy. He glanced at Char, and the light was skating off her glossy hair. She smiled at him and touched his hand on the steering wheel.

'I feel great,' she said, 'as if I want to catch this moment and hold on to it forever.'

'Me too,' he laughed.

They stopped at a pub in a small village and sat outside in the garden. Their table was next to an old stone wall that glowed golden in the sun and seemed to have absorbed the heat of the day. They ordered lobster salad and a bottle of white wine and they sat, eating and drinking, watching the sun turn red and begin to dip below the hills.

'I suppose we'd better start back,' Buddy said after the meal.

'Oh no, I don't want it to end. Why don't we stay up here overnight? I saw a bed-and-breakfast place just outside the village. It looked lovely, an old farm. It would be so great to wake up and go out for a walk in the fields tomorrow. Besides, you've been drinking – you can't drive! Oh, come on.'

There was no resisting her, and they walked back through the village to the farm. They turned into the farmyard and went round to the back of the house where an old collie dog guarded the open door. The dog stretched and stood up as they approached and, as Buddy bent down to stroke it, a voice called from the other side of the yard. A middle-aged woman came out of a barn, carrying a tin bowl full of eggs.

'We're looking for bed and breakfast,' Charmian explained.

'Fine. Let me just put these inside and I'll show you the way – the rooms are in a separate building that we've had converted. Come on, Jester.'

The collie led the way across the farmyard to an old stone barn. The walls were covered with roses and the scent hung in the air as they climbed the outside stone staircase to the first floor. The woman opened the door and the dog ran inside, skidding on the shiny, wooden floor of the long corridor.

'No, Jester, come back here,' the woman called as she led them inside. The dog came back and jumped up excitedly. 'He always gets skittish when he comes up here. Now then, ermm . . .?'

Charmian smiled. 'We'd like separate rooms, please.'

'Oh fine,' the woman said, opening the nearest door. 'There's this room, and the other is just down the corridor. They've both got shower and toilet so . . . well, you can just choose. Feel free to walk round the farm. There's a lovely view from the orchard. Breakfast is at any time after eight, in the main house. Well, I'll wish you good-night.'

They looked at the rooms and then went outside for a stroll. Night was falling fast but it was still warm, and they stood in the orchard, looking across the valley to the misty blue hills and the thin line of orangey light that clung to the horizon. Birds were still singing in the trees further down the hill; Buddy and Charmian sat on the grass and listened to the amazing sounds as birds called to each other. The notes tumbled together and rose up out of the deepening blue of the valley.

Slowly the light thickened until the trees disappeared. The birdsong grew quieter, then stopped. A hush fell all round them and they lay on their backs, watching the stars brighten and begin to wheel across the sky. The cooler night air started to sink down on them, and Buddy could feel the warmth of Charmian's shoulder against his.

'Mm, smell that air,' Charmian said as she took a deep breath. 'It's gorgeous – roses, cut grass. It's like the whole smell of summer. So rich.'

She took another deep sniff of the air and then sneezed.

'Too rich for your town nose,' Buddy laughed as she sneezed again.

He got to his feet and pulled her up. She held on to his hand as they turned back towards the house. He had to let go of her hand to open the gate out of the orchard, and he was wondering whether to take hold of it again when she slipped her arm round his back. He put his arm round her shoulder and they strolled across the farmyard. Jester came running up to them, his tail wagging the whole of his rear end.

Buddy bent down and scratched the collie behind his ears while Charmian squatted down and patted him. After a moment the dog ran back towards the house and, as they stood up together, Charmian pressed close to Buddy and kissed his lips. It was a gentle kiss and gone before he could respond.

She turned and started up the stairs. He stood

watching her go, not knowing what to do or say. She disappeared through the door.

By the time he got up the stairs she was already opening her bedroom door. She smiled.

'Good-night,' she said. Then she went in and closed the door behind her.

Buddy went into his room and got undressed. He had a shower, running it from hot to cold and back again, enjoying the water pouring on to his skin. He dried himself, standing in the dark, looking out of the window at the velvety night and the shimmering sky. Even in his bed he could see the sky, and he lay, watching one particular star edge closer and closer to the top of the window.

The door handle rattled and the door opened. He sat up and started to swing out of bed. Charmian was standing in the doorway, the light from the corridor streaming in behind her. She stepped into the room and closed the door. In the darkness he couldn't see where she was, but he stood up. He'd left the window open and he could feel a night breeze run across his naked body.

'Buddy,' Charmian said from the darkness. 'I know we've never talked about this but . . . when we were fourteen I was crazy about you . . . in love, I think. Then we had to move away and . . . I thought it was just a crush or something, and anyway . . . Look, what I'm trying to say is, since we met again I found out that I still do — love you. I don't know . . . The thing is, if you want me to go . . . I'll go.'

'No,' Buddy said, and his heart was pounding, shaking his whole chest. 'No, stay.'

He put out his hand and saw her move out of the shadow and into the faint light from the window.

149

She stopped just in front of him and pulled the straps of her dress off her shoulders and let it drop to the floor. Her skin shone grey-blue and her body was cooler than his as she pressed herself against him. He turned and slid into the bed.

She stood for an instant, then lifted the covers and slipped in next to him.

Chapter Twenty-Two

It was hard to say goodbye to Charmian, and all week he thought about her and wanted to see her again. He rang Jenny and explained that he couldn't see her any more. She didn't sound very upset, and he realized how shallow their relationship had been.

How different with Char. Everything was right. It all felt complete. He admired her. He respected her. They could talk like he'd never talked with anyone else. It was physical as well, of course. Oh yes. Oh yes. More than ever before. The friendship, the talk, the understanding, the happiness at being together – it all made loving her body even better. Just thinking about that night made him feel weak with longing. Swoon. It was a good word for the way his head and his heart spun when he thought about her.

And the ridiculous thing was that she didn't know what he felt. When he saw her the following weekend, she kept asking if he was sure.

'Of course I'm sure,' he kept telling her.

'I don't know – I feel I sort of pushed it. I mean I

knew . . . I've known since we met up again. But you never showed anything.'

'Because I'm dumb. I'm stupid. I'm blind. I needed a push.'

'There you are – you think I pushed you.'

'I don't mean like that. Oh come on, Char. Look in my eyes. Look straight in my eyes. This is how much I love you.'

He rolled his eyes round and round then crossed them, until she started to laugh.

'It's just a joke to you,' she giggled.

'No, it's not. Everything else is a joke. But not this. This is the most serious thing in the whole world and yet it makes me so happy that all I can do is go around smiling like an idiot. Look, look at my lips. See? They can't help it, they just keep turning up at the sides. They've just got to smile. They're crazy lips. Completely crazy. Look, they're going again. They're going to smile. Quick – the only thing that can stop them being crazy lips is if you put your lips against them. Like this . . .'

He wanted to swing from lampposts. He wanted to climb trees. He wanted to sing. Yeah, make up songs and sing them just to her. He wanted to run across the grass. And laugh and jump up and down. And touch her. Be with her. He wanted to hold her. Kiss her. Make love to her. Smile at her. Look at her. He felt light and stupid and wonderful.

He behaved like a loony all day, and she laughed and joined in; but when they kissed goodbye at the end of the evening she became all serious again.

'Really, Buddy, I wish I . . . I wish it hadn't been me that . . . came into your room. I feel I kind of trapped you.'

151

'Charmian Rybeero, cut it out! Trapped me. You're nuts. You make me swoon. Isn't that a great word? Swoon. You're the most wonderful, fantastic thing that's ever happened to me. I could die now and it wouldn't matter.'

'Don't say that!' Her arms went round him and she squeezed so tightly that he knew she was really afraid.

'Hey, don't worry,' he said. 'I'll be here panting on your doorstep, the minute you get home next week. In fact I'll meet you from work.'

She stepped back. 'You've forgotten.'

'What?'

'Buddy, I told you ages ago. I've got this three-week manager's course in Scotland starting on Saturday.'

'Oh no! I forgot. Don't go. Tell 'em you're ill or something.'

'Buddy, I can't.'

'But that means I won't see you for nearly four weeks. A whole month! I can't stand it. I'll come up to Scotland.'

'Don't be stupid. Anyway, we'll be working all the time, it's really intensive.'

The news filled him with gloom, and suddenly he felt he had to get away or he would become really miserable.

'I'm going,' he said, giving her a last little kiss. 'I'll ring you. 'Bye.'

It felt like a terrible wrench, getting in the car and driving off, and it had all happened so fast. Char looked sad and she didn't wave back when he stuck his hand out of the window. He looked in the rear-view mirror when he got to the corner but she was already out of sight.

Perhaps being in love meant it would always be like this, saying goodbye: a terrible tearing feeling in the chest.

He rang her every evening during the week and then wrote to her every day while she was in Scotland. He got a couple of postcards from her, telling him how hard the course was. They even had to go on an outward bound weekend, camping and living rough. 'Dead useful stuff for working on the perfume counter when I get back!' she wrote.

She just signed Char on the cards. No 'Love' and certainly none of the stupid, lovey-dovey stuff he found himself putting in his letters.

'I want to be your teddy bear,' he wrote in one of them. 'I know it sounds dumb, but I do, I really do. Just like Elvis in that song. I always thought it was stupid, but now I know it's not. I want to be your teddy bear, waiting patiently on your pillow until you come to bed and hug me. You've done this to me. I go around thinking all these stupid things and it's like every love song I've ever heard. I'm a walking cliché of LURVE! But it's all true. I try and write songs about it, but all I can think of saying is – I love you, I love you.'

In another of them he put a whole page covered with Xs and wrote 'There are four hundred and seventy-three kisses on this page. Not enough. I'll give you more when I see you.'

In fact he didn't give her one.

He tried to, but she wouldn't let him.

She came back from Scotland late on a Sunday evening and they'd arranged to meet the following Saturday, but he couldn't wait. On Wednesday afternoon he drove the hundred and thirty miles to her house. He arrived early and parked the car down the road so he could surprise her when she turned the corner on her way home from work.

At just gone six he saw her in his side mirror. She was walking slowly, head down, and she looked tired. He smiled in anticipation. She'd soon cheer up. He waited until she was level with the car, then swung the door open.

'Dadaaaaaah!' he yelled as he jumped out.

She spun around in surprise, and he caught her in his arms and leaned in to kiss her. She twisted her head away and pushed him back.

'What are you doing here? I didn't say you could come.'

'What is it?' he asked, feeling the blood drain away from his face.

She looked at him and her eyes started to fill with tears.

'I don't want to see you.'

'Why?'

She shook her head and a tear spilled from her eye and rolled down her cheek so slowly that it looked like oil on her skin.

'Char, what is it?' he asked, putting out his arms and trying to take hold of her.

She pushed him away again and leaned back against the hedge. She smeared the tear away with her hand and held her head up proudly, forcing herself not to break down.

'It's my fault. It's not your problem. It's only me to blame.'

'Char, what? What's your fault?'

The tears brimmed in her eyes again, but again she held them back with a proud shake of her head.

'I'm pregnant.'

Once or twice since that night, he had thought of the possibility and had sworn at himself for not using anything. But he'd swept the worry aside. It was so unlikely. Just one night. The chances must be tiny. No, it was all right. Next time he'd be more careful.

'I'm pregnant,' she said again. And every single one of the problems – telling parents, no university, getting married, finding somewhere to live – hit him. Like a punch in the chest. And he did everything wrong.

'Oh my God.' His first words. She was looking at him closely and, as he spoke, there was a flicker in her eyes.

'Have you told anyone?' His first question. Another flicker in Char's eyes, then she looked away from him. She raised her chin again proudly.

'I told my mother,' she said.

'What did she say?' These weren't the things he should be asking.

'She said she was ashamed of me and not to tell my father because it would probably kill him.'

'Oh my God.'

Her eyes were red, but there were no tears in them, only proud defiance. And he had to look away. Down the road, where things were going on as if nothing had happened. Cars racing past on the main road. Swifts swooping among the chimney pots. A kid bouncing a ball against a wall.

'What are you going to do?' he asked.

'If you mean, am I going to get rid of it? – the answer is no.'

'I didn't mean that . . .' But it had crossed his mind.

'Look,' she said, 'I've told you it's my problem. Not yours. I just want you to leave me alone, OK?'

He looked at her. Did she mean it?

'OK?' her voice was a harsh whisper. She meant it.

He nodded. She turned and walked away. He watched her go. She went into her house. Char and their baby. He did nothing.

Chapter Twenty-Three

Charmian had said leave her alone, so he tried to leave her alone. He longed to be able to see her and talk to her but he forced himself to stay away. He just couldn't stop thinking of her, though, and after eight days he gave in and rang her.

'Char, it's Buddy.'

There was silence at the other end. There were so many things he'd thought of saying to her, but suddenly he couldn't remember any of them. The silence went on.

'Char, I'm sorry,' he said finally.

'Well, I'm sorry you're sorry.'

There was another long pause. He could hear her breathing quickly and he wondered if she'd started to cry.

'Are you absolutely sure that, you know . . .?' he began.

'That it's yours?' Charmian cut in.

'No! That you're pregnant?'

'Yes, I'm sure – I had a test. And yes, it's yours.

I've never had sex with anyone else. Whatever you might think, I don't usually throw myself into bed with people.'

'Don't say things like that. Look, do you want to . . . Do you think we ought to . . . get married?'

'Well, that's a romantic proposal if ever I heard one. Let's put it this way – have you told anyone about this?'

'No.'

'Why? Because you were hoping I'd have an abortion?'

'No! Because I was ashamed, I suppose.'

'Ashamed?' her voice was hard and angry.

What did she want him to say? Everything he said seemed wrong. 'I don't mean ashamed. Embarrassed. Wondering what people would say. You know what I mean.'

'No, I don't. I've got a baby inside me. I didn't think it would happen like this, but there's no way I want this baby to feel that I'm embarrassed by it or ashamed of it or worried what people might say. I want it to feel wanted and loved, not . . . Look, Buddy, I told you before – this is my responsibility.'

'Char . . .'

'Don't ring me again.'

She put the phone down. The line went dead and Buddy could hear the thumping of his heart. He clenched his jaw tight to stop the stinging of tears in his eyes.

She had made him feel such a coward. She was right. He had wondered if the baby was his. He had thought about abortion. He had been more worried what people would say than about the baby. He hadn't even thought about the baby.

Well, the first thing he had to do was start talking about it. He had to tell his parents. His mum first.

He could feel the blood pulsing in his neck when he heard her come in from work. She popped her head round the door and asked him to make a cup of tea while she was changing. He went into the kitchen and got things ready.

She came in and sat down at the table. He handed her a cup of tea and sat down opposite her. He counted to ten. But said nothing. He lifted his cup to drink, but his hand was shaking so badly that he put it down again.

'Mum . . .'

She looked at him and for an instant he almost said something else, anything else, but he forced himself to say, 'Charmian's going to have a baby. It's mine.'

She closed her eyes and sighed wearily, 'Oh no.'

He had imagined that she would be shocked and angry, but she just sat there and let him talk. And when he'd told her everything, there was no blaming from her, just a concern to get practical problems sorted out.

'Well, whether Charmian wants you involved or not, you're going to have to provide for the little one. God knows if you'll have enough money left to do your university course.'

He didn't say it, but he didn't give a damn about the university course. All he cared about was Char.

'Why's she cutting me out like this, Mum? I just don't understand.'

'Maybe it's her way of coping. I don't know. If she decides to look after the baby on her own, there's nothing you can do about it, and at least it means you can get on with your own life. The last thing you need now is a baby tying you down. Think about it.'

He tried to think about it, but he couldn't imagine what it would be like having a baby around. All he could really think about was the pain of not being with Char. Everything had been so good – how could it suddenly turn so bad?

Having told his mum, he thought he'd got the worst over and that telling his dad would be much easier, but he was wrong. For a start, he could hardly get a word in edgeways when he went round to the caravan because his dad had his own news.

'Guess where I'm going next month. Memphis! To visit Elvis's house. Just think of it! Des King's organizing it all and we're hiring a minibus so we can tour around. And at the end we're gonna drive down to Florida and go to Disneyworld. What d'you reckon? Fantastic, eh?'

'Yeah.'

'Trip of a lifetime. I bin wanting to go to the States ever since I first 'eard rock'n'roll in the Fifties.'

'Dad –'

'I used to dream about driving along in a Cadillac wiv some beautiful young girl. Open top, sun shining, Buddy Holly on the radio. Fantastic! 'Ere, why don't you come wiv us?'

'I can't. Dad –'

' 'Course you can. Des'll fix it.'

'Dad!' he yelled.

'What?'

Buddy took a deep breath and blurted out his news. He thought his dad might laugh, or crack a joke – that's how he dealt with everything. But not this time. There was a terrible silence.

'How? How could you be so stupid?' his dad finally said in a whisper. Then his voice rose in anger. 'I thought you were clever. But oh no, you go and get yourself caught in the oldest trap on earth. You dumb little . . . I mean, my God, it's not as if you can't buy condoms everywhere, not like in my day. But you 'ave to go and take every risk under the sun. Risk falling for a baby. Risk pickin' up some disease. You stupid . . .'

'Dad, there's no risk of disease. It was the first time – for both of us.'

'Oh, so you thought you'd celebrate and 'ave a kid!'

'It wasn't like that. It was a mistake.'

'You can bloody say that again. God, I never thought we'd end up with black blood in our family.'

'There's no such thing as black blood or white blood. There's red blood, and that's all. We're all the same.'

'Oh yeah, I suppose you think that's a dead clever answer. We're not all the same. You know what the kid's gonna be, don't you? Not black, not white. Poor little thing's gonna be stuck in the middle – rejected by both sides.'

Buddy got up and moved to the door. He couldn't take any more of this. He opened the door, went out, and slammed it behind him. The caravan rocked. Rocked, like his whole life seemed to be rocking.

Nothing was sure any more. Did he want to go to university? Did he want to make music? Did he want a baby? Did he want to get married? Did he want to get tied down or did he want to be free? The only thing he could be sure of was what he felt about Charmian. He loved her. Maybe even that would change. He thought that she had loved him, but now she didn't even want to talk to him.

He rang her twice but put the phone down when her mother answered. Then, a week later, he rang again. This time Jules answered, and Buddy took the plunge.

'You've got a lot of nerve,' Julius said when he heard his voice. 'I ought to smash your face in for what you've done to my sister. My mum's nearly gone out of her mind worrying about it, and my dad's had to have extra pills for his heart.'

'Jules, please listen. I'm sorry if your parents are upset. I wish it had never happened. I never wanted a baby . . .'

There was a rattle as the receiver went down.

'Jules?'

'What?'

'I thought you'd put the phone down.'

'It was the extension. Must have been Char – she's the only one upstairs. So it's obvious she doesn't want to talk to you, isn't it? None of us do. We're in different worlds – you stick to yours and we'll stick to ours.'

'Jules, that's not true. What about when we were kids? We were friends.'

This time Julius did put the phone down, and the line went dead.

He tried writing a letter to Charmian, but he just couldn't find the right things to say. In the end he wrote a short note saying that he missed her and that, whatever she decided, he would give her money to help bring the baby up. He waited two weeks, then gave up waiting for a reply.

All the time he had believed, deep down, that it would all work out, but suddenly he slipped into a terrible depression. When he walked round town, everything and everybody seemed so ugly. People rushed around buying things they didn't really need. He looked in cafés and saw them stuffing their stupid faces with food. The noise and ugliness and stupidity were too terrible and he couldn't bear to go out. He lay in bed in the quiet house. He stared at the ceiling and felt empty and grey. Nothing mattered.

Two days running his mum came home from work and found him still in bed. The first time she didn't say much, but the second time she lost her temper. When he still wouldn't get up, she stormed out of the room and he heard her go downstairs and phone someone. He lay there, hoping that she had rung Charmian and that, by some miracle, she would come round. But she hadn't rung Charmian, she had rung his dad.

'You – out of that bed!' his dad ordered as he came through the door, half an hour later. Buddy didn't move, so his dad came over and grabbed the edge of the duvet. 'Look,' he said, 'I'll put up wiv almost anyfing from you, Buddy. But I ain't gonna let you lie in bed feelin' sorry for yourself. So, you get up or I pull you out.'

The look on his face showed that he meant it, so Buddy slid out and sat on the edge of the bed in his boxer shorts. His bedroom was chilly and he shivered.

'Get dressed,' his dad ordered.

'Dad, just . . .'

'Get dressed or I'll knock your block off. You know I'm strong enough, and I'm telling you I'm angry enough. Do it!'

Buddy didn't argue. He grabbed his jeans and a sweatshirt and put them on. Then he followed his dad downstairs.

They sat in the front room with his mum and had what his dad kept calling 'a family discussion'. There wasn't much discussion, though, because his dad did most of the talking. His mum said one or two things, but Buddy didn't say a word, mainly because he was worried that if he opened his mouth he would begin to cry. For the first time in years, his mum and dad were together and trying to sort things out for him.

'I don't know what to tell you about Charmian,' his dad said, 'cxccpt to say that when your 'eart gets broken it hurts like hell and you think it's never gonna get better. But it does. Bit by bit you get over it. Ain't that right, Carol?'

His mum and dad looked at each other, and she nodded.

'As for what you do now The Bosses 'ave broken up – go on wiv the music or go to university – well, you ain't been 'elped by me and your mum poking our oar in. So, I'm gonna shut up. You can do what you want and I ain't gonna put no pressure. Carol?'

'Me, too,' his mum said. 'You do whatever you want. I'm happy if you're happy.'

'OK, son?' his dad asked.

He nodded. It was more than OK. Nothing had changed. The problems were still there. But it was as if some huge, dark weight had been lifted off him.

'Right,' his dad said, getting up. 'I'm off. Family

discussion over. And if you stay in bed later than eight-thirty tomorrow, I'll knock you into the middle of next week.'

He was back again the following evening, but this time it wasn't for a family discussion. He'd had a word with Des King and it wasn't too late to change the travel arrangements. He wanted them both to come on the trip to the States.

His mum shook her head, 'Terry, it's a nice thought and I really appreciate it, but the idea of being stuck with a group of Teds going round Grace-land . . . well, you know what I mean. But I think Buddy ought to go. It'll take his mind off things and give him a break.' She put her hand on Buddy's shoulder and squeezed. 'Honest, love, it'll give you time to sort things out.'

'She's right, mate. A couple of weeks in the States wiv the lads, and everyfing'll look different. It'll be ace. And just think of all that music over there. We can see a different band every night.'

It was true. The Mississippi Delta. The land of the Blues. The land of Rock'n'Roll. It would be stupid to miss the chance. He didn't fancy being stuck with Des King and a group of Teds, but on the other hand . . .

He remembered the idea he'd had about all the doors that you could open or not. He had two doors in front of him now, one marked GO, the other marked STAY. Where did each one lead? He reached out and opened one.

'Yeah, I'd love to come,' he said.

Chapter Twenty-Four

The evening before his trip to America, Buddy took his mum out for a meal to thank her. For the last two weeks she had come home early every day and had involved him in helping to draw up a questionnaire for a big market research programme. Then she'd sent him to try it out on local businesses, before she presented it to her client. He knew that it was all an attempt to keep him busy and stop him feeling low. In fact, although he still worried about Char and missed her terribly, he hadn't felt helpless and depressed since that evening his dad had come round.

And now he was getting really excited at the idea of the holiday in the States.

'Don't you wish you were coming?' he asked his mum as they sat, drinking coffee, after the meal.

'No. There are loads of places I'd rather go. But America's always been your dad's dream. He said he'd take me there for our honeymoon – but we didn't have enough money, so we ended up in Torquay for five days. Typical!'

Buddy always loved hearing about the old days, so he kept asking questions and, for a change, his mum seemed to be in the mood to answer them. She talked about how she'd met his dad.

'First thing he ever said to me? Walked up to me at a dance and said, "Wotcher, darling. Wanna dance with the best-looking bloke in the room?"

And the thing is, he *was* the best looking bloke in the room. I fell for him like a ton of bricks! I was only seventeen and my mum and dad were dead, so I suppose I was looking for someone to hold on to.'

Then she started telling him about earlier times. How her mum had died when she was nine and how she'd been brought up by her dad, until he was killed at work when she was fifteen.

'That's why I left school so early. I mean, I wasn't very good at it and I wasted my chances there – but that's my biggest regret, that I didn't stay on and get my exams.'

She even told him about her earliest memories when she was a kid: staying with her gran in the country where the loo was just a wooden seat above a hole in the ground in a little hut at the end of the garden. And falling down and hurting her nose on a thing called a 'cakewalk' at a fair. And wanting to be a Brownie but her parents couldn't afford the uniform. And her favourite doll, called Loopy.

He felt really close to her, and when they left the restaurant he put his arm round her shoulder as they walked to the car.

He just couldn't get to sleep that night; he lay, looking at his room in the light from the street lamp outside. He'd slept in this bed for as long as he could remember. The sheets and pillowcases used to have planes and trains and soccer players on them. Up to the age of nine he used to cuddle his furry toy rabbit, Flops, in this bed.

He'd been ill with measles and mumps in this bed. He'd heard his dad playing his old Buddy Holly records from this bed, and he used to sing along with them until he fell asleep. He'd lain awake in this bed, listening to his mum and dad downstairs. He'd heard them talk and laugh, and he'd heard them row. He'd been lying in this bed the night his mum had left home when he was thirteen, and he'd thought it had been his fault. He'd lain awake in this bed worrying when his dad was out stealing for Des King. He'd learned to play guitar in this room. He'd written his first songs here.

He had a sudden panic that he would never sleep here again, never see this room again. Perhaps the plane would crash tomorrow. He would die young, like Buddy Holly.

The sky outside grew grey with the first light of dawn and he finally fell asleep.

His mum drove him to the airport the next morning and neither of them said much on the long journey. Buddy's insides were churning. He didn't want to go, and when he kissed her goodbye and watched her drive away he wished he was going home with her. She waved as she went round the corner and disappeared.

The minute he got inside the terminal building, he saw his dad and the others – it was impossible to miss them. They were all wearing their full Teddy Boy gear: drainpipe trousers, drape jackets with velvet collars, bootlace ties, thick, crêpe-soled shoes and fluorescent socks. They all had big sideburns and their hair was quiffed and shining with brilliantine.

Buddy had got used to seeing his dad looking like that, but even he blinked when he saw five of them together. Des King was the only one not in Ted gear and, despite the fact that he was dripping with flashy gold chains and rings and had a huge cigar stuck in his mouth, he looked positively ordinary next to the others.

'Right, let's get the introductions over,' his dad said. 'You know Des, of course.' Buddy nodded at King, and a familiar tremor of doubt ran through him. Did King know? Had he guessed that Buddy had once tried to get him caught by the police? He never showed the slightest sign, but Buddy always felt uneasy in his company.

King smiled a big smile and gripped Buddy's hand very tightly.

'And you've met Dougie and Vince, ain't you?' his dad went on.

'Yeah. Hi, Dougie,' Buddy said, shaking hands with the tall, thin Ted with the pale-blue drape jacket, then turning and shaking hands with Vince, who was wearing a black drape with red velvet collar and cuffs.

'And this is Little Pete,' his dad said, pointing to the small man whose hair was quiffed at the front but who had a huge bald patch at the back. He wore a grey drape with black velvet on the collar and cuffs which, along with his pinched, miserable face, made him look a bit like an undertaker.

Buddy shook hands with him. Little Pete's hand was icy and slightly damp, and he squeezed Buddy's hand painfully.

'And, lastly, we've got Evan. Evan's met Jerry Lee Lewis and Gene Vincent.'

'Really?' Buddy said, shaking hands with the fat man in the maroon drape with the black velvet trim.

'Yeah,' Evan said. 'I only shook hands and said hello, like, to Jerry Lee; but Gene stayed at my house when he played Swansea on his last tour before he died. Well, he was that broke, like. The promoters were ripping him off, see. Tragic, it was.'

Wherever they went, people stared at the five Teds, so Buddy walked some distance away from them and hoped that no one would think he was with them. As soon as they got through the security checks and into the departure lounge, the Teds headed for the bar. Everybody else ordered beer, but Little Pete and Evan had triple scotches, which they gulped and then ordered some more.

'They got the jitters about flying,' Dougie laughed.

'Nah,' Vince said. 'Any excuse to get tanked up with those two.'

Vince was right. After they downed their third triple scotch, Little Pete and Evan went off to the Duty Free shop. Buddy spotted them, ten minutes later, lifting the plastic bags to their lips and taking big gulps from their duty-free bottles. By the time the flight was called, they could hardly stand. They reeled their way to the plane, slumped down in their seats, and fell asleep.

Buddy envied them. He was feeling more and more nervous and he wished he could be unconscious, too. He looked out of the window at the ground. Perhaps he had already walked on it for the last time. As he thought that, he found himself saying to himself: so what? If you're going to die, you're going to die. There's nothing you can do about it. It's not such a big deal. Just accept what happens.

A shiver passed through him, and all his fear went. He felt calm and peaceful. As if he had handed his life over to something bigger than himself. Suddenly he knew what Charmian had meant when she talked about the answer to things being bigger and more complicated than human beings could understand. For an instant, just an instant, it felt as if he was in contact with that bigger thing; then the moment passed.

As soon as they were airborne and the NO SMOKING signs were turned off, his dad lit up.

'I thought you'd given up,' Buddy said.

'I have. But I've got to smoke while I'm in America. It's what I used to dream about. Driving a Buick or a Chevy, me looking like James Dean wiv a girl leaning against my shoulder and a Lucky Strike in my mouth. Dead cool.'

The pilot announced that they were flying over the Bristol Channel, and Buddy looked out of the window. They were above the clouds and he couldn't see the ground, but he wondered if, down below, Char could hear the distant drone of the plane.

They were about an hour out from Atlanta when the chief steward brought round the green visa forms for entering the USA. Everybody was in the middle of filling them in when Little Pete's high voice called out.

'Here, Terry – have you seen number B on page two? If you've done more than five years in nick, the Yanks won't let you in.'

Buddy saw a couple of people turn and look.

'That's all right,' Evan laughed. 'Tel's only done four years eleven months. Isn't that right, boyo?'

It was just a bad joke, but Buddy did a quick calculation. Did they count the sentence or the time served? When Buddy was nine, his dad had done three months; then, when he was fourteen, he'd got eighteen months, but he'd only served just over a year. Either way, it was well under five years.

Buddy had just completed his form when he saw Des King get up and walk back to Little Pete and Evan. King smiled as he bent over, and he kept smiling the whole time he was talking to them, but Buddy could see by the expressions on their faces that he wasn't being friendly. Des King could freeze most people when he wanted, and he was freezing the two Teds now. King stopped talking, and Little Pete and Evan nodded glumly.

'They say they're sorry, Tel, and it won't happen again,' King said quietly as he slid back into his seat.

'You're a pal, Des,' his dad said.

It was something that Buddy could never understand, their friendship. Sure, they'd known each other since school, but Buddy had seen King force his dad to go on stealing when he wanted to quit. Eventually his dad had been caught and imprisoned, but he'd never grassed. Since then, King had done everything to help him – but, even so, Buddy was amazed that his dad had never shown the slightest trace of resentment. Whenever Buddy asked him about it, he just smiled and said it was all about loyalty.

The plane touched down at Atlanta airport exactly on time. As they wheeled their trolleys along the corridor towards the Arrivals Hall, a lady was coming in the opposite direction. She had a smile on her face and Buddy thought she was laughing at the way the Teds were dressed, but when she drew level she stopped.

'Are y'all from England?' she asked.

They nodded.

'I'm just on my way there. And if all the guys are as good-lookin' and dress as sharp as y'all, I sure am gonna have myself one hell of a ball. Hey, what's the weather like back there? Rainin', I bet. I read all about that. Well, welcome to Georgia, y'all, and you just have the best trip, you hear?'

She smiled and walked off, and they stood looking at each other in amazement.

'It's like the movies,' his dad said. 'It's just like the bloody movies! I can't believe it. I'm here. Thirty-five years too late, but I've finally made it. And I'm gonna love every minute of it!'

Chapter Twenty-Five

'It's a Chevy! I'm gonna drive a Chevy,' his dad whooped as they piled into the mini-van at the rental car-park. He stuck a Lucky Strike in his mouth and lit it. 'Do I look like James Dean, or do I look like James Dean?' he asked, posing with his hands on the driving wheel.

'Yeah, OK, you look like James Dean,' Des laughed.

They pulled out of the parking lot and on to the four-lane highway that led away from the airport and round the outskirts of Atlanta. The tall buildings of the city centre shimmered in the heat haze, and the air streaming in through the open windows of the mini-van was thick and warm.

'OK back there, y'all?' his dad asked in a phoney American accent. 'This is your tour guide, welcoming y'all to Georgia. We're cruising down Interstate 20 towards Alabama. Just y'all settle back and enjoy the ride, now.'

There was a big poster by the side of the road advertising a golden oldies radio station, and they tuned the van radio in to it. It was playing songs from the Fifties, and the Teds started singing along to the records. They knew all the words, and Little Pete knew the facts about every song: title, artist, date of release, highest position in chart, record label.

'How do you remember all that stuff?' Des asked.

''E just makes it up,' his dad laughed.

'I do not make it up,' Little Pete said. '1956 to 1962. I know every Top Thirty hit. I ought to go on Mastermind. I'd win hands down.'

'Yeah,' Vince laughed, 'he can remember all that stuff, but he can't remember to do up his flies.'

Little Pete looked down at his flies and saw they were closed. Vince roared with laughter.

Singing, squabbling, boasting, teasing each other, playing jokes on each other. Buddy couldn't get over how much it was like being on a school coach trip. Except these kids were nearly fifty years old.

'Look at that,' Dougie said when he glanced up from his card game and saw the name of the town they were just passing. 'Leeds? We took a wrong turning. We're on the M1!'

'Bloody Yanks,' Evan said. 'Can't they think of their own town names? I mean, we don't go around calling our towns Chicago or Los Angeles, do we?'

'What about the Los Angeles in Lancashire, then?' Vince said.

'Don't be daft, there isn't one,' Evan said. Then he looked puzzled. 'There isn't, is there?'

Vince roared with laughter.

It was gone nine in the evening before they stopped at a motel in Jasper. They'd been on the move for nineteen hours, and everybody felt so tired that they all went straight to bed. Sleep hit Buddy at once, but he woke in the middle of the night. He had been dreaming about Charmian and he lay awake, thinking about her, for a long time before he slipped back into sleep.

Everybody felt a bit slow the following morning, so they didn't get on the road until nearly eleven. They drove up Highway 78, listening to another oldies radio station and, as they entered the city limits of Tupelo, Mississippi, the D J played Elvis Presley singing 'All Shook Up'.

'Cor, fancy that,' his dad said. 'Just when we arrive where Elvis was born 'e comes on the radio. Makes your 'air stand on end, don't it?'

' "All Shook Up",' Little Pete informed them. 'Elvis's first Number One in the UK. Reached the top spot in July 1957.'

As they cruised along the tree-lined avenues, following the signs to Elvis's birthplace, Des turned the radio off and they all fell silent.

'He must've walked along these streets when he was a kid,' Dougie said in an awed voice.

The actual house came as a real shock – it was just a tiny, two-roomed wooden shack that Elvis's father had built with his own hands. They bought tickets from an old lady who took them inside and it was lucky there were no other visitors because the seven of them almost filled the place. There was hardly anything to see – just a bed and a chest of drawers in the bedroom, and a stove and a table and a few chairs in the kitchen – but his dad and the others kept going backwards and forwards between the two rooms, trying to imagine what it must have been like for the young Elvis. A photo of him above the fireplace in the bedroom showed him as a two-year-old wearing dungarees and a battered old hat.

'They must've been so poor,' Buddy said to his dad.

'Oh they surely were,' the old lady said, overhearing him. 'Elvis said in an interview, "I could never be so rich that I would forget what it was like to be poor." And he never forgot his roots. Never.'

Evan had to turn away and blow his nose, and Buddy could see that a couple of the others had watery eyes.

'Did they have a toilet?' Buddy asked in the silence.

The Teds looked at him as if he had sworn in church, but the old lady took it in her stride.

'They had a small piece of land out back where they kept a cow and some chickens,' she said. 'I guess they would have had a little privy out there.'

'Like Mum's gran,' Buddy whispered to his dad.

Just up the hill from the cabin there was a museum, and they went and looked at all the things on show. There were records and clothes and news-paper cuttings, but the thing that most impressed the Teds was the hammer that Elvis's father, Vernon, had used to build the house.

After that, the others went over to visit the Elvis Presley Chapel, but Buddy had had enough. He strolled back to the little cabin and sat in the shade on the steps of the verandah. He was just wondering if the young Elvis had ever sat on this exact spot when his dad came and sat next to him.

'Fantastic, eh? 'Ere, did you see them photos of Elvis wiv a crew-cut when 'e was about twelve? They looked just like you when you 'ad that 'orrible skinhead cut.'

Buddy remembered that haircut. He'd had it when his mum left home, and he'd kept it until his dad was put in prison.

As if he'd caught Buddy's thoughts, his dad said, 'Elvis's poor old dad went to prison while they were living in this 'ouse. Forging cheques. They must've been dead broke.'

'Yeah.'

'Elvis always loved 'im, though,' his dad said, looking at Buddy.

'Yeah, I know,' Buddy said.

They drove round Tupelo to look at Elvis's first school and the shop where he bought his first guitar, then they booked into a motel for the night. They went out to eat at a steak house, then decided to stop for a drink at a bar. The trouble started almost as soon as they walked in. Four big men were there, playing pool, and they looked up and laughed when they saw the Ted clothes.

'What is this? A fruits' convention?' one of them asked in a loud voice.

Dougie bristled and Buddy's dad put a restraining hand on his shoulder.

'He thinks we're poofters,' Dougie said.

'So what?' his dad said. 'Just ignore it.'

They ordered their drinks, but the four men kept

making loud remarks and Dougie and Vince got more and more angry. Finally the four men settled down and concentrated on their game, but when Little Pete went to the loo he had to go past the pool table.

'Ooh, where's the sweet thang going?' one of the men said, barring Little Pete's way with his pool cue. 'The ladies' powder-room is over there, sweetie.'

Little Pete had been drinking heavily and, instead of ignoring the man, he pulled the pool cue out of his grasp and swung it at him. The man dodged the cue, grabbed hold of Little Pete and head-butted him in the face. Blood poured from Little Pete's nose and he staggered and fell. Before Buddy could stop him, his dad was striding towards the men, followed by Dougie and Vince. Buddy got up to follow, but Des held his arm.

'Four against four – leave 'em to it,' Des said.

'Yeah, but . . .'

Before Buddy could finish speaking, the fight had started. His dad hit the man who had butted Little Pete, sending him crashing back against the pool table. Vince and Dougie began punching two of the others while Evan jumped on the fourth man's back and knocked him to the ground.

Thirty seconds later, it was over. The owner of the bar switched the main lights on, stepped from behind the bar with a shotgun in his hands and pointed it in the general direction of the fighting.

'The cops are on their way, boys,' he shouted. 'If you don't want them to haul you away in a body bag, y'all better stop right now.'

The fighting stopped at once and they all stood there, breathing heavily and looking slightly stupid in the harsh, bright light of the overhead neon. Three minutes later, two police cars came swinging across the parking lot, their lights flashing and sirens howling. Four cops burst into the room, their guns at the ready. Buddy found himself putting his hands up in the air, like everyone else.

One of the cops spoke quietly with the owner for a few minutes, then walked over to the pool table.

'OK, boys, y'all beat it on home to your families now,' he said pointing to the four local men. Then he turned to the five Teds. 'You weirdos are comin' with us.'

Buddy and Des tried to talk to the policeman but he warned them to stay out of it unless they wanted to be arrested, too. They stood on the sidewalk outside the bar and watched as the Teds were put in the cars.

For the second time in his life, Buddy watched as his dad was driven away in a police car.

CHAPTER TWENTY-SIX

Buddy and Des went down to the police station, but they were told that the five were being held over-night. When they drove back at nine the following morning, the Teds were already standing on the steps, waiting for them. They were grinning and didn't look any the worse for the night they'd spent in the cells.

'Put your foot on it, Des,' Evan said as they piled into the mini-van. 'They've given us an hour, like, to collect our stuff and get out of town or there'll be more trouble.'

'Well, there'd better not be,' Des said, pointing his finger at Little Pete.

'It wasn't my fault,' Little Pete whined.

'You drink too much,' Des snapped as he eased the van out into the traffic.

'Be fair, Des,' his dad said. 'They nicked us 'cos they didn't like our clothes or the way we talk. It was just prejudice. Good job we weren't black as well.'

After a second he realized what he'd said and he looked across at Buddy.

'Still,' Vince chuckled, 'it was a bit of a laugh. The cells were all made of steel bars like in the cowboy films. I had a long chat to the bloke in the cell next to me. He said he was in for murder. Seemed like a really nice geezer. Mind you, I didn't get too close to the bars on his side!'

As they drove away from the police station, Evan started singing the Elvis song, 'Jailhouse Rock', and Little Pete told them it reached Number One in January 1958.

They got to Memphis at the end of the morning and the Teds wanted to go straight to Graceland, but Des had planned a general sightseeing tour. They drove to the centre of town then marched around after Des all afternoon while he pointed out the sights and read out bits from a guide book. The only visit the Teds were really interested in was when they went to Sun Studios where Elvis had made his first records. There wasn't much to see, but there was a really strong atmosphere in the small studio.

'I wouldn't mind recording here,' Buddy told his dad. 'It's got a good feel.'

'Could be arranged,' his dad said, and a little smile crinkled up his eyes. 'I'm glad you're still interested.'

They went down to Beale Street in the evening because Des had read that it was the centre for good restaurants and music clubs. They strolled along, looking at the various places, until Evan suddenly shouted and pointed to a restaurant across the street. The neon sign read 'Jerry Lee Lewis' Spot'.

'There's live music later, too,' Evan said, as they looked at the menu in the window. 'What d'you say, lads? After all, I met him, you know.'

'Yeah,' Vince said. 'And look what it says on the window – "Jerry Lee may visit anytime". He'll probably walk in tonight and say, "Evan, y'all, didn't we meet in Swansea, back in 1964? The drinks are on me."'

'Don't be daft, he wouldn't remember me after all this time,' Evan said. Then he peered in through the window and added, 'Still, you never know.'

The Teds piled in through the door, but Buddy grabbed hold of his dad's arm and held him back.

'Listen, dad, I need a break from all this. How about if I find somewhere else and meet you back here at midnight?'

'Yeah, sure,' his dad said. 'Take care, though.'

It was great to be on his own. He could hardly believe it: here he was on Beale Street, the heart of Memphis music. The sidewalks were bustling with people, and the sound of music drifted out of every bar. He strolled along, occasionally stopping at a bar door to listen to the band playing inside. And, finally, he came to B. B. King's Blues Club.

He'd listened to a lot of B. B. King records with Glenn, so he went straight in. The room was dark and crowded but he made his way to the bar and ordered a drink just as the band came onto the raised stage. A thin, young, black man, probably no older than Buddy, took the mike. The light from the blue neon guitar above the stage reflected in his eyes and they looked nervous. Buddy knew exactly what he was feeling – that moment before starting to play, when anything was possible: it could be great or it could be terrible.

'Good evening. My name's Floyd Haley and I'm from Austin, Texas. It's an honour for me to be here at BB's for the next three nights and to have the privilege of playing with this great band. I hope you enjoy the show.'

He counted the band in and swung into a wonderful five-minute guitar solo that made Buddy smile with pleasure. This guy could play! And then his voice – deep and powerful and so filled with emotion that Buddy felt as if his heartbeat was being altered by the sounds. For an hour and a half he was lost in the music and, when Haley said, 'Goodnight. Thanks!', Buddy was on his feet, clapping and cheering with everyone else.

And, more than anything, he was full of a desire to get back on stage and play again.

The visit to Graceland took the whole of the next day. For a start, there were thousands of visitors and they had to queue for over an hour before they could get in. Then his dad and the others didn't want to miss a thing. From the moment the shuttle bus swept them over Elvis Presley Boulevard and in through the big gates, they were thrilled by everything they saw.

Their tour guide of the mansion soon picked out their accents.

'Y'all from England?' she said. 'Well, you sure are welcome here to Elvis' home. I know that Elvis would have just loved your wonderful suits – as you'll see during your visit, he always liked colourful clothes himself.'

The Teds took photos of everything: the huge yellow-leather sofas, the chandeliers, the mirrored walls and ceilings, the three TVs that Elvis had used to watch different football games at the same time. Photos of stair-rails. Photos of each other. Photos of the guide. Even photos of photos on the wall.

'Just think,' his dad said as he posed for a photo leaning on the pool table, 'I'm touching something Elvis touched.'

When they got to the Trophy Room, the guide left them, saying that they could visit it at their own pace. Buddy groaned, knowing what that would mean. And he was right. It took them an hour and a half just to look at all the gold discs, while Little Pete told them all the facts and figures he knew about them. Then they spent another hour peering at the stage suits and letters and jewellery and other mementoes.

Finally they came out of the buildings into the Meditation Garden, where Elvis and his family were buried. It was a circular area with a small pond in the centre. The fountains in the pond, and the shady trees and bushes, made it feel cool, and the lines of people filing past the graves were as hushed as if they were in a cathedral.

The Teds had clubbed together to buy a wreath of white flowers in the shape of a guitar, and they placed it next to Elvis's grave. They stood for a while with their heads bowed, and the only sound was the splash of water as the breeze blew the spray from the fountain back and forth on the pond. Evan was crying openly and the others had tears in their eyes.

'Come on, lads,' Des King said. 'You're holding everyone up. Anyway, I don't reckon he's in there. His whole death was a put-up job to let him get away from all the publicity. He's probably on some private island feeding his face with cheeseburgers.'

A couple of tearful ladies standing in the queue gave him a filthy look, but at least it broke the Teds' mood and got them moving again.

They took a shuttle back across the busy road, had a late lunch, and started on all the other attractions: Elvis's planes, Elvis's cars and motorbikes, and a half-hour film on Elvis's career that the Teds insisted on watching twice. Even after all that, they still hadn't had enough; they went in and out of all the gift shops, buying badges, postcards, key rings, and anything that had Elvis's name or photo on it. Little Pete even bought a plastic bubble with a model of Graceland in it. All the way back to the motel he kept shaking it to watch the snow whirling in the liquid and settling on the house.

In the evening they all wanted to go back to Jerry Lee Lewis' Spot, so Buddy left them and went straight to B. B. King's Club and ate there. Floyd Haley's set was completely different from the previous night but, once again, Buddy was knocked out by it and just longed to get up on stage and jam with him.

'You're joking,' Buddy said at breakfast the next day when his dad and the other Teds told him that they were going back to Graceland. 'I've got Elvis coming out of my ears.'

'It's a once-in-a-lifetime chance,' Dougie argued.

'Yeah once, not twice,' Des King replied. 'Still, if you want to, go ahead. Buddy and I can do something else.'

Buddy didn't fancy spending the day with Des King, but he really couldn't face another visit to Graceland, so he agreed. The others went off in a taxi, and he got into the mini-van with Des.

They drove along the Mississippi to look at the Pyramid and Mud Island, then Des suggested going to the Memphis Pink Palace Museum. They spent a couple of hours looking at the exhibits, and Buddy was surprised at how much Des knew about American history. At the end of the visit they went into the Planetarium and, as they sat waiting for the show to begin, Buddy asked why he'd organized the trip.

'Oh, for the lads, really. They've all worked with me at one time or another.'

'What, at the breaker's?'

'No, I'm talking about the bad old days when we weren't all so law-abiding,' Des said in a low voice. He turned in his seat and looked straight at Buddy. 'Talking of which, there's something I've always wanted to ask you. You were the one who rang the cops, that night your dad got nicked at 56 Croxley Street, weren't you?'

Buddy's heart started to pound. He nodded.

'You were trying to set me up, and he got caught by mistake – is that it?'

Buddy nodded.

'Yes, I thought so. Well, no hard feelings. I was out of order with your dad back then. I should've let him out, like he wanted. I've tried to make it up to him since. You know that?'

Buddy nodded.

The lights went down and the stars started to spin across the ceiling above them. Buddy settled back in his seat and felt his heart gradually slow down to normal speed again.

As soon as they got back to the motel, they bumped into his dad, and one look at his long face told them that it hadn't been a good day.

'Oh, I 'ad a row wiv Little Pete and Evan,' his dad said when they asked him what was wrong. 'All I did was say that Buddy Holly wrote 'is own songs and Elvis didn't. Well, they took it the wrong way and started 'aving a go at me. I couldn't believe it. But then Vince makes it worse by taking the mick out of Evan. You know Vince, never knows when to stop. Well, suddenly Evan flips out and belts 'im one, right in the kisser. So Vince lets fly and belts 'im back.'

'Where was this?' Des asked.

'In the Meditation Garden.'

'You're kidding me.'

'No, honest – it was a nightmare. Vince really socked 'im and Evan went crashin' over the railings. Couple of wreaths went flyin', and Evan ends up lying right on top of Elvis's grandma's grave. I tell you, people went ape. Then the guards turned up, took one look and kicked us out. Anyway, Little Pete and Evan 'ave gone off to Jerry Lee's again, and Vince and Dougie 'ave gone to some Mexican place.'

'Oh spare me,' Des said. 'I think I'm staying in tonight and sending out for a pizza. I'll see you.'

'What are you doin'?' his dad asked Buddy when Des had gone.

'I thought of going back to B. B. King's. The food's great and there's this brilliant singer . . .'

'All right if I string along?'

'Yeah, of course.'

They arrived early at the club and got a table directly in front of the stage. Just as they were finishing their meal, Floyd Haley wandered in and placed his guitar on its stand, then he sat down at the table next to theirs and ordered a beer. He lifted his dark glasses on to his forehead and looked around the bar.

'Hey, you back again?' he grinned when he saw Buddy. 'You were here the other nights, right? Groovin' down there by the bar.'

'Yeah. They were great shows.'

'Well, right on. Hey, mind if I join you?'

He came over to their table and they introduced themselves. He told them that he'd been playing professionally since he was seventeen, mostly around Texas, and that this was his first time in Memphis. Buddy was a bit embarrassed when his dad started going on about The Bosses and their hit records but Floyd seemed really interested and said that he was still trying to get a record deal.

'So, you're from Texas,' his dad said. 'Ever been to Lubbock? It's where Buddy Holly lived. I named Buddy after 'im.'

'That so? Yeah, Lubbock's a cool place. But Austin is where it's at for music. I'm not just saying that 'cos it's my town. It's cookin'. You ought to come out there some time. Hey, you and me could jam some,' he said, turning to Buddy.

'I'd love to,' Buddy said, 'but we're going to Nashville next, and then down to Florida.'

They chatted a bit longer then the band started to come on stage and set up. Floyd finished his beer, said goodbye, and went up to join them.

It was another blistering set, and even his dad had to admit it was good. Floyd dedicated one of the songs to 'my British friends here tonight' and, as he left the stage at the end, he bent down and shook their hands.

When they got back to the motel, they bumped into Little Pete and Evan who were getting their keys at the desk.

'Wotcher,' his dad said to them. ''Ow was Jerry Lee's tonight? We've just seen this ace bloke at another club.'

The two of them turned and walked away without saying a word.

'Ow, my gawd – still 'aving our little sulk, are we?' his dad called after them. 'Cor, they're worse than kids, them two. Oh well, goodnight, mate. See you in the morning.'

About half an hour later, Buddy was lying in bed, reading, when there was a knock on his door. It was his dad, his eyes shining with excitement.

''Ere, I've bin thinkin'. This lot are gettin' on me wick. What about you and me 'iring a car and doin' our own fing? Drive down to Lubbock, together. It's nuts coming all this way and not going to the one place I really want to see. Des won't mind, and the others can go take a jump. I mean, stuff Disneyworld – who needs Mickey Mouse when we could 'ave Buddy Holly? What d'you say?'

Nashville and Disneyworld, with the Teds boozing and quarrelling all the time, or Texas with his dad? There was no contest.

'Yeah, let's go,' Buddy said.

At just after midday the next day they drove across the Mississippi Bridge in a bright red Chevy convertible. The sun was shining, the hood was down, the wind was blowing their hair, and they were heading West.

CHAPTER TWENTY-SEVEN

From Memphis they drove three hundred miles across Arkansas and stayed the night, just over the State line, in Oklahoma. The next morning, Buddy was surprised to see his dad come out of his room dressed in jeans and a check shirt rather than his usual Ted gear.

'Yeah, gotta get in the mood. I mean, drapes and drainpipes won't look right in Texas, will they? This is me Cowboy Look!'

To complete his 'look', he stopped in one of the towns on the way and went into a clothes store. He came out ten minutes later, wearing a stetson hat and a pair of cowboy boots.

'How'd I look, pardner?' he said, doing a sideways leap over the car door and landing in his seat. 'Let's get this wagon on the road!'

Hour after hour they drove on Interstate 40 across the dry Oklahoma plain, his dad leaning back with one hand on the wheel and the hat rammed down on his head to keep it from blowing away. The cruise control switch on the Chevy meant he could take his foot off the accelerator and let the car purr along at the 65mph speed limit.

'Ain't this just the life, pardner?' he said, grinning from ear to ear. 'Got a little song I just made up for the occasion. What d'you think?'

He started tapping his hand on the top of the dashboard and singing in his best Elvis imitation.

'I'm doin' the Oklahoma rock and roll
In my open-top Chevy with the cruise control
Keep on heading out to the West
'Cos that's the land I love the best.'

'Yeah, brilliant, Dad!' Buddy laughed.

'Don't you be gettin' sassy with your old pappy now, boy!' his dad said in a croaky old cowboy voice. 'Ah bin hittin' these here trails since before you was borned. Yes, sir, ah've seen it all – rustlers, rattlesnakes and stampedes that'd curl your hair and darken your pants! Ah remember me a time when ol' Jake "Thunder" Perkins – we called him "Thunder" on account of him likin' baked beans so much. Well, old "Thunder" come ridin' in one day . . .'

He went on and on with the story about 'Thunder' stampeding the cattle until Buddy was creased up and rolling around in the front seat, begging him to stop so that he could get his breath back.

They crossed the Texas State line towards the end of the afternoon and by the time they drove into

Amarillo the last of the flaming red sun was just dipping behind the horizon. His dad spotted a motel called The Big Texan and they pulled off the highway into the car-park. It was a huge place with a motel, restaurant and gift shop, and it was all built to look like an old cowboy town.

They booked into the motel, had a shower, and then strolled across the courtyard into the restaurant. It was a gigantic room with over a hundred tables, all of them full. A small band was playing country music on a stage in the corner, and the whole place was decorated as a western saloon.

'Look at this offer,' his dad said, pointing to the menu. 'You get a seventy-two-ounce steak free if you can eat it within one hour. How much is seventy-two ounces?'

'Dad, don't even think about it . . .'

'That's only four and an 'alf pounds. I bet I could manage it.'

'Dad!'

But there was no arguing with him.

Buddy ordered an eight-ounce steak with french fries, and he felt totally full after he'd eaten it, but his dad's steak was nine times as big. He started off well and after twenty minutes he had eaten nearly half of it but then he began to slow down. Sweat started to run down his face and he took longer and longer to chew and swallow each mouthful.

'Come on, Dad – just leave it,' Buddy said when there was about a quarter of an hour to go.

The steak was still twice as big as Buddy's entire meal. His dad was beginning to look really red in the face and he had undone his shirt and the top button on his jeans.

'Can't stop now,' he mumbled. 'I gotta pay for it if I don't finish it. Besides, everyone's looking – can't let 'em think us Brits ain't up to it.'

It was true, people were all turning to the table to see how the challenge was going and a few of them started to call out encouragement. The more they shouted, the more he ate.

The minutes were ticking away, and a couple of waiters came up and stood by the table, looking at their watches.

'Five minutes left,' one of them said.

'Come on, boy. You can do it,' someone yelled.

'My wrist aches – I can't even cut the bloody thing,' his dad whispered, as he sawed away at the meat and shovelled another bit into his mouth.

'Oh God, I'm gonna die,' he groaned a couple of minutes later as he lifted another forkful.

When the waiter announced that there was a minute to go, people began to stand up all over the room to get a better view. There were only another couple of mouthfuls left, but Buddy could see that his dad could hardly swallow the piece he had in his mouth.

'Thirty seconds.'

He put another piece in his mouth and began to chew. There was now just one large piece on the plate.

'Twenty-five . . . Twenty . . . Fifteen . . .'

His dad gulped and tried to swallow the piece in his mouth. He gulped again and it went down, painfully.

'Ten . . .'

He forked the last piece into his mouth. And pointed to his empty plate.

'Sorry, it's got to be swallowed,' the waiter said. 'Five . . .'

There was no time to chew it and his dad started to try to swallow it whole. But it just wouldn't go.

'Four . . . Three . . .'

Buddy picked up his glass of beer and handed it to his dad, who took a gulp.

'Two . . . One . . .'

'Gone!' his dad shouted as the steak swirled down his throat with the beer.

People started cheering and clapping, and he had to stand up and take a bow. The manager of the restaurant came over and got him to sign his name in a book of successful challengers. Buddy counted them quickly – fourteen in the last two years. His dad kept smiling while people were still looking at him, but the minute they lost interest he got up slowly.

'Gotta go,' he said between gritted teeth.

Buddy followed him out and then led him across the courtyard to his room.

'Leave me alone,' his dad groaned as he collapsed on the bed.

His belly was swollen like Evan's, and Buddy couldn't help laughing as he went out and closed the door.

Buddy got up early the next day and went for a walk across the dusty yellow ground behind the motel. The sun was already warm, but a cool breeze was blowing across the plain and sweeping little eddies of dust into the air. He came to a railway line and stood counting the wagons as a freight train rolled by: one hundred and twenty-nine. They rattled by and away across the enormous plain, finally disappearing into the vast distance.

He walked back to the motel and went into the café for breakfast. He sat at the window, looking out at the cars and trucks speeding by on I-40. So many people travelling. And it was the same on roads all over this huge country. All over the world. Millions and millions of people on the move. So many people were alive with him on the globe. So many, it was impossible to imagine. All living their lives, all seeing it just through their eyes. That truck-driver in the blue shirt speeding by, for instance, not even aware that someone called Buddy Clark had just watched him go by. What was that truck-driver's life like? And did it matter if he lived or died? Did it matter if anyone lived or died? Could each one of the billions of people on this planet matter? Or were they no more important than flies or ants?

And soon there would be another human being on the planet. A baby. Char's and his baby.

A wave of longing rushed through him. What was Char doing at this moment? What was the time back home? Was she thinking of him? She didn't even know he was in America. Maybe she wouldn't even care. And all the time, that new life was growing inside her.

His dad still hadn't got up by 10.30, so Buddy went to his door and knocked. There was no reply from inside. He knocked again. Still no reply. He went to the window, but the curtains were drawn. He banged on the window. Nothing moved inside and he had a moment of panic.

He went back to the door and pounded on it.

There was a click as the inside lock was turned

and then the door opened. His dad peered blearily out at the sunshine, groaned, and went back into the room.

'Blimey, it doesn't half pong in here,' Buddy said as he followed him in.

'Just call me "Thunder",' his dad said, collapsing on to the end of the bed. 'That steak really did me guts in. Never again!'

It took his dad ages to get going, and they weren't back on the road until after midday. Even then, he felt ill, so Buddy drove the hundred and twenty miles to Lubbock.

They got a motel room right opposite the Buddy Holly statue, and for the next two days they toured round the town, visiting all the places connected with him: the schools he went to, the church he used to attend, the radio station where he did his first live broadcasts, and the small, one-storey house he was living in when he had his first Number One hit.

'We're actually 'ere,' his dad said as they cruised up and down the wide, straight avenues. 'Lubbock, Texas. Buddy Holly's town. Seeing things he saw. Walking down the streets he walked down. It's a dream come true.'

The only disappointment was his birthplace. They searched up and down 6th Street and then realized that it had been demolished. They stood in front of the litter-filled empty lot, and his dad shook his head.

'Fancy knockin' it down. They're nuts, these Yanks. It ought to be a national shrine.'

They got lost trying to find Lubbock Cemetery and drove round and round a poverty-stricken area near the railroad yards. There were burnt-out cars on nearly every block and the buildings were boarded up and scrawled with graffiti. A group of winos stood, staring at them, as they waited at a red light, and Buddy was glad when the light changed. There were people slumped in doorways and badly dressed young kids running in the streets. The houses were run-down and in the window of one of them was a big sign which said, 'No More Killing'.

It was their first glimpse of another side of America, and they were both glad when they found the right road and saw a sign for the cemetery.

Buddy Holly's grave was marked by a simple stone slab set into the cracked brown earth. The grass round it was parched and shrivelled, and some-one had left a pathetic bunch of five plastic tulips. Carved into the stone was a guitar and the words 'In Loving Memory of our own Buddy Holley. September 7, 1936. February 3, 1959'.

'Blimey, they couldn't even spell his name right,' Buddy said.

'No, that's the right spelling. It only became Holly wivout an "e" when someone spelt it wrong on the record contract,' his dad said.

He bent down and brushed some of the dust off the stone. He'd bought a dozen yellow roses in town, and he laid them across the stone and stood up.

'It's not much of a grave, is it? I mean, compared wiv Elvis – all them flowers and the fountains and everyfing.'

'I like it,' Buddy said. 'It's simple. More normal. Like he was a real person, not some sort of god.'

'Yeah, that's right. A real person. You can 'ear it in 'is voice. It's like it's coming straight from 'is heart into yours. I reckon that's why people still love 'im today.'

'Yeah, he was great.'

'They changed my life – 'im and all them others. You got no idea what it was like, growin' up in England back then – grey, gloomy, cold, damp. 'Orrible! It was like being ground down by everyfing. Then along comes Rock'n'Roll, and it was like the sun comin' out. Suddenly you knew it didn't 'ave to be 'orrible. It could be fun and alive. Yeah, that's what they did – they gave us 'ope. Especially 'im, especially this one.'

His dad's voice choked and he looked down at the grave and shook his head gently.

'Well, Buddy Holly, you probably can't 'ear me wherever you are, but . . . you mean a lot to me. Blimey, I named me own son after you – that's 'ow much you mean. Anyway . . . I've come five thousand miles to say thanks.'

When they realized that there were only four days of the holiday left, they looked at the map to plan their route to Orlando to meet up with Des and the others and catch the plane home.

'Right,' his dad said, 'we bomb down to Houston tomorrow, nip along here to New Orleans the day after, then into Florida and down to Orlando. Easy!'

The first part of the journey was fine – along a straight, fast highway. It was just as Buddy had always imagined Texas: cactus, tumbleweeds, a huge blue sky arching over the burnt red plain, and the occasional oil-well pumping away in the distance. But south of Abilene the road was smaller and it began to twist and turn across rolling hills. Many times they were held up for ages behind slow-moving trucks or tractors, and by nightfall they were still over a hundred and fifty miles from Houston.

'That's all right,' his dad said. 'We'll stay the night in Austin. That guitar bloke, wotsisname, said it was a nice place.'

The motel owner told them that 6th Street was the best place for food and music, and, as soon as they got there and stepped out of the car, they could feel the atmosphere. It seemed that every building was a bar or a restaurant and, in every one of them, people were playing music. They ate at a place called Minnie Mae's and listened to a country music band, then they wandered down the street and went into another bar.

Three guitarists were sitting on the small stage, playing acoustic blues to a packed audience. They sounded good, but Buddy was so intent on ordering some drinks at the bar that he didn't really look at them. He had just managed to get a couple of beers when the song came to an end.

'Well, well, well,' someone said over the microphone, 'it's the British invasion. So you made it here after all.'

Buddy looked towards the stage and saw Floyd Haley grinning at him. Buddy raised his glass to him and then went over to his dad while the music started again.

'Fancy that, eh? Old wotsisname,' his dad said. 'Cheers.'

Floyd and the others were obviously just jamming with each other, choosing the songs on the spur of the moment and seeing where the music took them. They were good, and it was a real pleasure to watch them trading ideas and having as much fun as the audience. After a couple of numbers, one of the guitarists went to the bar for a drink and Floyd picked up the spare guitar and held it up.

'How about it, Buddy?' he said into the microphone.

'Yeah, go on,' his dad said, giving him a push.

Buddy made his way through the crowd and up on to the stage. He took the guitar and sat down on the spare stool. Floyd counted them in and they launched into a fast blues. Buddy just followed them, strumming rhythm chords, until Floyd tipped his head to show that he wanted him to play a solo. His heart gave a lurch, but he soon lost himself in chasing the melody line around the strings. As he finished, there was a burst of applause from the audience and Floyd gave him an approving nod.

'Hey, you're OK,' Floyd whispered when the song ended. 'Let's do some more.'

They played another four songs together, then Buddy handed the guitar back to its owner and picked up the harmonica next to Floyd's stool.

'OK?' he asked.

'You bet,' Floyd said.

Halfway through the next number, Buddy put the harmonica to his lips and began to blow a wild solo, whooping and stretching the notes until everyone was on their feet, rocking to the beat. He played another three numbers, then thanked the guitarists and stepped off the stage.

'Let's hear it for my friend from Britain,' Floyd called, and the audience clapped and cheered him as he made his way back to his dad.

'That was fantastic,' his dad said, patting him on the back.

'It sure was,' Floyd said, coming up to them. 'Hey, let's go outside and cool off.'

They bought some beers, then stood on the sidewalk and chatted. They told Floyd what they were doing there and he talked to them about the music scene in Austin.

'Told you it was cookin', didn't I? Why don't you stick around and groove?' Floyd said.

'We can't,' Buddy replied.

'Too bad. Hot musicians. Great studios. Can't tempt you, huh?' Floyd grinned.

Buddy laughed and shook his head.

They said goodbye and drove back to their motel and went to bed.

They were up early the next morning and drove to the outskirts of town before stopping for breakfast. His dad was very quiet while they ate, and Buddy wondered if he wasn't feeling well.

'No, I'm OK,' he said. 'It's just . . .'

'What? Dad?'

'I think we ought to stay. Now don't tell me we can't – we can. I can ring the airline and postpone the flight. I've got plenty of money saved up from Arctic.'

'Yes, but . . .'

'Buddy, what did you feel like last night on stage?'

'Great, but . . .'

'It's where you belong, mate – on stage. Singing, playing, making records. All this stuff about going to University is crap, and you know it is.'

'It's not just University, Dad. OK, you're right, I don't want to do that really. I want to make music – it's what I was born to do, I know it. But there's other things, too.'

'What?'

'Charmian. I love her, Dad. I really do. And I want to be with her.'

'Yeah, but she don't wanna be wiv you, does she? And anyway, I'm not saying live 'ere for ever. I'm saying stay 'ere for a bit. Play music. Maybe make a record over 'ere. You want to, I know you do. I could see it when you was on stage last night. You know this is the place.'

'But Charmian . . .'

'She ain't gonna go away. She's gonna be there. And maybe it'll work out when you get back, I don't know. But this might be the one chance you get to do stuff over 'ere.'

He took a sip of coffee and looked at Buddy over the rim of the cup.

'Well?' he asked.

Chapter Twenty-Eight

Rolling Wood Trailer Park
Ox Spring Road
Austin
Texas 78706
USA

28th September

Dear Char,
    I hope you got my cards from Memphis and

Lubbock so that at least you know I'm over here in the States. It started off as a holiday but we've been over here nearly two months now. We're living in a big rented caravan (they call it a mobile home over here) on the outskirts of Austin, overlooking the Colorado River. Austin's a fantastic place. There's some beautiful countryside and everything seems geared to having a good time – there's just a million things to do.

The best thing is the music. It's amazing. So many bands, so many brilliant musicians, so many places to play. That's why I'm here really. For the last six weeks I've been playing all day, every day. I bought myself my two dream guitars – a Fender electric and a Gibson acoustic – and I've been writing new songs like mad and then playing them with this bloke I met called Floyd Haley. He's an incredible blues guy. He knows everyone on the music scene here and he's been fixing up gigs and getting ace musicians for me to play with.

We've even been into a small studio to record demos of the songs – just him and me and a drummer. What I want to do is record them all properly and get an album (or two or three!) of material. Floyd's going to be the producer – he's got great ideas, and we kind of balance each other. He's so bluesy, but my stuff is more rock/pop and I think the combination is going to be really new and exciting. I hope!!

The big problem is money. It'll cost a lot to record the stuff properly even though we want to do it sort of 'live' – one take, with everyone playing live, and no overdubbing. So we're sending the demos to Bobby Rosen at Saroudan to see if he'll give us an advance to finance it all. That's my dad's job. He's having a wonderful time, running around being my manager, ringing Rosen and making friends with all the people in the music biz over here. They all think he's some kind of nut – this weird English bloke dressed up in cowboy hat and boots – but he charms the socks off them!

Anyway, we're having to watch the money carefully 'cos we're living off our savings. Dad had to take his beloved red convertible back to Alamo Rentals and he's driving around in a cheap old banger he bought. I mostly go everywhere on an old bike – not too bad now the weather is cooling down a bit.

I told you I've been writing a lot – over thirty songs already. The ideas just seem to be pouring out of me and there are so many things I want to say. I've written songs about things from the past. There's one called 'Dark House' which is sort of about Ralph James Campbell – you remember the simple bloke in 56 Croxley Street who got caught by the cops with my dad? But most of the songs are about you. Well, us, really. All three of us.

I keep thinking of all the things we did together and the things we talked about. You've made me see everything differently. The nights are incredibly clear here and sometimes I just lie outside near the river and look up at the stars and think about what you said once about how the Universe made you feel so small and humble. I can remember your exact words – 'We're so tiny and insignificant, and yet we're important because we're a part of it all.'

You're right. I know it now and it makes me feel so calm. The whole of Creation is so immense and complex and extraordinary that we'll never understand it really. I keep thinking about how scientists say that the Universe is expanding and I think, yeah OK, but what is it expanding into? What's there, just outside the edge of the Universe? Nothing? And trying to think about Nothing makes my brain scramble. What is Nothing? And I realize that my brain is too small to understand it. It can imagine Things but it can't imagine Nothing. It can't cope – it just goes haywire.

And you're right (you're right about everything!) when you say that all the attempts to explain it – like religions and science – are just pathetic attempts to try and explain it in human terms. Human terms just aren't good enough. The only way we can imagine a God is by thinking of Him (or Her) as some kind of very, very clever Human Being who's like a Father or Mother. That's the best our brains can imagine – but it's not good enough or big enough to REALLY explain it.

All my life I've worried about WHAT IT ALL MEANS, and I've kept asking WHY. Why am I here? Why do things happen? You've helped me to see that the best thing to do is to look at things and be filled with wonder.

Like I'm filled with wonder when I think about that life growing inside you. What a miracle.

Char, I did everything wrong – I know that now. I said the wrong things and I was stupid and shocked and scared. But now I've had time to think, I know that I love you and I want to be with you all the time. You've changed my life, the way I think, everything. I miss you terribly. And I want us to have the baby and be together. Maybe you were shocked and scared, too, and that's why you told me to go away.

I'm having a great time here but if you told me you wanted me, I would drop everything and fly straight home to be with you.

I love you, Char. Please, please write to me.

Buddy.

Chapter Twenty-Nine

Buddy was sitting on the step of their mobile home, strumming his guitar. Even this early in the morning the October sun was incredibly warm, although the leaves on the trees had started to turn red and brown.

'Blimey, I don't 'alf look old,' his dad said, looking at himself in the mirror just inside the door. 'I go around feeling like I'm twenty-one, then I see meself in the mirror and I look about three 'undred and six.'

'Don't be daft – you look great for your age.'

'Oh thanks – for my age! The worst fing is, I look more and more like my old man. Not my eyes or my mouth or my nose, just . . . somefing. Weird. We used to fight like cat and dog, and I end up lookin' like 'im. You don't remember 'im, do you?'

'No.'

'Docker, 'e was. Cor, 'e 'ad some muscles, I can tell you. A clip from 'im and you knew it all right. Strong as an ox. And then one day 'e just keels over. Like 'is dad before 'im. All die young, us Clarks.'

'Oh great!'

'When you gotta go, you gotta go, eh? Talking of which – I gotta go. MTV are doing a TV special about music in Austin next month, and my very good friend Max Truman is choosing the acts. So I'm off to twist 'is arm to see if I can get you on the bill. Catch you later.'

He roared off in his rusty old Buick and Buddy strolled over to the trailer park office to see if there was any mail. It was over two weeks since he'd written to Char and he felt sure the reply would come any day now. Joe Lye, the manager of the trailer park, checked the mail rack. No letter.

Just after midday he strapped his Fender across his back and cycled through Zilker Park then along the river into town. As he turned into 4th Street, Floyd was waiting for him outside Dillo Studios. They weren't the biggest studios in town but there was a good vibe, and the engineer, TJ, was Floyd's friend. He gave them a really cheap rate while they were making the demos, and they'd promised that they would make the album there if they got a record deal. TJ believed in them and liked the music they were making so the atmosphere was always relaxed and he never bothered how long it took to get things done.

Floyd didn't say anything, but as soon as they started to play Buddy knew something was wrong. Floyd's guitar playing, normally so bright and positive, was moody and dark. When they'd jammed for nearly an hour, Buddy asked him what was up.

'Had some real bad news, man. My cousin Antone got wasted down in Houston last night,' Floyd said. 'He was dealin' crack on a corner, and some other dude thought he was on his territory so he drove by and blew him away.'

Floyd took off his shades and rubbed his eyes. They were bloodshot.

'Wow. How old was he?'

'Antone? Fourteen.'

'Fourteen!'

'He was a great kid. Lived with us for six years when his parents split. Then he went down to Houston to be with his mom. Got himself a bad crack habit, and started dealin' to pay for it. And now he's gone.'

'Oh God, that's terrible. Hey, maybe we ought to skip it today.'

'No, no. I wanna play. Maybe write something. He was a cool kid – he'd dig to have a song written about him.'

Buddy began playing a slow chord sequence and Floyd started picking notes, trying out melody lines. They watched each other closely as they played, nodding briefly when they approved of something and using glances to encourage each other. As the mood built up, Floyd caught a brief melody line that he kept repeating. As he played it once more, Buddy began to hum it. Then suddenly he sang a line,

> 'There's a cool kid on the corner
> With empty warehouse eyes'

Floyd nodded and said, 'Yeah, go on.'

The lines poured out, and in an hour they had a song.

They gave the signal to T J and he began to roll the tape. Floyd played a long, sad introduction and Buddy caught the mood as he started to sing. He closed his eyes and imagined the young Antone's life – saw him: a kid in pain as his family split up, living away from his mother, and then finally caught up in the trap of drugs. Buddy's heart swelled with sadness but he held it all back, didn't try any obvious tricks with his voice, just let the words come naturally and tell their own story.

Floyd took over at the end, rolling the melody into a long, heart-breaking solo, filled with loss and tenderness. The notes trembled, fluttered like a bird caught in a cage, and then slowly died away.

'Oh boy. Oh boy,' T J whispered through the control-booth microphone. 'What a song.'

Floyd went down to Houston for two days to attend Antone's funeral and, while he was away, the long-awaited reply came from Bobby Rosen. He had listened to the demo tapes and had been impressed with the new songs but 'in the light of the difficult market, I don't feel I can offer a contract or an advance yet. I look forward to hearing the finished tapes and will reconsider the position then.'

'Stupid git!' his dad fumed. 'How the bloody 'ell

does 'e expect us to finish the recordings if we 'aven't got any money?'

The rest of Rosen's letter went on in great detail about the wonderful reviews that Mike and Jason's first album had been getting and how Saroudan were hoping that their single was going to be a big hit.

'Talk about rubbin' it in. Makes you sick!' his dad said, screwing up the letter and throwing it across the caravan. 'Still, it's Rosen's loss. I'll just flog it to one of the record companies in Austin.'

For a couple of days he went round all the contacts he'd made in the record business in Austin, but it was the same story: people thought the material was promising, but they wanted to hear finished record-ings before they decided.

'No one's ready to put their money where their mouth is,' his dad said gloomily. 'Looks as if we'll 'ave to raise it ourselves.'

'How?' Buddy asked.

'Well, I've got fifteen grand or so in the bank.'

'That's not nearly enough.'

'It's a start.'

'Besides, you can't chuck all your money away.'

'It's not chucking it away. It's an investment. Anyway, I'll 'ave a chat wiv Floyd and T J.'

T J agreed to go on charging the absolute minimum for the studio with a guarantee of a slice of the profits if the album was bought by a record company. The major expense, though, was going to be the musicians.

'We gotta use the best or we're just wasting our time,' Floyd pointed out. 'They don't come cheap. And they want money up front – they'll never do a slice-of-the-profits deal like T J.'

'So, 'ow much?' his dad asked.

'Well, it depends: if we record all the songs and if I go for the full arrangements and if I –'

'Just tell me 'ow much!'

'Including T J's minimum, we gotta be talking thirty to forty thousand dollars.'

His dad gulped. 'OK, I'll get it. I'll get my money transferred over 'ere so we can get started. Then I'll go out and find some more investors. Either that or I rob a bank!'

Buddy and Floyd spent days playing all the demos and discussing how they wanted the finished tracks to sound. They were listening to one of the tracks and trying to decide whether it needed a horn section when his dad came into the studio. He was dripping wet and he laid a letter down on the table.

'This came for you,' he said to Buddy, then turned to Floyd. 'Looks like we can start any day – I phoned my bank today and the money's on the way.'

Buddy looked at the letter. Rain had dripped on it, blurring the address slightly, but it was Char's hand-writing. A shiver ran up his spine.

'Cool,' Floyd said. 'We're about ready to roll. Hey, Terry, man, I saw you in Threadgill's last night.'

'Yeah?'

'Yeah. I was driving by and I seen you sitting in the window with a whole bunch of Austin's baddest dudes. You ain't planning that bank job with them, are you?'

'Nah, just some business associates. Gotta go where the money is.'

'Yeah, 'cept that kinda money buys a lot of guys a neat little hole in the head.'

'Don't worry, I can take care of meself.' His dad laughed, then turned to Buddy. 'Not opening your letter, then?'

'Yeah – I'll be back in a minute.'

He went out into the corridor and pushed open the emergency exit to the alleyway. Rain was pouring down and he stood in the doorway looking at the water cascading from a broken gutter. Then he took a deep breath and opened the envelope.

Dear Buddy,

I don't know what to say. Your letter made me cry. The baby is OK. I've had tests, and everything is fine. I felt sick at first but I'm OK now.

You say that if I ask you to, you'll drop everything and come home. I DON'T WANT YOU TO COME HOME. You say I've changed your life – well, I don't want to change it. You were doing OK until I came along. I saw your eyes when I told you about the baby. And I heard you tell Jules on the phone that you wished it had never happened. Sometimes it's best to trust your first feelings. I don't want you to give up anything for me. I know what it's like to have to give things up. I had to give up going to University when Dad got ill, and I know how badly I resented it.

Please don't write again because it upsets me too much.

Charmian

CHAPTER THIRTY

Buddy kept re-reading Char's letter, trying to interpret the meaning of every word. Sometimes it seemed hopeful – that, if he could just talk to her, everything would be all right. But at other times he could only see those clear messages that didn't need any interpretation: Don't come home, and Don't write again.

In the end he showed the letter to Floyd.

'Hey, man, don't ask me about love! I fouled up on every relationship with every chick I've ever had. They all say I love my guitar more'n them – and I say, right on!'

'Seriously, Floyd. Just reading it – what do you think?'

Floyd looked at the sheet of paper again and shook his head. 'I'd say this chick been put down a whole lot in her life and she ain't looking to have it happen all over. You say she black? Well, that figures.'

'You mean she thinks I don't love her?'

'I mean, deep down she don't believe no white boy really want a black girl like her.'

'No, that can't be true,' Buddy said. 'She's so together about stuff like that.'

'Maybe she got herself a whole lot of pride 'bout who she is inside, but she still ain't shook off what the whole damn world been telling her about the colour of her skin. That kinda stuff goes deep.'

'But do you think she loves me?'

'Hey, man – what do I know? You gotta look the sister in the eye and check it out.'

As soon as he said it, Buddy knew that Floyd was right. It was no good thinking of trying to write to her or phone her. He had to see her, talk the whole thing through and explain things to her properly, face to face. He had to go home.

His dad came into the studio that evening and when they finished work, he invited Buddy and Floyd out to eat. As they strolled along to his dad's favourite Mexican restaurant on the corner of Fifth and Lamar, Buddy made up his mind – he would tell him tonight. He was bound to be disappointed, so it would be good to have Floyd there as an ally.

His dad took ages looking at the menu and chatting to the waiter, Jorgito, and then he ended up ordering what he always ordered. Buddy waited until Jorgito came back with a bowl of blue corn *nachos* and a big pitcher of beer. His dad started scoffing the *nachos* and Floyd poured the beer.

This was the moment. 'Dad, I've decided to go home.'

His dad gulped his mouthful of *nachos* and looked at him. 'What's up? You feeling ill? Maybe you're just 'ungry.'

'No, I don't mean back to the caravan. I mean back to England. Now. This week. I've got to see Charmian, sort it all out.'

His dad took a swig of beer, then wiped the froth off his upper lip with the back of his hand and shrugged his shoulders, 'Well, if that's what you want . . .'

'You don't mind?' Buddy asked, surprised.

'Of course I mind,' his dad said. 'I mean, blimey, I bin working me socks off getting my savings over so you and Floyd could get recording. Now it's arrived, and you decide to pack it in. Not to mention that I finally got Max Truman to put you in this TV Special on MTV. So now I'll 'ave to ring 'im and tell 'im you're pulling out of one of the biggest shows of the year. Of course I bloody mind, but if that's what you want . . .'

'Dad, I know what you've been doing and I'm dead grateful, you know I am; but I've got to see Charmian. Floyd agrees – don't you, Floyd?'

'Hey, hold it right there,' Floyd said. 'Sure, I said you gotta see her. But I didn't say nothin' about splitting now, hell no. I been busting my butt to get the best guys in town lined up to play with you. They're hot and ready to go, so, hey . . .'

Buddy looked at both of them, and he knew he had lost. Things had got too complicated. Too many people were involved. Too much work had been done.

He got up and headed for the restaurant door. The back of his throat was burning and he didn't want anyone to see his tears. But as he reached the door his dad was there, putting his arm round his shoulder and going outside with him.

'Come on, Buddy,' his dad said as they leaned against the wall and watched the tail-lights of the traffic that was cruising smoothly up Lamar Boulevard. 'I know 'ow you feel . . .'

'Dad, don't start giving me sympathy,' he said bitterly. 'I know what you think about Char. I know you don't want black blood in the family.'

'Buddy –'

'Don't worry, I'll stay. I'll do the recordings. But don't think I don't know.'

'Buddy, you're wrong, and you know you are. OK, I've got a big stupid mouth and I said somefing well out of order but I take it back. I didn't mean it and I wish I'd never said it. If you want to marry Charmian, then that's fine by me. I swear to you, Buddy, I never want to make you miserable. Never. All right, I don't want you to go 'ome now but it's got nuffin' to do wiv Char.'

His dad walked away a couple of paces, then came back and put his hands on Buddy's shoulders.

'Please, Buddy – you've gotta believe me. Look, I'm going to ring your mum tomorrow and tell 'er to get in contact wiv Charmian. Get 'er to explain fings. You know what women are like: they can talk about stuff like this. She'll get somefing sorted. Then, once you've got the recording done, we'll go straight 'ome. I promise. OK?'

Buddy nodded.

The recording started, and Buddy was pleased to lose himself in all the hard work and the wonderful music.

Floyd had picked a basic band – himself, Buddy, a bass player called Steve, and Travis, the drummer they'd used on the demos – but he called in other musicians for nearly every track.

Each afternoon the four members of the band started by listening to the demos of the two songs they were planning to record and then they spent a couple of hours playing through them and getting the basic guitar, drums and bass parts worked out. Then the other musicians arrived in the evening, and they began rehearsing the whole sound while TJ set up the mikes and screens to get the sound balance right.

They were recording 'live' and, right up to the last moment, Floyd was often changing the arrangement, suggesting that the piano should come in here or the sax player should take a solo there. Sometimes he'd even suddenly decide that the song needed another instrument – a harmonium on 'Dark House' or extra percussion on 'Broken Cup'. He'd dash into the control booth to phone one of his musician friends and they'd turn up half an hour later, to be plunged into recording a song they'd never heard.

It was a dangerous way of doing things but it was fantastically exciting. There was always an electric tension in the air when the tapes finally started to roll and they began to play, but the danger seemed to bring out the best in people and they made music that was raw and edgy and alive.

They usually needed a number of 'takes' of the song before Floyd was satisfied, but he never allowed the music to settle into a pattern. He wanted it to sound improvised and spontaneous, so he often threw in new ideas between 'takes' so that the music would sound fresh each time.

It was nerve-racking, but Buddy loved walking this knife-edge and he found his singing and guitar playing was being stretched all the time and that he was being inspired by the musicians round him.

His dad was as enthusiastic as anyone. 'This is the way to do it,' he kept saying. 'Just like they did it in the old days. Elvis, Buddy Holly – all their best stuff was done live like this. They didn't want it perfect –

they wanted it to feel real. That's why it still sounds so good today.'

It was exhausting work but, even when they finished at three or four o'clock in the morning, Buddy was always still too wired up to sleep, so he and the others often went to eat and drink at a nearby café that stayed open all night. Even when all the others had gone, he and Floyd lingered on to talk about the next day's session, so he often didn't get to bed before six in the morning.

Buddy woke up at midday. The caravan was quiet and he realized that his dad was out. He lay there with the tune of one of last night's songs playing over and over inside his head. Then he remembered what day it was. It was his birthday. He was twenty-two years old. No time for celebration, though – it was another day in the studio. Another two songs to record.

He got out of bed and went for a cool shower to shock himself wide awake. Strange that his dad was out. He'd never forgotten his birthday, even when he was in prison, and Buddy had expected to wake and find him there, singing 'Happy Birthday' in his terrible, off-key voice and perhaps giving him a present. But there was nothing, not even a card.

He had coffee and some scrambled eggs and bacon in a diner on 6th Street and then went round to Dillo. He was early; the only person in the studio was TJ, setting up the mikes for the day.

'Hey,' TJ called in greeting, then went on untangling cables and testing the amps.

'You sleep here or something?' Buddy laughed.

'Pretty much,' TJ chuckled. 'My babe keeps threatening to cut out on me if she don't see me more often. What do I care? – I tell her we're making history here. She thinks I'm jiving her, but I'm not. We're making history. You're gonna be famous, Buddy. And I'm gonna have every band in the world just begging to come here to record!'

'Yeah, I've heard it all before,' Buddy laughed, and he plugged his guitar in and sat down to play.

He couldn't keep a stupid grin off his face as he played, though. It was true that he'd heard all that kind of hype before. People in the music business were always saying that this song was a sure Number One, or that this album would ship a million copies in two weeks – but TJ wasn't like them. Buddy trusted his opinion. Besides, he didn't need anyone to tell him, he knew it already: something special was happening.

It was like those wonderful moments when The Bosses had found a magic 'thing' on stage, that thing Rosen had called 'chemical'. It was happening here. Somehow, something magical was going on. All the elements – the songs, the musicians, Floyd's ideas – were coming together and creating music that was better than the songs, better than the musicians, better than Floyd's ideas. Music that cut through and woke up something inside you. Music that made you feel as if you were trembling on the edge of understanding.

It might not make him famous or make every band in the world want to record here, but maybe there would be people who would hear the music and be touched by it.

He couldn't ask for anything more.

Floyd, Steve and Travis turned up at about two-thirty, and they jammed for an hour or so. They played easily, singing old songs or making up new ones on the run, sparking each other with impromptu ideas that made them smile with pleasure. Then they began work on the two songs they were planning to record.

They had a break at six, then went back into the studio and met up with the pianist, the sax player and the accordion player who Floyd wanted to use on the two songs. They rehearsed the songs with the full band, and by nine o'clock they were ready to record.

'OK,' T J announced over the speaker, 'the tape's rolling. This is "Dying Without You" Take One.'

Floyd counted them in and they started to play the intro, thirty-two bars of slow, rolling rhythm with the sax playing a soft, silvery variation on the main tune. The sax faded away, Floyd strummed shivering chords on the guitar, and Buddy began to sing the first words:

> 'Looking at those blue hills
> Those blue hills of the evening
> When the birds stopped their singing
> And a hush fell from the stars.
> Didn't know it was . . .

There was a crash as the door was flung open. Buddy opened his eyes with a start and everyone stopped playing. His dad was standing in the door-way, a huge grin on his face.

'Terry!' Floyd shouted, furious that the mood of the song had been broken.

'What the hell are you doing, Dad? We're record-ing. Didn't you see the sign lit up outside?'

' 'Course I saw it, but I just couldn't wait. It's your birthday and I've been to Houston airport to get your present.'

He stretched his hand back into the corridor and pulled someone into view.

It was Charmian.

Chapter Thirty-One

The first few days with Charmian were difficult and disappointing. The tight recording schedule meant that work had to go on as usual and they also had to find time to rehearse the two songs for the TV Special.

They got Char a room at a hotel on 6th Street, not far from Dillo Studios, and she came to the recording sessions; but she was still tired from the flight, and his dad always drove her back to the hotel before they'd finished. Buddy was thrilled that she'd come to Austin, of course – but they got so little time on their own and there was so much that they needed to say to each other.

It was his dad who changed the situation.

'I'm movin' out of the caravan,' he announced. 'There's another one free at the other side of the trailer park and I've rented it. I reckon you two ought to 'ave somewhere to be alone. All right, darling?'

'Thanks, Terry, that would be great,' Char said, reaching over and patting his hand.

His dad moved out the next day and, when Buddy

got back after the session that night, Char was lying, asleep, in one of the bunks. It was very late so he crept into the caravan, trying not to wake her. He took off his clothes quietly and got into his own bunk.

'Buddy?' she murmured sleepily.

'Yeah?' he whispered.

There was a silence, then he heard her get up and walk across to him.

'I don't want to be on my own,' she said.

He reached up and took her hand and she slipped into bed with him. The bunk was narrow, but he shifted over as far as he could and she lay on her side, her head on his shoulder, with the firm swelling of her belly pressed against him.

She fell asleep almost at once, and he lay there with her in his arms, listening to her soft breathing and thinking about the baby inside her, just there where her belly touched his hip. Five months old. A tiny life. Did it know he was there? Could it feel him?

A couple of days later there was no recording, just a rehearsal to work on the songs for the TV programme. The rehearsal went so well that they packed up at lunchtime and, at last, Buddy had some time off to be with Char.

His dad lent him the Buick and they drove north through the hill country and stopped at a huge lake. The November sun was shining warmly and they strolled, hand in hand, along the shore, looking at the yachts and windsurfers out on the water.

'I can hardly believe I'm here,' Char said, letting go of his hand and putting her arm round his waist.

'I'm glad you are,' Buddy said, turning and giving her a kiss on her cheek. 'What did your mum and dad say when you told them you were coming?'

'Well, they weren't very happy, but your mum spoke to mine for ages on the phone and she finally agreed. My dad wouldn't even say goodbye to me when I left.'

'Oh, Char,' he said, pulling her close. 'Why can't they be happy about it?'

'I don't know. My dad's changed so much since he got ill. He and Jules have terrible rows. So my mum gets upset about that. I think she sort of relied on me to keep things happy, and then this happened and she felt as if everything was falling apart. Especially when I kept changing my mind.'

'About what?'

'Oh, you. The baby.'

'What, you mean you . . .'

'Thought of not having it? Once or twice. And don't tell me that wasn't the first thing *you* thought of, because I saw it in your face.'

'I thought of all sorts of things,' he admitted.

'Yeah, so did I. But I didn't want you to be like me. I wanted you to be pleased and sure and positive and . . .'

'. . . And I wasn't. I'm sorry.'

'It wasn't your fault. How could you be sure, when I wasn't?'

'I am now. You know that, don't you?'

Charmian nodded, and he stopped walking and pulled her around and kissed her. There was the stamp of running feet and he looked up from Charmian and saw two silver-haired men jogging towards them along the shore. Their faces were red and sweaty, and Buddy was shocked by the hatred in their eyes as they went by, turning their heads to stare.

'What's up with them?' he said, watching them jog away.

'What?' Char said.

'Those guys, they . . .' he stopped as, with a sudden chill, he realized what it was. They'd been staring with hatred because he was white and Char was black.

'What?' Char repeated.

'They looked as if they were gonna burst a blood vessel if they ran much further,' he laughed, not wanting her to know.

He pretended he was feeling a bit tired, so they turned around and walked back to the car. The loveliness of the lake and the hills couldn't make up for the ugliness of those two men and he wanted to get away from them. Char and Jules and Floyd had had to put up with looks like that all their lives. He remembered the first thing his dad had said when he heard about the baby – 'The poor thing's gonna be stuck in the middle' – and Buddy suddenly realized how much hatred the baby was going to face.

When they got back into the car, Buddy put his hand on Char's round belly.

'What's that for?' she chuckled.

'To tell it I love it. To let it know I want it. Maybe it sensed all those feelings we had about . . . not wanting it. And I just want to tell it everything's OK.'

'Don't worry. She knows how much she's loved. I tell her all the time.'

'She?'

'I found out when they were doing the tests.'

'A girl! I'm going to have a baby daughter!'

They drove back towards Austin, and Buddy stopped as close as he could to the summit of Mount Bonnell.

'Do you think you can manage to climb to the top?' he asked. 'It's not really a mountain, just a hill really, but there are over a hundred steps from here.'

'Of course I can climb. I'm not ill.'

'But is it OK for the baby?'

'Don't worry, she's a strong girl. Isn't that right, kid?' Char said, patting her belly gently.

There was a party of young schoolchildren at the top of the hill running around, taking photos, and leaning over the rails to look at the Colorado River far below. Buddy and Charmian sat on one of the rocks, watching them and listening to their laughter and excited cries as they raced around. Finally their teacher got them into line and led them away down the steps.

The air was crystal clear and the distant skyline of Austin stood out sharply in the late afternoon sunshine. They wandered round the top of the cliffs, looking down at the luxurious houses nestling on the river banks. A speedboat skimmed its way downstream. A cool breeze suddenly swept past them and Charmian shivered.

'Let's go down,' Buddy said, then took both her hands in his and faced her. 'But before we do, I've got something to ask you.'

'What?'

'Well, the last time I asked this I did it all wrong, so this time I'm going to do it properly.'

He got down on one knee and kissed her hand. His heart was knocking crazily in his chest.

'Buddy!' Char laughed.

'No, don't laugh. I know it's corny, but this is how I feel. I want to show you how much I love you and I want to ask you: will you marry me?'

She pulled him to his feet and her eyes were shining. She put her arms round his neck, kissed him, then looked straight at him and said, 'Yes, Buddy Clark, I want to marry you. With all my heart I want it.'

That evening they took his dad out for a meal and told him the news. He immediately ordered a bottle of champagne and raised his glass to them.

'Well,' he said, 'I won't pretend I 'aven't 'ad me doubts 'cos you know I 'ave. But I've seen Buddy goin' nuts wivout you, Char, so I know what you mean to 'im. And the fact that you came all this way must mean you love 'im. What am I talkin' about? I know you love 'im – I only 'ave to look at you together. Although what you see in 'im, I'll never know! Anyway, what I want to say is – I'm really 'appy for you, and I wish you everyfing you wish for yourselves. Cheers!'

Char was just raising her glass to her lips when his dad leaned across and took hold of her arm.

''Ere, darlin', you can't drink that now you're in the family way.'

'I'm only going to have a sip, Terry,' she smiled. 'Don't worry, I'm looking after your grandchild properly.'

'Grandchild! Oh, leave it out. Me, a grandad, I ask yer! What's the nipper gonna fink? It'll never believe that a young bloke like me could be its granddad!'

'It's not "It", Dad. It's a girl.'

'A girl? Oh gawd, a little girl. Oh, your mum's gonna be over the moon – she always wanted to buy dresses and all that stuff for a daughter. Now she can do it for a granddaughter. A little girl! That's great.'

Buddy was amazed to see the daft smile on his dad's face and the glisten of tears in his eyes.

''Ere, you know what you've gotta call 'er, don't you? Holly!'

'Oh, Dad, do me a favour.'

'Why not? Holly Clark. It's a lovely name. That's what I was gonna call you if you'd been a girl.'

'Yeah, but both of them together. Buddy and Holly. We can't!'

When they were in bed that night, Buddy turned on his side and looked at Char's profile in the moonlight pouring in through the small window above them. He reached out and ran his finger across her forehead and down her nose to her lips. She kissed his finger and he saw her lips part in a smile. He put his head on her shoulder and buried his face against her neck, smelling the faint trace of perfume on her skin.

'Buddy,' she murmured. 'What do you think of that name?'

'Holly? No, Char, we can't.'

'It's a nice name. And the funny thing is, as soon as your dad said it, she moved inside me.'

'It was just a coincidence.'

'I don't believe in coincidence. Everything is meant to happen.'

225

'You don't really believe that, do you?'

'Sometimes, yes. Sometimes, you just get a glimpse of how everything's . . . all tied up together, all linked. And when you can see it like that, life is incredible. You and me, for example. That wasn't chance. We were meant for each other.'

She turned towards him and kissed his lips, slipping her arms round his waist and pulling him tight against her.

CHAPTER THIRTY-TWO

The TV Special was a live concert, spotlighting the music scene in Austin. All the best local bands were playing, and there were guest appearances by big stars who had started their careers in Austin. Top of the bill was one of Buddy's favourite old blues singers, Nighthawk McShale, and he was thrilled when McShale came up to him after the afternoon rehearsal and congratulated him on his performance.

'You sing pretty good, boy,' the old man said, laying his leathery old hand on Buddy's shoulder. 'And yo' friend plays a mean guitar.'

'Floyd, yeah he's great,' Buddy said, and then didn't know what else to say. He wanted to say that he loved McShale's music and had been inspired by him but he just stood there staring dumbly at this legend of the blues.

Finally, McShale opened his mouth and let out a deep, rumbling laugh. Buddy glimpsed two gold front teeth gleaming at him, then the old blues singer ambled away down the corridor. Buddy dashed in the other direction and burst into his dressing-room where Floyd was talking to his dad and Char.

'You'll never guess what!' he shouted. 'Nighthawk McShale stopped me and said he liked me. Nighthawk McShale! And he said my friend Floyd plays a mean guitar.'

'Well, let's just 'ope the rest of the world agrees wiv 'im when they see you on TV tonight,' his dad said. 'If we don't find some investors pretty soon, we're gonna 'ave to pack up recording 'cos my money's nearly run out.'

The rehearsal had gone well and Buddy was feeling confident as they stood on the side of the stage, waiting to go on. Then the compere announced the band's name and, out of nowhere, a wave of panic swept through him. His heart was hammering and his hands shook as he plugged his guitar into the amp. Floyd counted to three and the band started to play the intro to 'Ordinary People'. Buddy took a deep breath, then turned to the mike.

He hit the first note and felt his voice crack. He turned away from the mike and coughed to clear his throat, but his vocal chords were all tensed up and his voice stayed tight and husky all the way through the song. He took a quick swig of water at the end of the song and started the next one, 'Rollingwood Blues'. His throat had cleared and he was just beginning to relax and enjoy himself when he broke a guitar string at the end of the first chorus. He pulled at the string to get it out of the way, then realized that he couldn't think of the words of the next verse – his brain was blank. He fumbled along, making up words for a couple of lines, until he suddenly remem-

bered the right lyrics. But all his confidence had
gone. He couldn't give the song the energy it needed
and he knew he was singing weakly. Even Floyd's
guitar playing was less powerful than usual and they
came off stage knowing that they had wasted a big
opportunity. The look on his dad's face said
everything.

The next day they went back into Dillo Studios and
tried to forget the disappointment by getting on with
recording. They finished the first song, 'Everyday
Miracle', really quickly, but the second song, 'Einstein And Me', was very complicated and things
went wrong on every take. They went on working
until five-thirty in the morning, but everybody was
getting short-tempered so they gave up. By the time
Buddy had some breakfast and got back to the
trailer park it was nearly eight o'clock. As he cycled
in through the gates, Joe Lye, the manager of the
trailer park, came out of the office and signalled him
to stop.

'I sure hate to do this,' Joe Lye said, 'but I gotta
ask you and your . . . girlfriend to pack up and leave.
You see, I've gotten some complaints from other
residents.'

'What complaints?' Buddy asked in surprise.

'Well, this has always been a place where white
folks could count on being around their own kind.
And when Mr Clark booked in here, he didn't mention nothing about bringing a . . . about your
girlfriend.'

Buddy was so shocked that he looked at Joe Lye,
unable to believe what he was hearing.

'It's not me, you understand – it's the residents,'

Lye said, looking away across the trailer park. 'And you don't have to go right away. I'll let you have a couple of days to find somewhere else.'

'I don't want a couple of days,' Buddy said, feeling his anger rise but forcing it back down into his chest.

He immediately cycled across to his dad's caravan and told him what had happened.

'I'll go and 'ave a word wiv 'im,' his dad said. 'Get somefing sorted out.'

'I don't want something sorted out, Dad! Don't you realize what he's saying? He's saying Char isn't good enough to stay here! We're going. If you want to stay, that's up to you.'

'No, you're right. Let's go.'

Char was still asleep and when Buddy woke her and told her what had happened, she seemed stunned by the news. She sat silently in the car while he and his dad got their things together and piled them in the back.

An hour later they drove past the office on their way out. Joe Lye was standing on the porch, and his dad slowed the car and wound down the window.

'Hey, Mr Clark, I didn't mean for you to go, too,' Lye said.

'I ain't staying nowhere where my daughter-in-law ain't welcome. So up yours, you racist git!' he yelled, then he gunned the motor and roared out through the gates in a cloud of dust.

They booked into a motel just off I-35 and unloaded the car. As soon as he sat down, Buddy felt totally drained and he decided he ought to try to get some sleep. His dad said he had some business to do in town and he asked Char to go with him.

'Come on, darlin', let's leave the superstar to 'ave

a kip,' he said, putting his arm round her and giving her a hug. 'We'll go and see if we can raise some cash. Maybe you'll bring me luck.'

Buddy went to bed, but he was still churning with anger, and the noise of planes landing and taking off at the nearby airport kept him awake until nearly noon. When he woke, it was five-thirty, and he jumped out of bed. He was late for the recording.

He had a quick shower, got dressed and was just going into the motel reception to ring for a cab when the Buick turned into the parking lot.

'Keep your 'air on,' his dad said. 'I called Floyd and told 'im you wouldn't be there till eight so we've got time to grab a bite to eat.'

They drove to a fish restaurant on 6th Street and ordered Southern Fried Catfish and a big bowl of french fries.

'Terry's found us somewhere to live,' Charmian said as they started to eat.

'Yeah, old Max Truman's off to Europe and Australia for a couple of months and 'e's gonna lend us 'is apartment on 25th Street, right near that little park up there. We can move in at the end of the week. Good old Max, eh?'

'It's hardly worth it,' Buddy said. 'If the money runs out, we're going to have to stop recording and go home soon anyway.'

'Don't give up so easy. I'm not gonna let the money run out, am I? I'll get it, don't worry.'

'How?'

'Never you mind,' his dad said, tapping the side of his nose. 'You just concentrate on the music.'

Floyd and all the musicians were waiting for him when he arrived, and they started work on 'Einstein

And Me' again. Floyd had had some new ideas for the song during the day, and they spent a couple of hours rehearsing this new, slower version. When they gave T J the signal to start recording, they got it right on the second take.

It was only just after midnight, but Buddy felt tired after the strain of the day so he decided to pack up early. He went to a bar with Floyd and told him what had happened at the trailer park.

'Welcome to Texas, man! They like us niggers to know our place. As long as we live in the housing projects and smoke crack and shoot each other, they're happy. Come too near their nice neighbourhoods, and their trigger-fingers start to itch.'

Charmian was still awake when he got back to the motel; lying in bed, staring blankly at the TV. She clung to him tightly when he got into bed and tears rolled down her cheeks and onto his shoulder. He couldn't think of any words that would help so he just hugged her and stroked her head until they both fell asleep.

A couple of days later, despite what his dad had said, the money ran out. He called a halt to recording until he could raise some more. He was out all day long, going round town to his contacts, while phone messages and faxes came for him at the motel office. In the meantime Buddy still met up with Floyd and T J at Dillo Studios, to start mixing the tracks they'd already recorded and to make plans for the rest of the songs.

They were all just on their way out of the studio one evening when there was the honking of a car horn from across the road. His dad's Buick did a big

U-turn and screamed to a stop next to them. The door opened and his dad leaped out with a big grin on his face.

'Get back in that studio and start work, you lazy gits – I've got the money!'

They went to the nearest bar to celebrate, and Floyd asked where he'd got the money from.

'Trade secret!' his dad laughed.

'Hey, come on, Terry,' Floyd said. 'Did you rob that bank, or what?'

Floyd and TJ went on asking, but he kept smiling and saying that he wasn't going to tell them. Buddy waited until they were alone in the car on the way back to the motel before he asked.

'Not you an' all!' his dad groaned. 'I've said it a million times already, leave that side of things to me. So just lay off, right?'

Buddy was angry but he didn't go on. He knew just how stubborn his dad could be. Besides, part of him didn't want to keep asking in case the answer was something he didn't want to hear.

He went to bed but he couldn't sleep. Surely his dad hadn't done something stupid? Why not? – he had in the past. Yes, but he'd changed. OK then, why the secrecy? That was just his style – a bit of a joke to make things seem mysterious and make himself look clever. For a while, yes, but not going on and on. The more Buddy thought about it, the more convinced he was that his dad had something to hide.

And then Buddy remembered Floyd saying something about seeing his dad in some café with – what did he call them? 'Austin's baddest dudes'. He tried to put the idea out of his head. He tried breathing deeply. He tried telling himself that his dad wouldn't be so crazy as to get involved with criminals over here. But none of it worked – the idea kept spinning around his brain and he had a sleepless night.

Early next morning, he knocked on his dad's door and woke him up.

'What's up?' his dad said, his eyes still half-closed with sleep.

'Where did that money come from?'

'Oh gawd, I've told you – just leave the financial side to me.'

'No. I'm not going back into the studios till you tell me. I'm not kidding, Dad. If you don't tell me, I'll go straight back to England with Char.'

'OK, OK. If you want to know so badly, I'll tell you. But you ain't gonna be pleased.'

His dad went over to his jacket and pulled out a piece of paper. It was a Bank Transfer Form made out to Terry Clark for £10,000. The signature at the bottom was D. King.

'Des?' Buddy said.

'Says 'e thinks 'e owes you. Well, now you know. So – do you go on recording or what?'

Buddy handed back the paper. Des King. Always Des King.

'Yeah, OK, we go on recording. But the minute we get any money for this record, we pay him back. With interest.'

His dad laughed. 'Don't worry. Des knows what 'e's doing – 'e asked for a two per cent cut of the profits!'

'He did what?' Buddy said. But he couldn't help chuckling. 'He doesn't change, does he?'

'Nah. Good old Des. I've changed, though – I beat 'im down to one per cent!'

CHAPTER THIRTY-THREE

Max Truman's apartment was enormous. There were four bedrooms, a huge kitchen and a beautiful living-room that ran the whole length of the building. All the floors were polished wood and the white walls had wall-hangings and paintings on them. It was light and airy and there was a feeling of calm everywhere.

Char fell in love with it at once and, while Buddy and his dad were unloading the car, she went round to the local delicatessen and bought some supplies.

'My mum never let me do much cooking at home, so I want to learn while I'm here. You're going to be my guinea pigs.'

'Blimey, Buddy, we're gonna be eatin' grass and pellets!' his dad laughed.

In fact, she turned out to be a great cook. She bought a Texas cookbook and tried all sorts of Tex-Mex dishes.

'You're gonna get fat, mate, if Char cooks like this all the time,' his dad said one day as he finished off a plateful of chicken *fajitas*.

'It's not going to be just me cooking, Terry,' Char said. 'Buddy's going to run the house and look after the baby some of the time while I'm studying.'

'That's right,' Buddy said. 'Char's going to do an Open University course when we get home.'

'Oh gawd, not another flippin' genius in the family – I'll be the only thicko. No, maybe Holly'll take after 'er granddad. Two thickos together.'

'No, she's going to be brilliant,' Buddy said, 'but she won't be called Holly, so just cut it out!'

The recording sessions went on getting better and better and nobody wanted them to end. Finally, though, they recorded the last two songs.

'Hey, man, I'm gonna miss this like crazy. Write some more,' the drummer, Travis, joked at the end of the last session.

'Are you kidding? We've got nearly forty tracks here,' Buddy laughed. 'I'm all written-out!'

'Don't look so miserable, Travis,' his dad said, getting up from the chair where he'd been sitting watching. 'It's not over yet. We've got a week's booking at Max Truman's club here in Austin and then five days at 'is other club in San Antonio.'

'What's this?' Buddy asked in disbelief.

'Yeah, I kind of promised it to 'im in return for usin' the apartment.'

'You . . . When's it for?'

'Just after Christmas till early in the New Year.'

'Oh no. I'm taking Char home for Christmas, and that's that.'

Char was still up when they got home. His dad immediately tried to win her round by saying that he'd only arranged the gigs so that they could live in the flat, but Buddy cut him short.

'You had no right to promise anything without asking me.'

'Well, the gigs are booked now,' Char said. 'And I quite like the idea of spending Christmas here, anyway. So I don't know what you're making such a fuss about.'

'I'm not making a fuss. It's just that . . . well, I thought we could get married before Christmas,' Buddy said.

'Get married here,' his dad suggested.

'Don't be daft,' Buddy snapped.

'It's not daft, it's romantic. Just fink – a wedding in Austin, Texas. Fabulous. We'll ask your mum and Char's mum and dad. They can fly across for the wedding and spend Christmas here. It would be ace. What d'you reckon, darlin'?'

'It would be fantastic,' Char said.

'Oh, I give up!' Buddy groaned.

'Good!' his dad said, and Char burst into giggles.

Charmian was on the phone to her parents and, even though she was out in the hall and Buddy couldn't hear all the words, it was obvious that it wasn't going well. His dad glanced up from the newspaper as Char's voice got louder.

'Mum, that's not fair,' they both heard her say.

His dad made a grimace towards Buddy, then went back to his paper.

They'd fixed the wedding for 22nd December, and his mum had accepted the invitation at once and was flying out a couple of days before the wedding. Buddy was really pleased that they'd all be together for Christmas, and he knew that Char would feel the same if her parents came.

She walked back into the room, and one look at her face told him what had happened.

'No?' he asked.

Char bit her lip and shook her head, and Buddy could see that she was on the point of tears.

'We're going out, Dad,' he said and grabbed Char's hand and took her out into the hall.

He slipped her coat over her shoulders and she followed, unresisting, as he led her down the stairs and outside. As soon as they got in the car, though, she started to cry.

'Dad says I've shamed the family,' she sobbed. 'And mum's just going along with him. It's like they're disowning me.'

'Of course they're not disowning you,' he said gently. 'They love you, you know they do. They're just upset. Look, we'll go home, get married there.'

'No. It wouldn't make any difference.'

They drove downtown in the pouring rain and parked by the side of the Colorado River. The tall buildings of the city were shrouded in a grey mist and Buddy stared at their dim shapes and held on to Char until her crying gradually ceased. Finally she sat up and wiped her eyes.

'That's it,' she said fiercely. 'I'm not going to cry any more. I'm not doing anything wrong and I'm not going to let them make me feel bad. They're the ones who are wrong. Mum knows it – I could hear it in her voice. But she just won't stand up to Dad. Well, if she wants to miss my wedding, that's up to her, but I'm not going to cry again.'

And she didn't.

When they got back to the apartment, she insisted on cooking a meal for the three of them and while they were eating she suddenly said, 'Who are you going to have as your best man?'

'I don't know. I thought of maybe asking Floyd.'

'You can't have him,' Char grinned, 'because I'm going to ask him to give me away. You can have your dad.'

'Yeah, OK then.'

'Yeah, OK then?' his dad said, punching his shoulder. 'What kind of invitation is that? I might only be second choice, you little toe-rag, but you're still gonna 'ave to ask me proper.'

'Right, then. Dad, will you please be my best man?'

'Buddy,' his dad said, then he choked and his eyes suddenly watered. He looked away and gulped, then he turned back with a careless grin on his face and said, 'Buddy, it would be an honour.'

Buddy went down to Dillo Studios every day to hear what TJ was doing with the mixes of the songs. Floyd was always there, and the three of them worked side by side, listening to the tracks, bringing the drums up a little here, laying the guitars a little further back there, emphasizing the sax on this song or the piano on that one.

It was great working with TJ and Floyd. They all loved the music and had exactly the same idea of how it should sound. TJ pinned a sign up above the mixing desk – 'LESS IS BEST' – and they tried to keep the music as close as possible to the original sound they'd made when they were playing in the studio.

'Real and simple,' Floyd said. 'Just let the soul of the music come through.'

The mixing took two weeks and, when it was finished, they listened to all the tracks, trying to decide which should be used on the album.

'Let's face it,' TJ said, 'there's enough for three

albums here. Three classic albums – and all made at Dillo Studios, folks! So which lucky company is gonna get them?'

His dad still had a bit of a grudge against Bobby Rosen for not financing the recording, but Buddy thought it would be best to stick with someone they knew, so they sent the tapes off to Saroudan. Luckily there wasn't much time to sit around worrying about what Rosen would think of them because they had to start work on the Christmas shows. Travis was still on drums and Steve was on bass, but they added a pianist, Lonnie James, and set to work rehearsing twenty of the new songs for performing live.

Two days before the wedding, Buddy and Char drove to Houston to pick up his mum from the airport; from the moment they got back to the apartment, she took over the arrangements for the wedding.

'You can't just have nuts and beer for the guests, Terry – you are terrible. This is a once-in-a-lifetime event and we've got to make it special. And where's the actual ceremony taking place, anyway?'

When she heard that the Justice of the Peace was going to marry them in Max Truman's apartment, she asked what arrangements they'd made. His dad said none and she almost went mad. She spent ages on the phone to caterers, photographers and florists, and she even hired some extra chairs. The next day she spent the morning tidying up, setting out the chairs and arranging the flowers. Then she announced that she and Char were going out.

'We're going to buy something for her to wear and we're not coming back. We're having a girl's night out and then going to a hotel – it's bad luck for the groom to see the bride before the wedding. See you tomorrow.'

The guests started arriving at about eleven-thirty. TJ and all the musicians who'd played on the recording sessions were there, and his dad had invited a few of the people he knew from the music business. Precisely at noon, the Justice of the Peace arrived, and shortly afterwards his mum came in and stood next to his dad.

'Floyd and Charmian are outside,' she whispered. 'We can start the music.'

Buddy nodded to Lonnie James, who sat down at Max Truman's grand piano and began to play the 'Wedding March'. The door opened and Charmian came in, holding onto Floyd's arm. She was wearing a white jacket and skirt and a pink blouse that matched the bouquet of roses she was holding.

They walked slowly up to where everyone was gathered, then Floyd solemnly took her hand, stood her next to Buddy, and stepped back. Buddy glanced sideways at Char, and she looked calm and beautiful. His hand brushed the back of hers and she smiled.

The Justice of the Peace made a short speech about the happiness of the occasion, then he led them slowly and gravely through the vows. Charmian repeated her vows almost in a whisper; when it came to his turn, Buddy found that his voice was husky with emotion. His dad winked at him as he handed him the ring, and Buddy's throat suddenly tightened as he took it and placed it on Char's finger. It felt like the most important thing he had ever done in his life.

'Well, I suppose I've got to make a speech,' his

dad said after the ceremony. 'But don't worry, I'll make it short. First off, it's really weird standin' 'ere at my son's wedding 'cos 'e still seems like a kid to me. But 'e's not, of course. Twenty-two, and already 'e's done so much to make me proud of 'im. Not just the music, although you all know how proud I am of that.

'But, like I said, it's not just the music, it's every-fing. I mean, I know all dads are proud of their sons but Buddy's 'ad to put up wiv me as 'is dad and . . . well, we've been through all kinds of stuff together and 'e's never let me down. Not once. I don't know what I've done to deserve 'im, but 'e's mine and . . . Anyway, what I'm trying to say is that Buddy's a fantastic bloke and 'e's chosen a fantastic girl to be 'is wife. I'm sure they're gonna be really 'appy together and I want you to raise your glasses and join me in wishin' them all the best. Buddy and Charmian.'

Everybody raised their glasses and repeated, 'Buddy and Charmian.'

CHAPTER THIRTY-FOUR

On Christmas morning his mum and dad went out for a walk round town while Buddy and Char cooked the meal. Buddy was standing next to the cooker, waiting for the vegetables to boil, when he glanced out of the kitchen window and saw his parents ambling back along the street. His dad was chattering away about something and his mum was looking at him with a smile on her face. They stopped as his dad waved his hands about in the air to emphasize what he was saying, and she suddenly burst out laughing and put her hand on his shoulder. She said something to him, and he started to laugh as well. They stood for nearly half a minute, laughing together, then they continued walking towards the house.

Buddy went up to Char, who was making the gravy, and he put his arms round her from behind and kissed the back of her neck.

'What's that for?' she murmured, tipping her head back in pleasure.

'Oh . . . just to say I love you and I'm happy.'

The turkey was delicious, and they all had so much to eat that they decided to go down to Town Lake after the meal to try to walk it off.

'Just fink,' his dad said as they strolled by the water, 'next Christmas we'll be doin' this wiv Holly in 'er pram.'

'Dad, I'm warning you,' Buddy laughed.

'All right, we'll be doin' this wiv Bertha or whatever 'orrible name you're gonna give the poor little fing. Or maybe she'll be walkin' by then.'

'Don't be daft – she'll only be nine months old,' his mum said.

'Yeah, but she's gonna be really advanced, our granddaughter. Blimey, don't 'alf make you feel your age, talking about a granddaughter. I feel just about grown-up enough to fink about being a dad wivout making too much of a mess of it. But bein' a granddad, it's ridiculous. I'll 'ave to go and buy meself some slippers and a walking-stick next!'

The *Austin Chronicle* called Buddy's gigs at Max

Truman's the 'hottest ticket in town', and all the shows were sold out in advance. As the club began to fill up on the first night, the band could feel the atmosphere even from backstage. People were still in a Christmas mood and they wanted to have a good time and, somehow, word had got round that they would hear something special at Max Truman's this week.

Buddy was nervous as he waited in the dressing-room, but only because the adrenalin was pumping and he wanted to get out on stage and play. At last the manager came in and told them it was time.

Floyd was first on stage and he plugged his guitar in quickly and went to the mike while Buddy and the others were still getting ready. As the welcoming applause died away, Floyd strummed his guitar and leaned into the mike.

'Good evening,' he said. 'You know why you're here. You've picked up that something's been going on here in Austin. And you're right. I've been around and I've played with some hot bands but, like the man said – this is something else. Ladies and gentlemen, it's my privilege to introduce Buddy Clark.'

Buddy hadn't expected Floyd to talk, and he was thrown by the big build-up and the wave of clapping and whooping that greeted him as he stepped up to the mike. He looked down and was even more thrown to see that Char and his mum and dad were sitting at the table just next to the stage. But what threw him most of all was the band. He counted them in for the first song, 'Throwing Stones', and was amazed by the wall of energy and aggression that crashed round him as they started to play.

He knew they were good, but he'd never heard

243

them play like this. It was like a tidal wave of sound and, as they built up to the first verse, Buddy found himself being lifted up and borne along with it. By the time it got to the moment for him to start singing, he found himself opening his mouth and screaming the words as if he was drowning and crying for help.

He knew that he couldn't go on singing with such intensity, nobody could. And yet he went on. Song after song. The band was playing with an urgency that drew out a wildness in his singing. Even the soft, tender songs were done with a toughness, a feeling of pain, and he could feel his voice racked and raw with the emotion in them.

When he sang 'Cool Kid' he felt as if his throat was being gripped by hands that were throttling him, and the words were jerked out between gasps. When he finished the vocal and turned to watch Floyd begin his solo, he saw the guitarist staring at him as if he had been hanging on to every word, though he had heard them dozens of times. Then he began to play a solo that was so achingly beautiful that Buddy felt tears pricking his eyes.

By the end of the two-hour set sweat was pouring from them and their clothes were soaked. The crowd screamed and stamped and shouted for more, so they came back on and did a five-song encore that lasted another fifty minutes. And the mad, crashing energy went on rising until the last note of the last song.

The response to the shows was overwhelming. The newspaper reviews talked about 'this brilliant band' and 'songs that eat into your heart'. They even heard that the $15 tickets were being sold for $60 on the black market. They were on a high, so Bobby Rosen's fax came as a bit of a disappointment: he liked the songs but he still wouldn't offer them a contract unless he could fix up an American deal.

While his dad spent hours on the phone discussing all this with Rosen, Buddy took Char and his mum out every day to show them the sights in the Texas Hill Country. They visited the nearby State Parks and walked along some of the beautiful lakes to see waterfalls and caverns in the rugged countryside. It was peaceful and quiet, and Buddy was happy to see how well his mum and Char got along. He loved just listening to them chatting about the future: where he and Char would live, how his mum could look after the baby for them sometimes, plans for going shopping together to buy things for the baby.

He tried to persuade his mum to stay longer, but she said she had to get back to work so, on New Year's Eve, they all drove down to Houston to see her off. He would have liked to stay with her until the plane left, but he had to get back for the evening show, so they said goodbye as soon as she had checked in.

''Bye, Carol,' Char said, giving her a hug. 'And thanks for all you did – the wedding and everything.'

'It was my pleasure, love. It was a lovely day and you looked beautiful. I'm so happy for you both.'

'Thanks for coming, Mum,' Buddy said, giving her a kiss and holding her tight.

'I'll miss you,' she whispered.

'Oh, we'll be home in three weeks. Then you and Char can start buying baby clothes and prams!'

'Well, actually, we might be a bit longer than

that,' his dad said suddenly. 'Now don't look at me like that, Buddy. Rosen reckons we ought to stay over 'ere for another month to do some PR work. Saroudan are sending the tapes to some American record companies and 'e wants us to meet them so they can see 'ow wonderful we are. And 'e wants us to go round gettin' the radio people on our side. Apparently it's dead important.'

'Dad, I've told you – after these gigs we're going home. I want to find somewhere to live before the baby comes.'

'OK, I'll just 'ave to ring Bobby and say no.'

'Yes, you will. So we'll see you in three weeks, Mum.'

''Bye, love, take care. And you, Terry.'

'Yeah, ta.'

His mum gave his dad a kiss on his cheek, then she made her way through customs and immigration into the departure lounge. At the last moment she waved, then she turned away and was lost in the crowd.

The last two gigs at Max Truman's were recorded by a local radio station for transmission later. His dad got hold of a tape, and the band listened to them in the apartment.

'Wow, awesome!' Travis said at the end. 'That could be a live album.'

'Maybe, we can send it to other radio stations, too,' Floyd said. 'You know how important they are.'

His dad gave Buddy a meaningful look, but he ignored it.

There was a five-day break before the gigs started

at San Antonio so it gave Buddy a chance to spend every minute of the day with Char. It was wonderful to wake up next to her and lie there, chatting, then having a lazy breakfast, before strolling round town together or sitting in a café watching people go by. Most of all, he loved just staying at home and reading quietly, side by side, looking up from time to time and watching her. Often, in the afternoon, she would curl up next to him on the sofa and go to sleep with her head in his lap. He would put his hand gently on the roundness of her belly and feel the gentle rise and fall of her breathing and, every now and then, the stir of the baby within.

'I don't want this to ever end,' Char said to him one day. 'I don't know if it's being with you or being pregnant or what, but I feel as if . . . I don't know . . . that I'm really living. As if I'm sort of in touch with something.'

The hair on Buddy's neck stood up in excitement as she spoke.

'Yeah,' he replied. 'I get that sometimes when I'm playing music. It's like . . . if you could just go a little bit further, you'd understand everything.'

'Yes, but not understand with your brain. It's something else, something inside you that feels like it's going to break out and join up with . . . everything.'

'But it never lasts, though,' Buddy said.

'It doesn't matter,' Char replied. 'Maybe it can't. Maybe it would stop you from living your ordinary life if you felt it all the time. But if you trust it, it's like a sign, a kind of message to tell you to keep going. To live properly and keep going in the right direction. Almost as if you belong somewhere else and that all the time you're heading there. Like going home.'

Late that night, Buddy woke up and got out of bed. Char went on sleeping, and he tip-toed out into the living-room. He switched on the light on the desk and sat down in an armchair. In the semi-darkness, just outside the pool of light from the lamp, he strummed his guitar quietly.

Out of the still of the night, the words started to come. He took a pen and paper and wrote down his song.

See it in the sunrise, clouds against pale blue
Flashing light on water, smoky rainfall too
The dancing of the atom, rocks and running streams
Long-forgotten stories, memories and dreams
The beauty of the children, the wisdom of the old
Changing of the seasons, always heading home.

From year to year
From day to day
From dawn to dark
From birth to grave
Always heading home
We're always heading home.

It's there in children's voices, echoes from the past
The music of the forest, the silence of the stars
The rhythm of the ocean, a call that can't be heard
A feeling something's missing, that can't be said in
    words
The way that all things balance, the fast one and the
    slow
The question and the answer, always heading home.

From year to year
From day to day
From dawn to dark
From birth to grave
Always heading home
We're always heading home.

CHAPTER THIRTY-FIVE

The gigs at Max Truman's club in San Antonio were
sold out every night and they got great reviews. As
soon as they got back to Austin they went into Dillo
Studios to record 'Always Heading Home'. Buddy
knew exactly how he wanted the song to sound: the
rhythm of Travis and Steve, way off in the back-
ground, like a softly pounding heart, while Floyd
and Lonnie James wove in and out of the melody on
guitar and piano. It took a whole night session to get
it right but the finished track was perfect.

His dad immediately sent it off to Saroudan and
he bet Buddy that Rosen would choose it as the first
single. TJ said that he'd played it to a number of
people from the record business in Austin who
thought it was fantastic.

Char thought it was wonderful, too, and it was while
they were talking about it one evening that she said
he ought to do the PR tour that Rosen had proposed.

'Has my dad been getting at you?' Buddy asked.

'Well, he's mentioned it a couple of times, but
that's not why I think you should do it. After all,
everything depends on getting an American record

deal. If you could tie it up now, it would save you having to come back just after the baby's born. Besides, it'll be a bit like a honeymoon, going round the States together.'

'But what about you? All that time on the road . . . anything could happen. Maybe it's not good to be trailing all over the place so near to the birth.'

'I'm fine. Look at me – I'm as fit as a fiddle. Honest, Buddy, I think you should do it.'

Buddy was sure his dad had been putting more pressure on her than she admitted, but she was right: it did seem silly not to finish the job while they were over here. He had a long chat with his dad and said that he was willing to do the tour.

'Five weeks, though, and no longer. I want to take Char home before the end of February so that she has a month before the baby's born. So don't try any of your tricks to extend it, OK?'

'As if I would,' his dad grinned. 'Honest, mate, you won't regret it. Bobby's sure we're gonna get a deal and 'e says it'll be a real bonus to get radio stations on our side. I'm gonna ask Floyd to come wiv us, 'cos 'e's got contacts all over the place.'

Three days later they crammed their luggage into the boot of the Buick and set off westwards, across the huge empty wilderness of West Texas, to El Paso. His dad drove, with Char up front next to him so that she had more room to stretch out. Buddy and Floyd sat behind, jammed in with their guitars and some bags that wouldn't fit into the boot, and they often played and sang to pass the time.

They stopped for a day in El Paso and a day in Tucson, Arizona, just long enough to contact the local radio stations and play a couple of songs live on air. In these first two towns, it was only Floyd's reputation that got them on the radio. By the time they got to Phoenix, though, Saroudan's publicity machine was contacting the radio stations and sending a tape of a couple of the tracks before Buddy arrived.

They stopped in Yuma and then drove into California, stopping in San Diego, then heading north-west through San Bernardino and Pasadena. Everywhere they went, the DJs were enthusiastic about the tapes and promised that they would play the album when it came out. As well as interviews and live sessions of some songs, Buddy often recorded plugs for the radio stations. He hated doing it, but his dad persuaded him that it was all good publicity, and he soon got used to rattling off the stupid scripts he was handed.

'Hi, I'm Buddy Clark on KLMD – the hottest place on the dial for the coolest music. Stay right here on 93.8 FM.'

They spent five days in Los Angeles, and his dad wanted to drive out to visit Disneyland, but they were too busy. In addition to all the radio stations and music papers he had contacted, Rosen had fixed up meetings with three major record companies who were interested in signing Buddy for American distribution.

Buddy felt a bit like some caged animal as he sat in offices while various record executives wandered in to look at him. They all said they loved the recordings they'd been sent, but Buddy didn't trust them and he left most of the talking to his dad, who obviously enjoyed all the flattering talk and the hype.

'Of course, I love it,' he said when Buddy asked him. 'Where else do I get treated like a big wheel?'

They were sitting in the offices of the third record company when there was a distant rumbling and the room began to quiver slightly. Everybody froze for a moment as a couple of books fell off the shelves. Then the shaking stopped and they started breathing again.

'Just a small one,' the record executive smiled.

'Blimey, I wouldn't like to be 'ere when there's a big one. It's like standing on top of a jelly,' his dad said.

Buddy got up and headed for the door.

'Where you goin'?' his dad called.

'To see Charmian,' Buddy said. 'I'll get a taxi. You can finish off here.'

Char was lying on the bed when he got back to their hotel room.

'I was so scared,' she whispered as he sat down and put his arms round her. 'All I could think of was the baby. She moved inside me as if she could feel the earthquake and didn't like it. I was worried I might start having her, there and then.'

'Ssh, it's OK, now. Look, why don't we call it a day and go home now?'

'No, I'll be all right, honest.'

Buddy wasn't sure. However, when they moved up to San Francisco, they had such a good time that he was glad he hadn't missed it. They crammed all of the PR business into two days and then had three days' rest. They stayed with Floyd's cousin near the Golden Gate Bridge and she showed them all the sights of the city. Buddy and Char's bedroom had a spectacular view over the bay and the bridge, and each morning they lay in bed late, just looking out of the window and enjoying being alone together.

It was cold when they set out on the next stage of the journey, eastwards across the Sierra Nevada. There was a spectacular storm raging in the mountains and streaks of lightning lit up the jagged peaks. Then, just as they crossed the highest pass, the car heater packed up. They were all shivering with cold by the time they got into Reno and stopped to have the heater fixed.

Again Buddy was worried about the effect of all this travelling on Char, but she said she was loving it and was determined to finish the trip.

The journey began to feel endless. Long, long hours on the road, singing and playing in the back of the car to pass the time. Arriving in a big town and trying to find their way through the network of road loops and interchanges. Then a search for a motel, meals in restaurants, meeting journalists, interviews and recording sessions at radio stations, a quick look round the town, and back on the road again. Salt Lake City. Denver. They headed east, leaving the Rockies behind. Kansas City. St Louis. They crossed the huge rolling centre of the continent before turning north towards Chicago.

Bitter winds swept in from the wild grey water of Lake Michigan, and Charmian stayed in the motel all the time while Floyd, Buddy and his dad did the tour of radio stations round Chicago. It was the first sign she'd shown of being tired, and Buddy decided that, with just over a month to go before the baby was due, it was time to go home.

'Buddy, we can't,' his dad said when he told him. 'You've got to 'ang on a little bit longer. Rosen's fixed up for us to play a showcase at The Bluebird Café in Nashville.'

'Dad, I've made up my mind.'

'Look, mate, a couple of the record companies are ready to bid for the American deal on the album and they're sending their top men to Nashville to see you. Rosen is arranging for Travis and Steve to come up just to do the one gig. We can't put it all off now. It'll be an extra five days, that's all. Tell 'im, Floyd.'

Floyd just shrugged, but Buddy could see that he thought they should do it. Five days. It couldn't make that much difference. There'd still be nearly a month before the baby was born. And Char kept saying that first babies usually came late, anyway.

Travis and Steve were already waiting for them when they arrived in Nashville, and that evening they went out to the Bluebird Café. It was small – a bar-café with tables and chairs and room for about 150 people at the very most, and the performing area was tiny – but there was a great atmosphere in there even when it was empty.

'It's the hip place in town,' Floyd said. 'This guy Rosen must know what he's doing.'

'Oh yeah,' Buddy laughed. 'Remind me to play you a song called "Driving" some time.'

They rehearsed for two days, learning to play the songs without Lonnie James's piano. Mainly, it meant rearranging them slightly, with more guitar work from Floyd and some extra harmonica playing from Buddy. It felt good to be playing together again and, after they'd got the songs sorted out, they went on jamming for the sheer pleasure of it.

The two record executives flew in on the morning of the gig, one from New York and the other from Atlanta. Buddy met them briefly, then left his dad to get on with the job of entertaining them until the evening. He and Char drove downtown and looked round the shops.

They stopped in a kids' clothes shop and Char spent ages buying clothes for the baby.

'Well, my, I guess you must be expecting a little girl,' the shop assistant said, wrapping the pink baby-grows and some pretty little dresses.

'Yes,' Char said, smiling.

'And are you the proud dad?' the assistant asked.

'Yes,' Buddy said, and felt a foolish blush creep up his face.

'The proud dad!' Char laughed when they got outside. 'How are you doing, Daddy?'

'I'm doing absolutely brilliantly, thank you, Mother,' Buddy said in a funny voice, then he caught her in his arms and kissed her.

Someone hooted from a car, and they looked round to see a taxi driver smiling at them.

'It must be love!' the driver called out of the window as the lights changed and he drove away.

'He's right – it must be love,' Buddy said to Char and kissed her again.

CHAPTER THIRTY-SIX

The Bluebird Café was packed and Buddy was pleased that he couldn't even see where the two record executives were sitting. Despite the freezing weather outside, the room was so hot from all the people that he started to sweat as soon as he got on stage.

From the very first song he was aware that this gig would be nothing like the ones they'd done in Texas. The wild, almost angry, edge had gone. Tonight, they weren't finding the pain in the songs, they were finding the calm, and a kind of sadness. He could feel it in his own voice and he could hear it in Floyd's liquid guitar playing. Most of all, he could see it in the audience. They were moving to the rhythm but they weren't lost in a pounding beat. They were listening, caught up in the meaning of the songs.

He couldn't work out how the change had come about: was it because of how he was feeling, happy and peaceful? It didn't matter. The songs were showing new sides of themselves. 'Dark House' was less about the frenzied fear of Ralph James Campbell and more about his loneliness. 'Cool Kid' was less about Antone's terrible death and more about the sadness of his young life.

Song after song was subtly transformed, until Buddy stopped noticing. Only dimly aware of the clear and beautiful sounds coming out of his own mouth, he let himself go into the swirl of the music. The songs went by – 'Destiny's Doors', 'Bend in the River', 'Everyday Miracle' – and he knew the audience was with him; but he wasn't thinking of them, he was searching. He was hearing the notes of the music weaving in and out of each other, each note made more beautiful by the existence of the one next to it. He saw the connections each note made with another and he saw how necessary and inevitable they were. Notes didn't happen by chance, they *had* to be.

It was easy to see it in a song if you concentrated and focused right. It was harder to see it in life. It was the same, though. Everything in Creation *had* to be, just like the notes in a song. When he got into the music, that's what he sensed, what he almost knew to be true. Almost.

Life was too big to come into focus, the way a song could. That's why he could never break through to see it whole. Perhaps in some other time he had seen it. In another life. Before he was born. Perhaps he would see it again. But, here, on this earth, he had forgotten. He could never remember what had been forgotten; but just knowing that it had been forgotten brought it closer. Until it was there, just out of reach. Waiting.

Floyd counted them into the last song, and Buddy started to sing 'Always Heading Home'. The verse built slowly, the pictures piling on top of each other, and he could feel the audience reaching up with him. As he hit the chorus and the guitar stroked out its ringing, golden chords, everybody seemed to take a breath and let it out in a soft shout of approval.

Back into the build of the second verse, and he was almost speaking the lines, while Floyd's guitar played the melody. The build and then the release into the chorus. Again the cries from the audience, but this time the chorus went on, round and round, chiming like bells until the whole audience was on their feet.

A nod to Floyd, and the song came to a shimmering halt.

The crowd erupted into applause as Buddy and the band bowed and went off backstage. Five minutes later, they were still shouting and clapping for more.

Just as they were about to go back on, Buddy turned to the band, 'Forget what we planned. I want to do some old rock'n'roll stuff for my dad.'

'A shot of rhythm and blues?' Floyd said. 'Right on!'

For a moment the crowd was stunned as the band belted into an old Chuck Berry song, but then they caught on. They'd been wound up tight by the show, now it was time to let go. This was fun, this was joy, this was release. On your feet. Dance. Shake your body. Celebrate. Let the good times roll.

Buddy Holly, Elvis, Little Richard, Jerry Lee Lewis – all the songs he'd learned as a kid came pouring out in a non-stop medley.

'These songs are for you,' he said, pointing to his dad.

His dad raised two thumbs and went on dancing.

Twenty minutes of roaring hits from the past. Unrehearsed and rough, but jumping like a firecracker. And the band pumping, watching each other like hawks to make the change from one song to the next, grinning with the pleasure of being together and having fun.

A final nod to Floyd, who turned to the drums and raised his eyebrows at Travis. Through the riff one more time. A long roll on the drums as the guitars scratched faster and faster, moving higher and higher up the frets, and the bass boomed along with them. An instant of silence. Then a rimshot crash on the drums as the guitars hit the last chord.

It was over.

*

Three hours later, the band and Char were alone in the café. The crowd had finally gone; the manager was in a back room counting the day's takings, and a dim red-and-blue sign above the bar was the only light. They had talked themselves out about the gig. They sipped beer and relaxed, each of them lost in thought. Tomorrow's parting was already coming between them.

Headlights swept across them as a car pulled up in front of the café. They picked up their things and walked outside.

'Well, Terry, what did they say?' Floyd asked.

'They both want the album, and they're ready to cut each other's throats to get it. Good job they're stayin' in different hotels! Bobby Rosen's gonna 'ave to sort this one out. But it looks as if we got ourselves a deal! Anyway, pile in.'

Char sat on Buddy's lap in the front, and the other three got in the back with the guitars. His dad drove slowly along the frozen roads, back into the centre of town.

''Ere, the one from Atlanta's got 'is own little plane,' his dad said, nudging Buddy with his elbow. 'Says 'e'll take us back wiv 'im if we want. What d'you reckon?'

'No.' His instant reaction, faster than the thought of why he said it.

'Well, I fink I might go wiv 'im. Might get a better deal, you never know. Are you sure you wanna drive? Come on, come on the plane wiv me.'

He almost said yes.

But he couldn't. It was there – the same old fear. And clearer and sharper this time. A small plane. Snow on the ground. February. Buddy Holly.

Perhaps he shouldn't let his dad go. But no, this stupid, mad, childish superstition didn't apply to his dad. Only to him. He hated it so much, this crazy fear, that he almost threw it away, almost defied it and said, Yes, he would fly. But he didn't.

'No, we'll go in the car,' he said. 'We can take it easy. It'll give me and Char a bit of time on our own. Eh, Char?'

She squeezed his hand and said, 'Yeah. I don't fancy a small plane anyway. It might not be good for the baby if it's not properly pressurized.'

It was decided. He couldn't change his mind now because Char didn't want to fly, either. And a great sense of relief hit him. Maybe it wasn't superstition. Maybe his fear had been right. Perhaps all his life he'd been heading towards this moment of danger. But he had avoided it. He was safe.

Fine snow was floating down from the sky and being whirled by the wind when they arrived at Memphis airport.

'Look, I'm gonna 'ave to go straight through,' his dad said. 'There's a special lounge for people on private flights, and I'm late already.'

'Oh, VIP treatment, eh?' Buddy said, then glanced out of the window at the snow. 'Are you sure about flying, Dad? The weather looks bad.'

'Nah, it's just a few flakes. It'll only take us about an hour. So, I meet you tomorrow evening at the 'otel in Atlanta, about eight o'clock, right? And in the meantime I'll fix the flight back to England.'

He turned to the three guys from the band and shook hands with each of them in turn.

'OK, you lot, I wanna say ta for all you've done

for Buddy and me – you've bin fantastic. We'll be in touch as soon as we've got a release date on the album – set up tours and publicity and stuff. The future looks good!'

His dad took Charmian in his arms and gave her a kiss, 'See yer tomorrow, darlin' – all right?'

He picked up his bag to go, then turned back, and Buddy knew what he was going to do. He reached up and ruffled Buddy's hair, then pulled his nose and chucked him under the chin. The old, old sign of his love.

'Cut it out, Dad!' he said.

'Oh, too old for that, are yer?' his dad laughed. 'You'll never be too old. 'Cos you'll always be my kid, right?'

He walked away. Buddy waited for him to turn back and wave, but he didn't. He pushed through the doors to the lounge and disappeared.

'We better go check in,' Floyd said. 'And you better hit the road.'

'Yeah,' Buddy said.

He wanted to say so much to them, but there were no words. They all looked at each other and smiled.

Travis and Steve gave Char a kiss and then shook Buddy's hand. Floyd kissed Char, then took Buddy's hand and pulled him into a bear-hug.

'Floyd, listen . . .' Buddy started, as they broke apart, but then he shrugged.

'No need to say it, brother. I know,' Floyd said. He put his hand one last time on Buddy's shoulder, then picked up his guitar and walked away with the others.

Char took Buddy's hand and gave it a squeeze.

*

Snow continued to fall from the leaden sky as they drove south out of Nashville on I-24. Gusts of wind buffeted the Buick and whipped the fine snow off the road and into the grass verges. Buddy glanced at his watch. If everything had gone well, his dad would have landed safely by now.

They could have kept driving and got closer to Atlanta that evening, but they didn't.

The road conditions were difficult and he felt so sad at saying goodbye to the others that he was glad to stop in Chattanooga. They found a hotel overlooking the Tennessee River, then they went for a walk along the riverfront. The snow had stopped but the wind was bitter, and they clung on to each other to keep out the cold.

Back in the warmth of their hotel room, they ordered tea and drank it, lying on the bed, then fell asleep in each other's arms. They woke at seven in the evening and went back out into the biting cold to look for a restaurant. The sky had cleared and the stars were startlingly bright above the river.

They ate in a family-run Italian restaurant, and the owner made a great fuss of Char, asking when the baby was due and bringing his wife and young daughter out to meet her. The owner kissed Char's hand and wished them both luck as they left.

They walked back to the hotel, glowing from the food and the friendliness of the Italian family, and went straight to bed. They watched TV for a while until Char went to sleep, then Buddy switched it off and curled up next to her.

His arm was resting against her belly and he felt the baby move a couple of times. He tried to imagine his daughter, and he suddenly realized that he kept thinking of her as 'Holly'. Trust his dad to come up with a name like that. It was a nice name but . . . He tried to think of other names but none fitted. He kept coming back to Holly.

Perhaps because of the sleep he'd had in the afternoon, he didn't feel at all tired now, and his mind raced. He thought about the music, and the journey across the States. About Floyd and the others, and the friendship and understanding they'd found through the music. About his mum, waiting at home. Perhaps she'd already found a flat where he could settle down with Char and Ho– the baby. And he thought about the Rybeeros. They'd be bound to change their minds when they saw how happy Char was. And when the baby came – their granddaughter – they would love her like everyone else. And Jules. His brother-in-law. His old friend. He saw him as he'd been at thirteen when they'd first got to know each other. Always jumping about, always full of plans and mad ideas. Surely all that couldn't be forgotten? No – they'd find a way to become close again.

And he thought about Char, felt her body, warm, against his. She said she'd been in love with him since she was fourteen. Why hadn't he seen it, back then? It would have given them so much more time together. Don't ask. Just accept. He loved her now. They were together now. That was enough.

They could have started early and got to Atlanta by lunchtime, but they didn't.

They got up late and decided to have a slow morning. It was only a 120-mile drive – they could take their time. They had a big breakfast and walked by the Tennessee River again. The sun was shining, sparkling on the frost-covered trees on the hill across the river, and the whole world felt crisp and clean.

They left Chattanooga in the early afternoon and drove south on I-75. They could have stayed on the interstate highway but they didn't. It was very busy and, just south of Calhoun, Buddy decided to leave it and take the smaller Highway 41 which ran parallel with the main road all the way to Atlanta. This road was virtually empty and they enjoyed cruising along it, with time to look at the rolling hills.

They could have driven straight through Cartersville, but they didn't.

They stopped for coffee and doughnuts and strolled along the main street to stretch their legs. There was a craft shop just down from the café, and Char went in and bought a small wooden doll with a pink-and-white gingham dress.

'It'll look lovely by the side of the cot,' she said to Buddy as they walked back to the car.

By the time they crossed the long bridge across Lake Allatoona, the sun had gone down and the last streaks of orange and red were fading in the sky.

'I'm tired,' Char said. 'Just think of how far we've driven. Thousands of miles. It's been fantastic, though. We've crammed so much in. It seems like a lifetime.'

'Nearly home now,' Buddy said.

'We're always heading home,' Char sang and then snuggled down in the seat and closed her eyes.

Buddy put his hand on her belly and she covered it with her hand and held it there. The baby moved. He pressed lightly.

'Hello in there, this is your daddy speaking,' he said.

Char smiled, already almost asleep.

'This is your daddy speaking,' Buddy thought. 'Welcome to the world, little thing. Little thing that's half me and half Char. What will you be like? What colour will you be? Who cares, as long as you're born safe. It's a funny old place, this world you're coming to, but you'll like it.'

A mile and a half down the road, the young truck driver put his foot on the accelerator as he crested one of the hills, and the truck kicked into the long descent. He could have left Marietta an hour earlier but he hadn't. He'd got caught up in a card game at the depot, and now he was late. He wanted to get back to Cartersville before his girl left to go out to work. They hardly got time to see each other since she'd started these night shifts.

He hit the bottom of the hill fast and the truck bucked as the wheels skewed slightly to the left. The dip in the road was a frost-hollow and the road surface had been icy since the sun had left it at three o'clock. The tyres started to slide, and the driver stamped on the brakes. The front wheels locked and the whole rear end of the truck slewed around.

The driver felt the truck tip and then he was slung to the roof as it crashed on to its side and slid along the road, sparks flying where the metal struck the tarmac. The slide seemed to go on for ever, with shrieking metal and the smashing of glass.

Finally there was silence and the movement stopped. He rolled out through the broken windscreen on to the road. There were cuts on his hands and his leg ached, but he was alive.

He looked at the truck. It was on its side, blocking

the whole width of the road. He looked at the top of the hill. The truck would be hidden from view until someone reached the top and started down. They wouldn't see it until too late.

Even as he looked, a light struck the upper branches on the trees on the top of the hill. He started to run: a car was coming. He had to get up there to warn them. Flag them down. He took four paces, then his broken ankle gave way under him. Pain flared up his leg. He crawled to the side of the road and began to scream.

'Stop!'

The Buick reached the top of the hill and dipped into the slope. The headlights beamed down from the sky, back on to the road and shone on something. The whole of the underside of the truck was black, but one of the wheels had buckled under and the chrome of the wheel trim reflected the glare of the light.

Buddy jammed his foot on the brake. The Buick skidded. The tyres smoked, gripping and tearing themselves to pieces to try to stop, but the momentum was too great. It didn't slew or slide, and Buddy saw that they were going to hit the truck head on.

And he saw, too, every door that had opened, every step that had been taken, to bring him to this moment.

At the last instant he shot his right arm out in front of Charmian and the baby.

CHAPTER THIRTY-SEVEN

For a moment, Terry didn't know where he was when he woke up. He'd been walking down a street with Buddy and they'd decided to go into a pub for a drink. A band had been playing in the corner and Buddy had got up to play with them. He had been longing to hear Buddy sing. Everything about him had been willing it to happen. And it had seemed so real. Even when he was waking and realized it was a dream, he was still longing for it to be real. Then he opened his eyes and looked across the room and knew where he was.

Grey, early morning light was coming in through the window. Buddy was lying in the bed. The distant sound of hospital life filtered through the door.

The dreadful pain gripped Terry's heart again. For a few brief hours of sleep he had been free of it, but now it was back, weighing him down, emptying his life of any meaning.

Anything was better than this pain. Even the terror. He had thought the terror had been unbearable.

The terror had started as a quiet nag of doubt in the hotel as he waited for Buddy and Charmian to arrive. Three hours after they were due he had gone down to the lobby and waited by the door, his heart leaping with hope every time the headlights of a car turned into the car-park. He had told himself not to worry, told himself every sensible reason why they might be late: breakdowns, traffic jams.

The nag of doubt had turned into an aching sense of disaster as midnight came, and they still weren't there. No message. They would have rung if they'd broken down. His mind raced over all the possibilities and kept coming back to the worst.

He had kept thinking of ringing the police, but he put it off as long as possible. Finally, at around two-thirty in the morning, he had called. His heart had been knocking so hard that he had seen his finger jolting with the pulse of his blood as he'd tried to press the keys on the phone.

He'd waited for ages while they'd checked the details of car crashes. No record of an accident involving a blue Buick in the Atlanta city area. They would get on to Highway Patrol to check the route from Chattanooga to Atlanta. Could the enquirer ring back in half an hour, please?

He had watched the minutes tick away on the clock above the hotel reception desk. The receptionist had asked if he would like a coffee. He had said no.

Five minutes short of the half-hour, he had rung again and asked for Desk Sergeant Larner. Yes, there had been an accident involving a young couple, out on Highway 41. He had no details of the car. The couple had been airlifted to Emory Hospital.

It was in the cab on the way to the hospital that the terror had really broken. He had found himself talking out loud, telling himself to calm down. His heartbeat had been pounding in his ears and he had barely been able to breathe. When he had tried to steady himself by taking a deep breath, his whole chest had shuddered with a sob. His mind had been ablaze with the fear, thoughts racing around in panic.

Oh yes, the terror had been awful. But at least there had been hope. Hope that it wasn't Buddy and Charmian. And how he had clung on to that hope. Right up to the moment he'd walked into the room, he had hoped it was someone else.

And then he'd seen his son. His beautiful, talented son, lying there, so still. The bandages round the top of his head, and the blankets and sheets raised off his poor, broken body by a hooped cage. And the drips and the tubes going into him. Below the bandages that covered his hair and his forehead, his face was uninjured. It was pale, so pale that his lips were almost white, but it was unmarked.

The fact that his face was unmarked had kept the hope alive. All morning he had stared at that unmoving, unmarked face and convinced himself that it would all be all right. There was hope.

Bit by bit, during the afternoon, the hope had died. He had slowly come to realize that no one was doing anything. A nurse came in every hour to look. A doctor came in and looked, and Terry had been scared to ask why no action was being taken. Why was nobody talking about operations to put things right?

In the early evening the doctor had come in again and Terry had taken him out in the corridor and started to ask all the questions. What was wrong with Buddy? Why didn't he move? Why wasn't anything being done?

When the doctor avoided his eyes and tried to stall, the final bits of hope began to drain from Terry's heart. But there must have still been a tiny fragment of hope left, because he had asked the question – 'Is there anyfing you can do for him, Doctor?'

Up to that moment there was still hope. The doctor could have said 'Yes'. But he said 'No'. He was kind and he gripped Terry's shoulder to show that he cared, and he said how sorry he was, but he said 'No'. The internal injuries were too severe. The liver, the spleen, the kidneys were all injured beyond repair. The hips, both legs and one arm were broken, and they couldn't even set them properly. There was spinal damage. All they could do was keep him sedated so that he wouldn't suffer.

And hope had finally died. And the pain that had gripped his heart, and gripped it ever since, was more terrible than the terror. More terrible than anything he had ever known.

He got up slowly from the chair where he'd been asleep and where his dreaming mind had teased him with pictures of a healthy, uninjured Buddy. He walked slowly over to the bed and looked down at the reality. The drips, the tubes, the bandages; the pale, unmoving face that was even paler in this grey early morning light.

He bent close and could just hear Buddy's faint breathing. He was still alive.

He sat by the bed and took Buddy's hand in his. It was cool and there was no movement. He stroked the hand and tried to will the strength and life from his own hands to pass into Buddy.

'Come on, Buddy,' he said. 'Come on, son. Wake up.'

The nurse came in and changed the drips and gave Buddy another injection.

'Can 'e 'ear me?' Terry asked. 'Do you fink 'e can 'ear me if I talk to 'im?'

'I'm sure he can,' she said.

'That stuff you're giving 'im, it don't make 'im unconscious?'

'No, it's just for the pain,' she said. 'You keep talking to him. It'll help him, to know that you're here.'

So he talked. About the day. About the past. About the future. About how much he loved him. And all the time he stroked Buddy's hand. And he tried to encourage him.

'Come on, Buddy. Wake up. Come on.'

About mid-morning, Buddy took one larger breath that came out in a long sigh and his hand moved slightly.

Terry rubbed the hand harder and bent close to Buddy's ear and spoke urgently, 'That's it. Move. Come on, Buddy. Move your hand. Come on, you can do it. Oh please, Buddy, please don't die!'

And then Terry's tears started to fall and his throat became too choked to speak. He got up and went out of the room. If Buddy could hear him, he didn't want him to hear that he was crying.

He stood in the corridor and tried to stop the tears, stop the shaking grief.

The nurse came and gave him a coffee. He drank it, but said that he wasn't hungry when she asked if he wanted to eat.

He was just about to go back into the room when he thought about the baby. He had seen her briefly yesterday, and the doctor had gone on about what a miracle it was that she was so healthy. Terry had looked at her and felt nothing. How could the doctor talk about miracles when Charmian was dead and his son was dying?

But now he had an idea, and he made his way down to the Maternity Department. The nurse wasn't very happy when he told her what he wanted to do, so he went to see the doctor in charge of the whole unit. She came and looked at the baby and asked about her progress and then she said yes. She lifted the baby out of the cot and put her in Terry's arms.

When he got back to the room, he had the impression that Buddy had moved slightly. One of his eyelids was not completely closed and his head seemed to be lying at a slightly different angle.

He sat down next to the bed and put the sleeping baby next to Buddy. Then he started to talk again. About the baby and how well she was and how beautiful she was. He lifted Buddy's hand and laid it next to the baby, curling it round so that it cradled the baby's head. The baby slept and Buddy lay still.

Halfway through the afternoon, a nurse came up from the Maternity Unit and took the baby away to feed her. Terry made her promise to bring her back, and an hour later she did. The baby was awake, her eyes half open and her little fists moving as Terry held her in his arms. He rocked her gently and after a while she went to sleep.

He put her next to Buddy and began to talk again.

'Come on, Buddy. Wake up. You've got to see your daughter. She's 'ere, right next to you. And she's so lovely, Buddy. She's perfect. Wake up and look at 'er. Your little daughter. She's right 'ere by your side.'

The nurse came in and changed Buddy's drips.

Terry stood up to let the nurse get nearer. He walked over to the window, cradling the baby in his arms. It was getting dark outside. The baby moved in his arms and kicked one of her legs, and he looked down but she was still asleep.

'Oh,' the nurse said and Terry turned. 'He's opened one of his eyes.'

Terry hurried over and saw that Buddy's right eye was nearly fully open. The nurse moved her finger from side to side but the eye did not follow the movement. She bent again to give him his injection, but Terry stopped her.

'Can you just wait a bit? Maybe 'e's tryin' to wake up and that stuff makes 'im sleep. Just a couple of minutes?'

Just as he finished talking, Terry saw Buddy's lips open and close slightly. The nurse saw it, too, and put her ear close to Buddy's mouth.

'I think he's trying to say something,' she said, standing up.

Terry handed her the baby and bent close to Buddy's mouth. There was nothing. Just the softest sound of breath.

'Come on, Buddy. It's dad 'ere,' he said, taking hold of Buddy's hand and gripping it tight. 'Come on, wake up. Your baby's 'ere an' all. Right 'ere, look.'

He took the baby and held her above the open eye. There was no movement.

'I'll be back in ten minutes, Mr Clark,' the nurse said.

When she'd gone, Terry sat down and started talking again. 'Come on, Buddy, wake up. Look at your baby. She's 'ere, can you see 'er? She's lovely.

Look at 'er. Come on, son. They're gonna come back and give you more of that stuff and you'll just sleep. You've got to look at 'er now.'

He shook Buddy's hand again, but that eye stayed blank and unmoving. He shook Buddy's hand again and gripped it tight. There was the faintest pressure back and Terry saw Buddy's lips open again. He put the baby on the bed and bent down until his ear was touching Buddy's lips. He heard the slow intake of breath and then the slow sigh as it started to come out. And through the sigh he heard the word that was being breathed.

'Holly.'

'Yes, Buddy. She's right next to you. There, can you feel 'er?'

He laid Buddy's hand on his daughter's head.

The nurse came back and gave Buddy his injection.

After a while, the right eyelid fluttered and closed. But Terry went on talking.

Another nurse came and took Holly away for the night.

Terry held on to Buddy's hand. That was all he could do for him now: hold his hand and love him while he slipped away.

It was just after ten when Terry felt Buddy's hand relax. He had gone.

CHAPTER THIRTY-EIGHT

It took ages for Terry to get through customs and immigration in Atlanta airport. At first the hold-up was about having stayed in the USA for longer than ninety days, then it was all about having worked without a work permit. As soon as he told them about Buddy and Charmian, though, they suddenly dropped their questions and stamped his departure form. But, even then, there was the endless paper-work connected with taking the bodies back home. On top of everything, there were forms that had to be filled in for Holly, and they had to look through all the documents from the hospital.

At one point he'd been worried that he would miss the flight, but the officials worked as fast as they could and he got on board just before it took off.

Holly slept in his arms, waking only once during the eight-hour flight. The stewardess brought a bottle of milk and offered to feed her, but Terry insisted on doing it himself.

Carol was waiting for him at the airport. She looked tired and red-eyed; when they went down to the gates and saw the two coffins being unloaded from the plane and put into the hearse, she leaned against his arm and sobbed.

When they got back to her house, she busied herself getting Holly's food prepared and then watched as Terry fed her and changed her.

'You've become an expert,' she said as he laid the sleeping Holly in her cot again.

They sat together and she asked questions about the crash and the time in the hospital, and he gave her the answers. It was hard to relive it all, but he knew that she needed to know. She cried again, and he put his arm round her.

'I've been in contact with the Rybeeros,' she said,

when she stopped crying. 'About the funeral arrangements. They'd like it if they could both be buried down there. They've got their church down there and they're so keen. I didn't know what you'd think.'

'I don't care where they're buried as long as they're together.'

'So we'll say yes?'

'Yeah,' Terry said. 'What about Holly – did they say anything?'

Carol nodded. 'They think it would be best if we looked after her . . . Mr Rybeero's illness and everything. They'd want her to go and stay sometimes, of course.'

'What do you mean by "we"?' Terry asked.

'I mean us. Together. She's going to need a mum and a dad, isn't she?'

Terry nodded. 'Yeah, she is. Do you fink we can do it?'

'It's what Buddy would've wanted.'

Three weeks after the funeral 'Always Heading Home' was released by Saroudan. Fuelled by all the publicity about Buddy's death, it went to Number One and stayed there for seven weeks. The album was released shortly after the single and it, too, went to Number One.

On the day the album went to Number One in the US Charts, they got a phone-call from Floyd: he was coming over to see them and Holly. He stayed with them a week and, just before he left, they asked him to be her godfather. He accepted.

Terry decorated Buddy's room and turned it into a

nursery for Holly. At the end of the year he began to put up the gold and platinum discs round the wall above her cot. There would be more when the second and third albums were released.

Terry also kept the hundreds of letters they received every month from fans all round the world who had been touched by Buddy's music. He stored them in files, which he stacked on the shelves in Holly's room.

He knew that one day she would want to read them.